"PERSUASIVE AND MOVING . . . there aren't many books that can change your life, but—like the events he celebrates, the sight of monarch butterflies or the sound of whippoorwills—*Country Cured* is good for what ails you."

—*Greensboro News & Record*

"A THOUGHTFUL JOURNALIST RETURNS TO THE RURAL HAUNTS OF HIS YOUTH, SKETCHING THE PEOPLE, PLACES AND CUSTOMS WITH SYMPATHY AND HUMOR."

—*Denver Post*

"Bledsoe's observant eye and imaginative mind respond to country living with an especially appealing balance of sensitivity and humanity, reflected in laments about gardens, the elemental power of storms, and the trials of a country writer."

—*Booklist*

JERRY BLEDSOE is an award-winning journalist and the author of several books including *The New York Times* bestseller, *Bitter Blood*. He received the National Headliner Award for his reporting of the *Bitter Blood* case. A native of Danville, Virginia, he now makes his home in Asheboro, North Carolina.

COUNTRY CURED

Reflections from the Heart

Jerry Bledsoe

A PLUME BOOK

PLUME
Published by the Penguin Group
Penguin Books USA Inc., 375 Hudson Street, New York, New York 10014, U.S.A.
Penguin Books Ltd, 27 Wrights Lane, London W8 5TZ, England
Penguin Books Australia Ltd, Ringwood, Victoria, Australia
Penguin Books Canada Ltd, 10 Alcorn Avenue, Toronto, Ontario, Canada M4V 3B2
Penguin Books (N.Z.) Ltd, 182-190 Wairau Road, Auckland 10, New Zealand

Penguin Books Ltd, Registered Offices: Harmondsworth, Middlesex, England

Published by Plume, an imprint of New American Library, a division of
Penguin Books USA Inc. This is an authorized reprint of a hardcover edition published by
Longstreet Press, Inc.

First Plume Printing, December, 1991
10 9 8 7 6 5 4 3 2 1

Portions of the material included in this book previously appeared in slightly different form
in the *Greensboro News and Record* and the *Charlotte Observer*.

 REGISTERED TRADEMARK—MARCA REGISTRADA

LIBRARY OF CONGRESS CATALOGING-IN-PUBLICATION DATA:
Bledsoe, Jerry.
      Country cured : reflections from the heart / Jerry Bledsoe.
          p.   cm.
      Originally published: Atlanta : Longstreet Press, 1989.
      ISBN 0-452-26706-4
      1. North Carolina—Social life and customs.   2. Bledsoe, Jerry—
Homes and haunts—North Carolina.   3. North Carolina—Biography.
I. Title.
F260.B574   1991
975.6—dc20   91-29516
                                                                 CIP

Printed in the United States of America

BOOKS ARE AVAILABLE AT QUANTITY DISCOUNTS WHEN USED TO PROMOTE PRODUCTS
OR SERVICES. FOR INFORMATION PLEASE WRITE TO PREMIUM MARKETING DIVISION,
PENGUIN BOOKS USA INC., 375 HUDSON STREET, NEW YORK, NEW YORK 10014.

For Aunt Vivianne

At a certain point in my adult life, along with my wife, Linda, I made a decision to move to the country. As with any major decision, the thinking that preceded action was complex; the motives, complicated. But in some fundamental way we were convinced that the move would be good because the country itself has powers — powers to heal, to restore, to cure us of what ails us, which is, in most cases, today an unwieldy phenomenon composed of a million tiny trials and tribulations that fall under that loosest of labels: modern life.

So we moved and have lived for many years, experiencing the joys of those curative powers we believed to exist. We've also found that the country provides space for the mind to call forth and examine images, scenes, episodes from the past, for us to lavish upon them a kind of attention that I suspect those who live more harried, cosmopolitan lives don't enjoy the luxury of.

As a writer, this way of life has proved right for me, and I find that my memories, long exposed to country living, have undergone a treatment, a process, if you will, very much like what happens to a good ham that is country cured. The slow aging of the meat, treated with just the right combination of spices and smoked at just the right temperature for exactly the necessary time, creates a special taste, one with a bite, a unique tang, that regular hams just don't have.

I feel that way about my memories and observations sometimes now. They seem richer, deeper, tastier, I guess, than they ever would have had I not chosen to place myself in the country setting that has nurtured and sustained me for all these years. This book, then, is my invitation to a ham dinner of sorts. I can imagine myself setting up the table on a broad front porch washed by the sweetest breezes spring has to offer. And on that table I carefully place my memories to share with you. I ask that they be blessed and hope that they will nourish you as they have nourished and blessed me, again and again.

Where I Come From

I turn onto the street, and the years peel away. I am twelve again, whizzing down the hill on my J. C. Higgins Special, no hands, my newspaper delivery bag flapping in the basket.

I was five when we moved to Fifth Avenue in Thomasville, a small town in central North Carolina famed for its furniture factories. How the street came to be Fifth Avenue, I don't know. There were no First, Second, Third, or Fourth avenues. I used to think my street was named for a candy bar, and it may well have been.

Although it was only a few blocks from downtown, across the mainline Southern Railroad tracks, Fifth Avenue was a dirt street then, dusty in summer, muddy in winter. It wasn't paved until several years after we moved there. Improvements also brought a sidewalk that became a downhill raceway for kids on skates, scooters, tricycles, and wagons.

Approaching Fifth Avenue on East Main Street, I might never have recognized the neighborhood. All the houses are gone: Shannon Lambeth's, Shirley Pierce's, Bertram Heathcote's (from Bertram's second-floor bedroom, on a clear day, we could see Pilot Mountain fifty miles away). In their place is a furniture showroom, a white and glassy behemoth, with a big parking lot behind that claimed the barber's house and Mrs. Chisholm's tiny store, where workers from the huge furniture factory on East Main once gathered for lunch. It also wiped out the tucked-away field of tangled growth where we used to cut limber saplings to make bows, harvest long, straight dried weeds for arrows, and build our best forts and hideouts.

But Fifth Avenue seems little changed. All the houses that I remember so well are here — Miss Dickens's, Mr. Marlowe's, Dr. Phillips's, the Smiths', the Gilliams', the Townsends'. They just seem smaller, as if in scale instead of real. But something isn't quite right. The street seems empty somehow. And it's not just that the spreading chinaberry tree, so easy to climb, is missing from Mr. Marlowe's yard. It takes a minute for me to realize just what is wrong.

There are no kids. Not one. And this is after school hours. Was I expecting to see Billy and Lyle Smith heading to their backyard clubhouse to show silent and grainy Castle films on their 8mm projector? Or Jimmy White — Whitey we all called him — throwing a football with his brother, Joe Bickett? Mark Whisnant running across the garden from his house carrying an armload of toy cars and trucks? My little brother, Larry, coming to tell me that I'd better get home — and *now*!

At the Joneses' house at the bottom of the hill, I slow instinctively, as I once did on my bike. The Joneses were our next-door neighbors. Mr. Jones was a milkman. He drove an old black Chevrolet — was it a '39? — that, appropriately, had a milky windshield.

The little house is still there. Number nineteen. I had been afraid it might be gone because I'd heard that it had fallen into disrepair. Somebody has been working on it. A paint bucket sits on the porch; a "For Sale" sign has been stuck in the yard. The house is empty. I had not expected this.

I pull the car to the curb.

This isn't our house. Others have changed it to suit themselves. The white weatherboards have been covered by an ugly, fake-brick siding made of asphalt. The brick porch pillars have been ripped out and replaced by wooden posts. Unfamiliar shrubs grow in the tiny front yard, but the spot that was always bald and pebbly remains so.

I can't get over how small the house seems. It was always one of the smallest on the street, but it seemed much larger than this. It stood on high, spindly brick pillars when my daddy bought it for twenty-five hundred dollars, the first house that he could call his own. It had just four rooms. The bathroom, with only a commode and a claw-footed tub, no hot water, was on the tiny back porch. My mother cooked on a woodstove. An old green icebox sat on the back porch near the bathroom. We hung a big green card on the door with instructions for the ice man, and on blistering summer days the arrival of his truck was an event. We kids gathered around to catch the wild chunks that flew from the huge, steaming blocks as the ice man split them with his pick. We'd wrap the precious coldness in newspapers and crunch it with our teeth.

My daddy underpinned the house with brick and enclosed the back porch to create a dinette. He removed the steep, rickety back steps and put a new rear entrance on one side of the house. He moved the kitchen into a former bedroom, installed cabinets, new plumbing, a sink, a refrigerator, and a kerosene cookstove. Later, when we got hot water and an electric range, we thought that we were really something.

Now, walking across the narrow yard for the first time since we moved away in 1956, when I was fifteen, I feel like a stranger. Hesitantly, I step onto the porch, and the swing appears. It is a summer night, brightened by fireflies, and we are there, my mother, Larry, and me, swinging and laughing, scheming and dreaming. New neighbors have moved into the apartment across the street. They have a TV, one of the first in our neighborhood. We can see its tantalizing flicker through a window.

"Miz Carter," my mother is saying in mock tones as we pretend to be standing in a group at the new neighbors' door, "could we borrow a cup of sugar—and your TV?"

I peek into a window. The house has been remodeled: new ceilings, new carpet, new paneling. The same in every room. All with a look of cheapness. But I see it as it was, the roses on the living-room wallpaper, the little fireplace, now covered over, with the coal bucket by the hearth. The dark linoleum floor.

I walk to the back of the house and again know the fear of tumbling down those missing back steps as I once did, the reason my daddy got rid of them. I see a chicken flopping in the day lily bed, its head dangling grotesquely after Mr. Beck, our other next-door neighbor, wrung its neck to make Sunday dinner. My dog, Penny, a sturdy terrier (dead how many years now?), strains at his chain, barking fiercely at the dying chicken.

The apple tree my daddy planted in the garden as a mere twig is now in its last days. The big willow by the drainage ditch is gone. I can't believe that the hill on which my brothers and I wrestled, practically a cliff to us, is a mere rise. And strange how the towering shrub to which my mother sent us to fetch switches so that we could pay for our misdeeds has lost its menace.

I stay for a long time remembering and leave reluctantly, looking back. Later, I stop at a phone booth and make a call.

"How much is that little house you have for sale on Fifth Avenue?" I ask the woman at the real-estate office.

"Thirteen-five," she says. "It's been remodeled throughout. It has electric heat, new bathroom fixtures, new kitchen cabinets, and a double stainless-steel sink. It's a real nice little house."

"It used to be," I say.

That trip—back to a place, *the* place we remember as home—is one we've all made. Whether the neighborhood is changed or remains basically the same, whether the house is still there or long gone, the place holds us, draws us backward to the people and events that define it, to the years that make us what we are.

My visit to Fifth Avenue triggered something in me. After my call to the realtor, with her carefully prepared and completely unknowing sales pitch, I knew that the best days of the neighborhood and the house were over—at least those best for me and mine. Memory is the only place they remain alive; words are the only way to capture them as they were when I lived them.

So I began to remember and to write, to search through words and stories for that inescapable yet almost indefinable place that takes up the biggest part of our hearts. I went in search of where I come from, knowing that to find that place is to find myself, to know and understand my world now.

When a house changes, when a business closes, more is lost than the building itself. People and things aren't all that disappears. In my old neighborhood, Noah Ledford's store is gone, and with it a way of life has passed.

The store was on Taylor Street, one block over from Fifth Avenue. It was a big building, two stories, painted green and white. Noah had the first floor. Apartments occupied the second.

A hosiery mill stood across the street next-door to a laundry. Two blocks north was Main Street School. Residential streets were all around. At lunchtime, the mill workers crowded into Noah's for cans of sardines, pork and beans, Vienna sausages, crackers, cakes, and soft drinks. Noah also made sandwiches for some, slowly pushing a big block of cheese and a fat roll of bologna through his electric slicer, deliberately slathering slices of Merita bread with mayonnaise and mustard.

In the afternoon, the laundry ladies came. They were fat and sweaty and wore kerchiefs tied around their heads. Their dispositions were jolly, and they laughed loudly and enjoyed teasing and joking with Noah, who was noted for being sullen and crotchety. They drank big Nehis in exotic flavors such as peach and strawberry, and, to the amazement of us kids, they munched on Argo starch from red boxes, eight cents each.

Twice a day the railroad men parked their switching engine on the track across the creek that ran beside the store and walked over for their breaks. They were big men, strong and ruddy. They wore sweaty, striped railroad hats. Red bandannas dangled from their hip pockets. They ate as much at breaktime as most men eat for meals.

Mainly, though, Noah's was a neighborhood store, a place where people stopped for a quart of milk, a loaf of bread, a bar of soap, or soft drinks. Men from the neighborhood often went there just to sit by the kerosene stove in the center of the floor and chat with one another.

Noah, who was called No-ee by almost everybody, rarely joined in. He was a little man, bent and gnarled by arthritis. It hurt him to walk or move quickly, and he seemed equally pained to speak. He had long, hairy arms and wore rimless spectacles that usually perched on the tip of his great beak of a nose. A forest of hair flared from his nostrils. I never knew his age, but he always seemed old to me.

There were many tales about Noah. We kids had all heard of the riches that he supposedly had secreted in the little back room of the store where he lived alone, an ardent bachelor. During the day, when business was light, he sat in an old straight-backed chair guarding the entrance to that room, an empty coffee can at his side to accommodate his snuff spittings. At night, when he closed the store, he drew the blinds and retreated to his back room with his radio. We all pictured him there cackling and counting his silver dollars and gold pieces. We spent many nights in futile attempts to peek around those blinds and catch a glimpse of Noah and his money.

Noah seldom left the store, but every Sunday afternoon he climbed into the backseat of one of Hegler's taxis and disappeared until late that night. There was much speculation about where Noah went on these trips. Adults tended to think that he went to see some family member that he never talked about or that he had a girlfriend. But we kids pictured him going off to bury his riches.

Noah had to have great riches, we figured, because his store was filled with such delights. The walls were lined from floor to ceiling with shelves holding canned foods and other merchandise. Noah plucked items from the higher shelves with a long-handled clasp.

A counter on the left held loaves of bread and packages of buns and rolls at the end nearest the door. In the middle, on heavy brown paper, were tomatoes and bananas under a scale hanging from the ceiling. The bananas were usually overripe and swarming with tiny gnats. The remainder of the counter presented an array of nickel and dime cakes sufficient to dazzle tastebuds and daze bellies. Behind this counter stood the long drink box, with its tempting variety of bottled soft drinks cooling in icy, bubbling water.

A counter at the back housed the cash register and a big selection of packaged fried pies and doughnuts, but it ended abruptly to make room for a refrigerated case with a big glass front. In this case were: milk, mostly in pint and half-pint cartons; the cheese and bologna for sandwich makings; and one-pound blocks of country sausage and liver pudding. A ring of cheddar cheese rested in a wooden box atop the case. Behind it was the ice cream box, from which Noah would fetch fruit-flavored twin Popsicles, Fudgesicles, and Dream-sicles on hot summer days when we could come up with a nickel.

The counter to the right was heaven to us kids. It stretched almost the length of the store, and on it were two low glass cases. The candy counter. We would scramble onto the benches in front of it, clutching a few pennies, and agonize over our decisions. Would we get Kits, Mary Janes, licorice twists, sour balls, caramel blobs, or candy cigarettes, pink-tipped and three to a pack? Would it be peanut butter logs, B. B. Bats, cinnamon bits, stick candy, Hershey Kisses, Twoffers, Fireballs, Saf-T-Pops, Tootsie Rolls or Double Bubble gum wrapped with funny papers inside? How about a set of buckteeth made of sweet, chewy wax? Orange lips? A mustache shiny black? Penny Nips — red, green, and yellow in crumbly wax bottles?

Noah always yelled at us about leaning on the glass and snapped at us to hurry and make up our minds. He didn't have all day to spend with three-cent customers. He was gruff, and a passing stranger might have thought him mean, but we knew better. We liked Noah, and we knew that under his gruffness he liked us, too.

Even after I grew up and moved away, I would drive back to Noah's store now and then for a soft drink and a chat about old times. Noah never changed. He was always as crotchety as ever, grumbling and snapping at a new bunch of kids, who, no doubt, thought that he hid riches in his back room. But his eyes told me that he was secretly happy to see me.

When I drove by and discovered the store closed and empty, I tried to find out what had happened. I talked to Mr. Beck, who had been our next-door neighbor on Fifth Avenue. After he retired from his job in the mill, Mr. Beck had helped Noah in the store at lunchtime for many years. He told me that Noah had had a stroke and was in a nursing home somewhere near Charlotte.

"Doesn't seem right, ol No-ee not being there," Mr. Beck said. "But then nothing much seems right around here anymore."

Somehow, of course, I had to earn the pennies and nickels and dimes I spent at Noah's store. That's the way the world I come from was: kids earned the money they spent. Every piece of gum, every bottle of Dr Pepper was a treat that tasted doubly good because we had worked to buy it. Like Mr. Beck, I sometimes get the feeling that nothing much is right with the world, especially when I see kids cruising malls with tens and twenties to burn on video games and Orange Juliuses. I start to wonder if any of them have ever known the heady pleasure of being in business for themselves at nine or ten.

When I was nine, I started hanging around newspapers, an activity that not only kept me in M&Ms but also led me to my life's work.

Lots of boys in Thomasville wanted paper routes in those days, and you had to be on your toes to get one. To land a daily route with one of the papers that came into town from High Point, Greensboro, or Winston-Salem, you had to be eleven, but the *Tribune*, Thomasville's twice-weekly paper, would let you start at ten.

I wanted to be sure that I got a route when I reached that age, so since I knew some of the older boys who were already carriers, I started presenting myself regularly in the back shop of the *Tribune*. I got to know the pressmen, the linotype operators, the circulation manager. Sometimes I would help "tail" the press, stacking and toting away the papers that it spewed out. On Thursdays, when the papers were fat with ads and came in more than one section, the additional sections had to be inserted by hand, and I joined in that tedious task.

My industriousness was rewarded with a shared route when I was still nine, carried on foot with a canvas bag across my shoulder. When I finally reached ten, I got my own route and my first bike, a J. C. Higgins from Sears, bright red, with a wire basket on the handlebars for holding papers.

A *Tribune* route paid only a nickel a week per customer, and I wanted to make more. So when I turned eleven, I jumped at the route offered by my school principal, who moonlighted as a circulation man for what was then the *Twin-City Sentinel*.

A *Sentinel* route was the least desirable of all the routes for out-of-town dailies because the paper had the least circulation in Thomasville, but I didn't care. I got the prime route, the one that included downtown and most of the northeast quadrant, and I became a circulation-building dynamo. My success was mainly due to the *Sentinel's* constant contests for its carriers. You could win movie tickets, footballs, trips to the fair, and all sorts of things by getting new subscribers. I won a lot of stuff because I was frail, wore patched dungarees, and could put a special tremulous plea into my voice.

"All you have to do is take it for three weeks," I'd say, almost always to the woman of the house, "just long enough to help me win the contest, and then you can quit if you want."

It was a strong and rare woman who could resist my pitch, and over a couple of years I signed up several a dozen times or more. I padded my own route from forty customers to more than sixty and even got new subscribers for other carriers. So effective was I that the *Sentinel* sent me and my buddy Charles Tysinger to Washington with a group of carriers to visit the White House during National Newspaperboy Week. My picture appeared in the *Sentinel*, peering out from under a replica of the Liberty Bell in front of the Treasury Building.

But a day came when I had a falling out with the *Sentinel*. A new subscription contest was announced. The winner was to get a fancy new bike. My old J. C. Higgins was cheap and nearly worn out. That new bike was mine. I knew it, and all the other carriers knew it.

A deadline was set. The winner had to get a minimum number of new subscribers. I hustled as usual. No other carriers even bothered. A couple of days before the contest was to end, I was the only carrier with enough new subscribers to win. I was eager to start delivering papers on my new bike. Then the word came. The contest deadline had been extended by a month. A circulation bigwig from Winston-Salem came to hold a pep rally. For some reason, Leroy West got all razzed up and started hustling. He beat me by two or three subscribers — and rode away grinning on *my* new bike.

I felt cheated. I cried that I was robbed. I threatened to sue. My mother gave my principal and several others a piece of her mind. All to no avail. So I quit and got a route with the *Greensboro Daily News*.

And Greensboro remains my newspaper home to this day, another piece of evidence that where we come from is pretty much who we are.

I was a good, hard-working kid, yes, but I wasn't perfect. Far from it. My childhood is littered with the same misdeeds as that of any normal boy growing up in a simpler day and age. Yes, I have misbehaved, played cruel tricks on my peers, deceived adults. I have even tasted the sweet sin of theft, and for me the taste was sweet indeed.

I've deliberately stolen only two things in all my life. These were multiple thefts, however, and I was never caught. Got away scot-free. Well, not exactly scot-free. I never got away from myself. Guilt about those thefts still dogs me.

I have previously confessed to one of these crimes, though never publicly. While I was growing up on Fifth Avenue, I and several other culprits who shall go unnamed here (let them deal with their own guilt) used to snitch grapes every summer from the vines of Miss Dickens, who lived at the top of the street. We could have stolen from other grape vines in the neighborhood, most of them closely guarded by crotchety old men, but Miss Dickens was blind. Her vines were a temptingly easy target.

Some years ago, when my first book came out, Miss Dickens showed up at the publication party at the Thomasville Library. The first thing I said to her, blurted with great relief, was, "I used to steal your grapes." She laughed and said she'd known it all along. Every kid in the neighborhood had stolen her grapes for years, she said. Because of Miss Dickens, I now turn my head when I see small figures darting among my own grape vines on late-summer evenings.

My other thefts were perpetrated entirely on my own. I think that anybody would have to admit that, if ever there were a perfect crime, this was it. My dad drove a truck for a wholesale company when I was growing up. He sold candy, chewing gum, cigarettes, headache powders, and various other notions and sundries to small stores. Sometimes I accompanied him on his rounds. Riding all day in a truck loaded with sweet stuff presented terrific temptation.

Getting at any of it was another matter. Because of the way things were packaged, stealing without detection was almost impossible. I discovered only one vulnerable item on the truck: Goobers.

Goobers — small, chocolate-covered peanuts — are still around. At that time they came in cartons of twenty-four little boxes, each of which sold for a nickel. But unlike the individual boxes of other goodies, such as Boston Baked Beans, Goobers were not wrapped in cellophane. You need only pull open the end flap of a box, and there were the Goobers, ready for taking.

Left alone in the truck, I would open each little box and take one Goober, only one. Nobody, I knew, would ever miss just one, and I had an unending supply of Goobers.

With a mind that could come up with that scheme, it's a wonder I didn't devote myself to a life of crime. But eventually guilt got the better of me, and shame overcame my sweet tooth. Even so, every time I've seen a box of Goobers through the years, I've felt a pang of conscience.

In *Adventures of Huckleberry Finn,* the young hero concludes that the conscience takes up the biggest part of a person and causes no end of trouble. When I was growing up, that certainly felt true. It really bothered me that I was taking one chocolate-covered peanut from each of the boxes my father would later sell to an unknowing customer. Even as I was diabolically scheming to do so, cunningly perfecting my method, I knew that I was doing something wrong.

It must be a natural part of growing up, that almost innocent walk on the wild side, tempting the fates and risking disapproval of parents and society in order to know what another way of life would be like. Those adventures were an inevitable rite of passage back when I was trying to make the leap from child to whatever came next. A major milestone in my naive flirtation with sin was the hootchy-kootchy show that came for an annual visit to the fairgrounds near Thomasville.

Like so many things, the hootchy-kootchy show is better left to memory, I think. From the perspective of settled adulthood, it's not nearly so exciting as it was to an uninitiated young man. In fact, it's downright depressing — except that it does remind you of what it once felt like, does transport you back in time to an evening when the women looked seductive instead of sad, when the air was filled with excitement and promise instead of resignation and defeat.

"Hey, watch the doorway. We're going to bring 'em out.... Okay, turn the motors on, girls. Turn 'em on. Watch it. We're going to do it. Right down here at the old College of Wiggle Knowledge ... burlee-que, girlee-que, striptease ... the hootchy-kootchy show, the girly-girly show ..."

The barker's spiel was the same. I hadn't been to a hootchy-kootchy show in at least ten years, and I probably wouldn't have put up my own dollar ("That's just twenty-five cents a girl," the barker reminded) to go to this one, but I had a free pass.

Inside the tent, a group of young men crowded around a chest-high stage. Its sides were shielded by drooping, faded curtains hung on plumbing pipes. In front of the stage was a row of low, wooden benches occupied by several people, including a few females. Except for the presence of female spectators, the scene was the same as it was for those hootchy-kootchy shows from my past. At the Midway Showgrounds, halfway between Thomasville and High Point, those shows had a genuine aura of excitement and eroticism. The tent where the "girls" performed was usually pitched at about the same spot where Oral Roberts put his healing walkway when he set up his own big tent at the showgrounds.

I was fourteen when I got my first glimpse inside a hootchy-kootchy show. A couple of buddies and I rode our bikes out to the showgrounds. We were afraid to buy tickets, so we sneaked around back of the tent, lay on our bellies, and peeked under the bottom. I got only a brief glimpse before a roustabout caught us and threatened to turn us over to the police and promised a bleak lifetime in prison if we were ever caught peeking again. I was scared half to death. Going to prison would have ruined my Sunday school attendance record.

The next year, when I was fifteen, my buddies and I used a more ingenious method of getting to see the show. We walked right up and bought tickets. To our amazement, nobody questioned ages. Oh, the excitement of seeing that first fully naked woman (you had to pay extra inside the tent for the full view), of hearing lewd talk all around! The memory is still vivid. But even more vivid is the memory of my guilt and my fear of being seen entering or leaving the show by somebody who would tell my parents. I was sure that on emerging from that tent of sin, my preacher, my teacher, my mother would be standing in line waiting to point an accusing finger at me and shake a head in disapproval and disappointment.

Nearly half a lifetime had passed since I sweated through those guilt-fed fears. Now the show was about to begin. As I took a seat on a bench near the back, a shrill female voice announced the first act. A rock tune blared from squeaky speakers; the lights went appropriately blue; a fat woman in a sequined gown waddled onto the stage.

One after another, four dancers clumped out with garishly painted faces and freakish wigs, stripped immediately to pasties and G-strings without the slightest pretensions to the art of striptease, then stood moving sluggishly, their sagging and bulging parts bouncing several beats behind the music. When the audience failed to greet their energies with enthusiastic appreciation, the dancers scowled, muttered insults, or feigned indifference. This wasn't the same. Not alluring. Or exciting. Or titillating. Or exotic. It was just . . . sad. I left wondering about the future of hootchy-kootchy.

I told a friend about this later. He is a few years older than I am, a long-time connoisseur of hootchy-kootchy. He'd been to this show, too, and had left after about half of it.

"You have to be fifteen," he said. "You have to be fifteen."

A few nights later, I was back at the fair and happened to pass the show. It was not yet eleven P.M. The barker was giving his spiel: "If you're under eighteen, you wouldn't understand it. If you're over eighty, you can't stand it. The show for red-blooded men and broad-minded women. . . . This will probably be our last show of the night. . . . Take it back, girls. Start it up. It's showtime . . ."

When the dancers went back, the crowd that had gathered to look them over and hear the spiel broke up, wandering on along the midway. Nobody approached the ticket booth. The barker turned to the wigged head of one of the dancers sticking out from the curtain. "Looks like we've already had our last show," he said.

It is one thing for the hootchy-kootchy to be gone forever. After all, it was never a permanent part of life, was only a dalliance, nothing more. It is quite another thing to discover that a significant portion of the very foundation of your experience is lost, has disappeared as surely as the magic of the hootchy-kootchy has evaporated.

No place is more integral to a child's sense of who he is, of where he belongs than his home, the place that he lives with his family. But following close behind is his school, that building he goes to when he leaves his home. A school is always much more than a building, just as a home is more than a house. A school is the people, the growing recognition of the mind and its powers, the sounds and sights of growing up and defining who and what we are. Long after we graduate and move on to other lives, the school itself looms large in memory, is a touchstone against which we measure all our efforts and relationships. But nothing lasts forever, not even schools. They too must depend on memory alone to keep them alive.

When I went back to Main Street School, it was the right time of year. The maples were changing colors on the big front lawn, just as they had been another fall, long ago, when I sat in Mrs. Burrus's third-floor English class, daydreaming when I should have been studying, watching through the tall windows as the trees changed, day by day. It was the right time of year for going back to school, but I was too late. What I was looking for didn't exist anymore. Once, a semicircular sidewalk (I had known intimately every crack and hollow spot in it, for I skated there regularly as a kid) began by the street at the front corners of the block-wide lawn and swept past the maples up to a flight of wide concrete steps that rose to the big glass front doors. Beyond the doors more steps led to the main hallway, the offices, and the auditorium.

On a steaming hot day in the summer of 1959, I stood by the office door at the top of those front steps awaiting a verdict. It was all up to "Bugs-and-Flowers" Miller (in his biology class he required every student to collect and identify, by scientific and common name, fifty insects and flowers, thus the nickname). Due to a ridiculous requirement of the Thomasville City Schools that certain subjects be passed and a minimum number of credit hours attained, I had not been allowed to graduate with the rest of my class. For weeks I had suffered through an elementary science course in summer school, seldom cracking a book, never listening to Bugs-and-Flowers as he droned away at the front of the class. I had been in summer school before, and I knew that it was designed not to teach but to punish and cleanse, and I—a prisoner doing time—had spent the weeks doodling, dozing, and thinking of going off to Florida and becoming a beach boy.

Bugs-and-Flowers grinned.

"I guess you know that you don't deserve it," he said.

I mumbled a humble acknowledgment.

"Here," he said, tossing me a packaged diploma, "take it and get out of here before I change my mind."

My graduation exercises.

I didn't think it significant then, but I was the last person to graduate from Main Street School, for the new high school was already nearing completion on the edge of town, and when classes began again at the end of summer, Main Street School, which was built in 1922 and had once sheltered students of all twelve grades, was to become Thomasville's first junior high school.

My only thought at that moment was to follow Bugs-and-Flowers's advice, and I fled, feeling freer than I ever had felt, down the steps, through the doors, bounding onto the sidewalk, and out across the big lawn where the maples looked cool and green. Never again, I swore, would I darken the doors of that building.

I kept my word, too, although I had never really meant the vow so seriously.

Now decades later Thomasville has a brand-new junior high, and when I heard that officialdom was thinking of tearing down Main Street School, I knew that I had to go back. I wanted to walk its long, dark halls again, to see in the emptiness the familiar faces and hear in the silences the sounds that are so much a part of me.

I intended to do it. I kept intending to right up until it was too late. Still, standing under the maples, with no school building left, dim echoes of the past came welling up.

"Leroy West, Darrell Hall, Jerry Bledsoe, report to the office immediately!"

The public address system would crackle throughout the school. Usually we heard it faintly from a far corner of the ball field, where we lounged contentedly under a big willow oak watching a girls' phys-ed class. We knew, of course, what it meant: Mr. Teat had discovered us missing again from chemistry lab, probably accidentally, for he was a man so deeply absorbed in science that his clothes were always mismatched and his fly frequently was open (he was not too absorbed, however, to eventually flunk us).

W. S. Horton, the principal, was an imposing figure with a worried, deeply lined face, and he would sit, as he always did, looking at my records and shaking his head. Then he would look up at me sadly and with a plaintive voice say, "You could do so much better if only you would try."

Late again.

I live only a block from the school on Fifth Avenue, and although I always take the shortcut across Billy Smith's backyard and through the big hole under the schoolyard fence, I always seem to be late.

Grammar-grade rooms are in the basement, and Miss Lillian Yow, my first-grade teacher, a short, plump woman with a kind face, who wears high-topped black shoes, somber dresses, and twists her hair into a bun, will be waiting for me at the entrance, far down the hall from the room, and she will run with me, past the cafeteria with its lunch smells already stirring, past the furnace room and the doors to the old waterlogged dungeon of a gym, urging, "Hurry, hurry!" and when the tardy bell catches me, as it often does, I will brace for a pain in the ear, for she is a pincher.

So many memories stirring with the leaves of the maples . . . memories of faces and names of teachers and classmates neither seen nor thought about for more years now than I care to count . . . and memories of the building itself, red-bricked and triple-winged.

It always reminded me somehow of a fortress. I knew every dark and exotic corner of it, and I loved it, played there after school and on weekends when I was a kid. I can still see it as clearly as I did then.

A bulldozer brought me back to the present, interrupting my reverie as it pushed through the gray earth, crunching over crushed bricks and shattered glass, all that remained of Main Street School. The empty spot where it had once stood seemed so much smaller

than the building I had known, smaller than the empty spot that I
felt within myself. Another crucial thing lost. Gone forever.

I have never been one to be much concerned about my roots,
figuring it was better not to know about my ancestry, lest it throw
me into hopelessness and despair. I never bothered to learn the
names of my ancestors beyond my grandparents. Johnsons, I knew,
were in the family, as well as Jacksons, Atkinses, and Draughns, but
that was the extent of my knowledge. Somewhere along the line I
did learn that Bledsoe is an English name. My son, Erik, came
home from school and told me that he had found Bledsoe in a book
about family names — ours comes from Old English, Blaeds-hoe,
according to Erik's book. It was supposed to mean prosperous. Erik
wanted to know what had happened, and I tried to explain that by
the time we inherited the name, the family bloodlines had
obviously been corrupted.

It is not a very common name, Bledsoe, but occasionally I have
encountered it in my reading and rambling. I remember reading
somewhere that a Bledsoe surveyed the original state line between
Virginia and North Carolina. Mark Twain sometimes mentioned
the Bledsoes of Tennessee, but he doesn't seem to have held them
in high regard.

I once passed through a little coal mining town named Bledsoe
in the mountains of Kentucky. There wasn't much there. The town
store had two nice outhouses perched rather precariously on a
hillside. I took a picture of them. When I questioned the people in
the store about the origins of the town's name, nobody knew. They
pronounced it "Bledsaw" and said there hadn't been anybody of
that name around for years.

Our own family lore has it that two brothers (nobody is sure of
their names) came into the hills of North Carolina during the time
of Daniel Boone. One stayed, and the other went over the mountains with Boone (who is also supposed to be tied into the family
somehow). Our branch of the family is the one that stayed. The
other branch, being more adventurous, went on to distinguish itself.

Of our branch, the most distinguished member I ever encountered was a fellow I met in a fancy restaurant one night. His name

was Marty Bledsoe, and he turned out to be a distant cousin of my father's. His work took him from table to table in restaurants and nightclubs all over the country. He analyzed handwriting for a small fee. I knew he was distinguished because he was wearing a tuxedo.

Such was the shallow, frivolous nature of my knowledge about being a Bledsoe until I met Bob Siegfried, who lives in Richmond, Virginia. Bob is perhaps the world's expert on Bledsoes, a distinction earned through thirty-five years of diligent attention to the Bledsoe situation. His charts on the family total more than three hundred.

I first learned of Bob and his interest in Bledsoes when I received his invitation to a meeting of the Bledsoe Family Historical Society, an organization that, until he wrote me, I didn't know existed. Before I got around to calling Bob, the meeting had been cancelled for lack of interested Bledsoes. Still, Bob and I had a good talk. He told me that he first became curious about the family because his grandmother on his father's side was a Bledsoe. Once he started tracing her lineage, the whole clan began to intrigue him. To him, we became one big jigsaw puzzle.

From Bob I learned that one Bledsoe from the past had been president of the Union Pacific Railroad. Even further back, Bledsoes had fought in the Crusades; they had even lived in Bledsoe Castle in Bedfordshire, England. All the American Bledsoes, as far as Bob can tell, descend from one George Bledsoe, who arrived in Northumberland County, Virginia, on the Chesapeake Bay, in 1653. George's offspring have, since then, distinguished themselves in a number of ways. They include noted jurists, professors, admirals, industrialists, U.S. senators, and even one vice-president — Richard M. Johnson, who served under Martin Van Buren.

As much as I appreciate Bob's knowledge, though, I find myself still not very concerned with such large, abstract exploration of my past. It's fun to find those things out, sort of like winning Trivial Pursuit, I guess. But in the long run I find, as I grow older, that what really interests me is more immediate, more personal, intimate, and detailed. These days, I find that I am, in fact, interested in my roots, if by roots we mean those closest to us who have nourished our experience and who grounded us in those things that really matter, that have always mattered and always will.

Bob has spent a lifetime digging deep into being a Bledsoe. Now I realize I too have spent a lifetime absorbed in my Bledsoe-ness. It's just that I have mined a narrower region. I do not know as much as Bob and probably never will. But what I know I know well, well enough to acknowledge that these people — these Bledsoes and the others who stand inseparable from them — they, too, are part of where I come from.

New Home Church of Christ sits in a field behind Manny Doby's house on a narrow gravel road in the foothills of the Blue Ridge Mountains near Dobson, the county seat of Surry County, North Carolina. For sixty-seven years it was a little white church with a bell in the steeple and towering oaks on the north side, where moss grows on the stone steps. But the congregation decided that the little frame building was no longer sufficient and set about building a new one. They put it right in front of the old one. The new church is compact, its walls are brick, and it, too, has a bell in the steeple. It really isn't that much different from the old one except that it is new and, thus, more desirable.

The cemetery, common to most country churches, lies beside the old building and behind the new, facing the morning sun. It is neatly trimmed, and many of the graves sport fresh flowers. The headstones offer a roll call of church membership past and present: Wolfe, Doby, Johnson, Hamlin, Davis, Snow, and Bledsoe. My grandparents are among the Bledsoes buried there.

Bledsoes were a part of New Home Church from its founding although none is active now because circumstances forced all of them, including my grandparents, to move away, in search of better lives, from the red tobacco fields on which they had barely thrived. But New Home is still the old home church for our clan of Bledsoes, and each year on the first Sunday of August we return for a reunion.

On this homecoming Sunday, the family members who have remained in the country arrive in dusty pickup trucks and park in the shade. The city folks drive up in shiny cars they leave to bake in the sun. Most family members, especially those, like us, who drive considerable distances, arrive just as the church service is ending. The preacher has given the call, and the congregation sings plaintively: "Why-y-y not, why-y-y not, why not come home to him now?" The plea wafts hauntingly out of the building and dissipates over the hills.

Five long tables borrowed from another church line the cemetery fence under the oaks, and several women, all strangers to me, do their best to keep them from being overrun by children and insects that have begun swarming in anticipation of the coming feast.

My daddy's first cousin Monroe Snow brings the soft drinks, in washtubs filled with big hunks of ice, in the back of his pickup truck. He always brings the drinks because he can get them wholesale.

Every woman arrives lugging food, big boxes of it. Fried chicken. Whole baked hams. Beef roasts cooked until they collapse at the touch of a fork. Potato salad. Deviled eggs. Snap beans boiled with great slabs of streaked pork fat and topped with whole pods of okra. Black-eyed peas and purple crowder peas. Corn on the cob and off. Monstrous pink tomatoes sliced into big slabs. Biscuits, some of them stuffed with slices of country ham and thick patties of homemade sausage. Huge hunks of corn bread, crusty brown. And desserts. Oh, the desserts! Cakes and pies of every description. The tables seem incapable of holding it all.

When the time finally comes to get at it, the preacher prays so long in blessing the food that I begin to wonder if somebody has failed to invite him to eat. After the blessing blessedly ends, it is "How are you?" and "I reckon I'll do," and "You're sure looking good," and "So are you," and "Come here, I want you to meet your daddy's daddy's brother's oldest boy's daughter from West Virginia," and " Have you tried Aunt Ider's pumpkin surprise? It's the best thing you ever put in your mouth."

When dinner, as the family always calls the midday meal, dissolves into restrained burps and congratulations, the women busy themselves at the table, cleaning up and seeing whose desserts haven't been eaten, while the children chase one another, throwing windfall apples from a gnarled old tree out back, and the men perch on upended soft-drink crates, talking and laughing and smoking.

"Going to be some mighty good singing here this evenin'," Cousin Monroe announces.

The gospel singing begins in midafternoon, and the church fills for it even though many of the young people opt for a softball game in an empty field beyond the cemetery. The Bledsoe family is amply blessed with preachers, and all of them show up for reunion. They call one another "Brother," and they always promise not to preach during the singing. But they just can't help themselves.

Woodrow Snow, another of my daddy's first cousins, slips in just a little preaching while his quartet performs. Between songs Gene Snow, yet another cousin, also a preacher and a member of a quartet, can't resist preaching just a bit about loving our neighbors.

"Lot of people, I despise their ways," he says, "but thank God I love their souls."

Uncle Rufus, my daddy's brother, who has his own quartet and his own church, doesn't even get into the first song before he sets in.

"I didn't come here to preach this afternoon . . . ," he announces, but then the Spirit hits him, and he's off for a good ten minutes, flailing his arms, striding back and forth, belting it out, hardly pushing for a breath. Uncle Rufus can really get going when the Spirit hits him.

A collection is always taken to help out Cousin Monroe with the cost of the soft drinks, which come, he says, to thirty-four dollars and something. He gets $36.85 and says that's fine. He says that he wants to thank everybody who gave and that he hopes the Lord will bless everybody who didn't have any to give.

"And if you had it to give and didn't, then we hope you stump your toe," he adds.

Then he announces that the extra money from the collection will go toward next year's drinks.

After the singing, people begin drifting off to their cars and trucks, pausing for hugs and handshakes and to tell one another how good it has been to see them and how they ought to get together more often. But finally we must leave New Home Church to old remembrances, to long-dead family members, who watch over its grounds for another year, keeping it ready for the ritual of our return. The church and the cemetery, the ceremony of the reunion are handed to us, ready-made connections to those we come from and those who share our heritage. But there are other valuable ways to make such connections, ways that are more independent, that require more effort on our part, perhaps, but that serve up their own rewards. This second kind of reuniting with our past is what drew my father and me back to his home territory. For years he longed to own land in the mountain county where he was born and reared. When he realized that dream, he wanted to share it with me, so we made a journey to that piece of the past he had managed to racapture.

The paved road ended at a small frame house with pigs rooting in the yard, and a gravel road angled off to the right through the woods toward the river. An old man wearing overalls waved from the yard as we passed.

The gravel road was wide, obviously maintained, but a short distance along it, we turned onto a narrower road, red dirt, rutted and no longer tended. Trees grew so close by its sides that it was wide enough for only one vehicle. For some reason, I thought of that scene from the movie *Deliverance*, the one in which the canoeists make their way down those ominous forest roads to the river.

The road forked. To the left it led to an abandoned homestead. A heavy wire suspended from two posts must have once blocked the road to the old place, but somebody had torn it down. Off a little spur to the right, a turn-around point, big piles of freshly dumped household garbage lay under the trees. The road to the river went straight ahead, but it wasn't really a road any longer. Small trees were growing from it, and it had eroded to the point that it was little more than a series of deep gullies.

"Are you sure this thing will make it?" I asked my dad.

"I've been in worse places than this with it," he said, stopping to put the vehicle into four-wheel drive.

The piece of his past my father purchased is a tract of wilderness along the river that includes the old homestead we passed. He had often described the place to me after his trips there—bear tracks he found, signs of many deer, big trout in deep pools.

"Is there rhododendron?" I had asked him.

"The river bank is thick with it," he replied. "It's like a jungle. You can't even walk through it."

So I told him I'd like to dig up some little ones, and we had come. He had even promised that no digging would be necessary, that I could just pull them up, roots and all, from the river sand.

As the van lurched toward the river, through mudholes and over gullies, tree branches slapped the windshield, and my father ducked reflexively. When people drove wagons and rode horses, this was a major road, but no more.

Dad stopped to show me an old church he had told me about. The sanctuary was close to the road, almost hidden by trees, just the skeleton of a tiny frame building, its roof now collapsed. But once the silence of these woods was filled with hell-fire preaching, hallelujahs, and old-time hymns. The graveyard was even closer to the road than the sanctuary. The one visible tombstone bore a forlorn epitaph: "Gone but not forgotten." Trees with thick trunks were growing from the grave.

Near the river a thicket of tall rhododendron had comandeered the road, making further passage impossible. We abandoned the van and made our way on foot the short remaining distance downhill to the river and its banks crowded with heath. The water was clear and swift, a beautiful, hidden, noisy, violent passage through the forest.

"Boy, I'd like to come back when these rhododendron are blooming," I told my father.

"You cast a fly into the pool right back up under that steep bank there," he said, "and you'd have a trout in a minute."

The loose sand relinquished the smaller rhododendrons and laurels with little effort on my part. The back of the van was quickly filled. Dad searched the sandbars and found the tracks of a mother bear and one cub, along with the hoofprints of many deer. On the way back up the hillside to the old farmhouse, we stopped and used shovels to dig some small white pines, ferns, and yuccas growing wild near the old church. All of these, along with the rhododendron and laurel, I later replanted at home.

The main part of the old house was made of thick logs, roofed with tin, now rusted. The chimney was rocks chinked with mud, and although it still stood, great sections had fallen. Onto the back of the house, a kitchen, a large pantry, and a big porch had been added, balanced precariously on stacks of flat stones, the unpainted wall boards gray with age.

When my dad bought the place, the house was filled with old furniture, including a wood range and a wood heater. His plan was to carry some of the stuff away (I myself had laid claim to one of the stoves), but we discovered that raiders had hit, stealing everything of value. The house was now filled with nothing more than junk and trash, so much that it was difficult to walk through it.

"Look at that," my dad said, pointing to a half-gallon blue Mason jar of corn on the cob. "I bet that corn was put up thirty years ago, and it still looks good."

From the litter I salvaged some burlap sacks to wrap around the rhododendron roots. There seemed to be a thousand empty liquor and wine bottles strewn about. On the back porch I found a liquor bottle with a recent date on the stamp and spotted drying vomit on the rocks that served as steps for the porch.

"Some old drunk's been sleeping in here," I said.

My dad went down the hill and wandered around.

"There's one clump of creecy greens down there that would make a mess," he said upon his return.

We stood for a few minutes looking at the old place. Once it was a well-tended farm, but nature had reclaimed it almost completely. Jonquils and forsythia bloomed near the house on this spring-like late-winter morning, and gnarled old fruit trees were beginning to bud. My dad was born on a place almost exactly like this, only a few miles away, and in that place he spent his boyhood.

I turned to him and said, "It must have been really beautiful once."

"It was," he replied. "It was."

Those branches of the Bledsoe clan—the stationary and the adventurous—that we can trace back to the early North Carolina

Bledsoes were made real to me by two women who loom large in many of my memories. From the perspective of adulthood, as I wander now and then through the events and the stories I remember, my grandmother—Ma-Ma, we all called her—and my Aunt Vivianne keep cropping up to remind me that those impulses to stay put and to reach outward are inherent in my very Bledsoe-ness. I cannot escape what they represent, nor would I want to. The lessons of their lives help me make sense of myself and the world I live in now. They are real women; their stories, rich with distinctive detail and idiosyncratic impulses. But they are also types, representations of the ongoing struggle in all of us, to place ourselves comfortably on the spectrum of what is safe and known and what is out there to discover if only we will take the risk.

Ma-Ma is my living symbol of the stable branch of our clan. For many years, my grandmother was a member of the same small Methodist church, and she never missed a Sunday if she could avoid it. Once, when she found herself without a ride, she hitchhiked to church. Made it, too.

She wrote to me about that episode and threatened to hitchhike to see me when the grapes were ripe if I didn't come to get her. So I called to arrange a trip with my Aunt Doris, a fellow grape lover, serving as chauffeur. I figured we could combine grape-picking with a birthday celebration for Ma-Ma.

"I'm getting just like a baby," Ma-Ma said with a laugh when I called to say that the grapes would soon be ripe and that she should plan to come help gather them. "My hair's falling out. My teeth already fell out. I can't talk. You know what they say, 'Once a man, twice a child.' There's something to those things they wrote two thousand years ago."

"Wait a minute," I said. "Let's back up just a little. You know you're never going to get anybody to believe that you can't talk."

Talk? Why, Mary Belle Atkins could talk up a storm. She could talk up a *hurricane*.

Despite the birthday that added another year and her observation that she was reverting to babyhood, she came and talked as usual. Talked for hours.

"You know," she said, "I can remember everything that happened from the time I was a little girl until I was about forty better than I can remember what happened last week. I can remember every little detail."

She went right on to prove it.

For the longest time, she had been telling me that she wanted to write a book about her girlhood. The problem was that she didn't think she could get the words right. But if I would help just a little with the wording, she thought she could do it, and she was sure that it would be a bestseller.

What she really wanted was to tell me and let me write it. So after that trip to celebrate her eighty-sixth birthday and to gather grapes, I sent her back home with a cassette tape recorder and a stack of blank tapes. I showed her how to operate the recorder and told her to talk into it every day and tell everything she could remember. I figured it was time to harvest those stories that only she could tell.

She was a little apprehensive about being able to work the thing, but I assured her it was simple and she could do it. I gave her careful instructions and repeated them several times, just to be sure.

A few months later, my brother Phil returned from a visit to Ma-Ma bringing the recorder. She'd sent it back, he said, because it didn't work. I checked it and discovered that the brand-new life-long batteries I'd installed before she took it were dead.

Phil didn't bring back any tapes with the recorder, but later, when Ma-Ma returned for another visit, she brought those back, too. She told me all about the troubles she'd had with the recorder. She'd talked on only one of the tapes, she said, but she didn't know whether anything was on it. After she left, I played that tape. A complete transcript follows:

Ma-Ma (in a very distant voice): "Jerry, can you hear me from there?"

Laughter from my twin cousins, Jan and Trish, her granddaughters.

Trish: "Yeah, he should be able to hear you from there."

More laughter.

Jan: "We don't want to start this now, we're . . ."

Ma-Ma (louder now): "Yes, I do! Jerry, I haven't talked on this any yet because every time I start talking it goes off, and then I wait for somebody to come and fix it, and then when they come, unless they set right here and hold it, it goes off. Them little wheels quits turning, and I haven't talked any about old times and the prices of things and how we lived up in the country, but if it's still going now, I'm going to try and talk some. Trish is holding it and if they'd stay a while but everybody that comes . . ."

Silence.

Click.

Click.

Silence.

Ma-Ma: "I'm going to . . . uh . . . (turning away from the microphone) hold it down here because I think I've got my hand the wrong way . . ."

Trish (explaining the on-off switch on the microphone): "If you hold it up here, you cut it off."

Ma-Ma: "I believe I do!"

Long pause.

Ma-Ma: "Now I'm going to try to talk about something you can put in the book from now on . . . (turning to Trish and Jan with a little giggle) I ain't going to talk to you no more. Listen, uh, well, last night, uh, uh, uh, yeah, Sunday . . ."

Trish: (indecipherable).

Ma-Ma: "My birthday was Tuesday, you know, and it was . . . ah, uh, ah, . . . and Betty (her niece) come over and she fixed it, and I started to tell, and Betty wanted to set down in here and listen and looked down and the thing was *off*. And, uh . . . so . . . I'm going to tell something now. I'm going to tell . . . I was borned, you know, in '94, 18 and 94, and I'm going to talk about how the people lived where I lived in the mountains of North Carolina in Surry County, and I'm going to tell how the people lived in them days and what they worked for and how a lot of people lived from now on. I think I'll tell some each day, if it'll keep running. I don't know if it will or not, but . . ."

Click.

Silence.
End of tape.

So my idea to have Ma-Ma preserve the memories and stories she'd been telling for as long as I can remember didn't work. I'd hoped to make sure that there'd never come a day when I wouldn't be able to hear her stories and her laughter, but she became another victim of high-tech failure. So did I.

That means I'll have to do the telling myself, from what I remember. I'll have to be her voice, let hers rise up from my own memories whenever it will.

I always called her Ma-Ma, the name I had for her when I was very young. She was the grandparent I had the longest, but I didn't spend as much time with her as I should have.

Well into her nineties, she insisted on living alone, fiercely independent, in a yellow house in Danville, Virginia. She was very proud of that house. She bought and paid for it herself.

She was born and grew up in a big white house built in 1837 (it's still standing) on a four-hundred-acre farm in the foothills of the Blue Ridge Mountains near Mount Airy, North Carolina. She bore eight children. One, known to the family as little Hazel, died in infancy. The other seven were brought to adulthood in a mill-owned house in the cotton-mill village of Schoolfield, on the edge of Danville.

"I cooked three big meals a day," Ma-Ma once told my wife, Linda, "and I thought Santa Claus had come when I didn't have to bake two kinds of bread at a meal."

Pa-Pa, who died when I was eleven, didn't believe that a woman should work outside the home or have money of her own. He believed firmly that a man was ruler of his family. He and Ma-Ma had some differences about that. After all of the children were grown, Ma-Ma asserted her independence. There was a separation. I was just a child then, and I never heard the details. But I do know that Pa-Pa moved back across the state line to another mill town called Leaksville, where he lived out his last days in a grungy room over a downtown cafe. Ma-Ma hit the streets selling Avon to take care of herself. She did well at it, too.

Two of my most vivid childhood memories are of the sweet perfumed Avon smell of her house and her laughter echoing through it. She always smelled of Avon, even when it had been many years since she sold any, and her laughter remained unchanged as well — always loud, raucous, and often employed.

The wonder was that Ma-Ma could still see life with so much humor after the staggering blows the years had dealt her. Her youngest child, Ray, died. I was the one to take her the news, and all I could do was hold her as she sobbed over and over, "Lord, why couldn't you have taken me and left him?" Four years later, cancer claimed her eldest child, Herman, and again we feared for her. She was eighty-six then, her heart no longer strong. But that was only one of her ailments.

"My hip is just going away," she told me with a laugh. "Look at that. Don't know where it's going. Look how my feet swell. I must weigh twice as much at night as when I get up in the morning. I fall down all the time. Just fall down. I fell down at the supermarket, fell right out in the floor and couldn't get up."

These were not complaints, mind you, merely statements of fact, delivered with amusement that she could find herself in such a fix. She worried about these ailments, though, at the same time she was making jokes about them, because she was afraid they could land her in a hospital.

"You know what can happen if you get in those hospitals," she said. "They can send you to one of those old nursing homes. Don't even let you go back to your own house. And you can't do anything about it." She snorted. "Might as well just let you go on out like the elephants to the dying grounds."

For Ma-Ma one key to avoiding the dying grounds was humor. Another was staying involved and busy: taking care of herself, going to church, participating in senior-citizens' activities. On occasion, she even found herself the object of romantic attention. She cackled when she told of one would-be suitor who showed up at her door.

"The last thing I need is some toothless old man hanging around," she said.

This particular suitor she found totally distasteful, and just reporting the incident was enough to get her riled up. According to her, he was a little guy who wore a heavy, double-breasted suit on even the hottest days. She had noticed him a few times when he had gotten off the bus near her house and gone to call on one of her neighbors.

One day, though, as she was planting flowers in her front yard, she saw him coming toward her. He stopped at her walkway and said, "How are you today?"

"I'm all right," Ma-Ma said. She was stooped over working and kept right at it, paying him no attention.

"I brought something," he said.

She saw that he had a paper bag in his hand.

"You did?" Ma-Ma said, continuing her work.

"It's for you," he said, opening the bag to reveal a box of candy. "Sweets for the sweet."

Ma-Ma always interrupted the story at this point with a shudder and a long "Ooooooh."

"Sweets for the sweet," she'd say with utter disdain. "I thought, 'Oh, murder!' I couldn't stand him. He made me sick. He was that kind that you couldn't stand, you know. Big ol' double-breasted hot coat. I knew he couldn't drive a car, getting off the bus like that."

"I don't eat candy," she told him, working right on. "I can't have candy. Doctor won't let me have it."

That rebuff sent him off, with his candy, but that wasn't the end of him. He later showed up at Ma-Ma's door with a friend, both of them carrying banjos. *Banjos*, of all things. She told him that she was sorry, but she just didn't have time to listen.

This guy was nothing if not persistent, though. One Saturday, my uncle Ray came from Raleigh for a visit. He and Ma-Ma were getting ready to go shopping, but she was waiting for a man who owed her money to come by and pay her. When Ray appeared at her bedroom door to tell her that a gentleman was waiting to see her, she thought it was that man, bringing her the money. Her smile quickly disappeared when she walked into the living room, however.

"There stood that same little ol' man with that double-breasted coat on and it hot," she told me.

"Is this your son?" he asked her.

"Yes, this is my son," she said coldly.

"Well, I'll go if your son's here and come back tomorrow."

"Why are you coming back tomorrow?" Ma-Ma asked.

"Well, I don't have to," he offered.

"I know you don't. And I wish you wouldn't."

The man mumbled good-bye and made a hasty departure. Ray looked shocked.

"I'm surprised at you, Mama," he said. "I didn't know that you would speak to somebody that sharply."

"Well, Ray, you don't know it all," she said. " That little ol' man, I can't stand him. *Come back tomorrow*! On Sunday. For what? Wears those awful old clothes. Can't even drive a car."

"Now listen, Mama," Ray said. "You don't lie, do you?"

"Of course not."

"Well, tell me what would you have done if he'd been a nicely dressed man with a Cadillac sitting out front?"

"I'd have said, 'And what time will you be here tomorrow?'"

For many years Ma-Ma made an annual trip to Florida to visit friends and relatives, but as she neared ninety, she had to give that adventure up, primarily because of her gout, a disease she didn't think she should have.

"Gout?" she had harumphed to the doctor who diagnosed it. "I thought only old men got gout."

"Old ladies get it, too," he replied with a quick grin.

The disease made it hard for her to negotiate stairs. She had to have support and winced with pain on every step. Although Florida, of course, is mostly flat, almost everybody that she went there to see seemed to have stairways that she couldn't avoid, so she began to conclude that trip was hardly worth the pain.

Besides, on the last Florida trip she made, the gout got her into quite a predicament, one that may have helped her make the decision to abandon Florida once and for all. She arrived at the airport for the flight back home to find that she would have to climb a ramp to get into the plane. Impossible, she told the airline clerk.

No problem, said the clerk. As soon as the other passengers were loaded, somebody would wheel away the ramp, guide the lift into its place, seat her in a wheelchair, and whisk her right up to the door. Two young male attendants in snazzy uniforms were assigned to see that she was comfortably and safely embarked. They were very pleasant, and she was flattered by their attentions.

The ramp was removed, the lift set in place. The attendants rolled her onto the lift and took up stations beside her. The lift started up. A female flight attendant was waiting in the open door of the plane, smiling down at her.

"Welcome aboa—," said the attendant as the lift reached the door. "Hey!"

The lift didn't stop. It just kept going.

"Whoa!" hollered Ma-Ma.

It kept going.

"Hold it!" yelled one of the male attendants.

It continued right on, halfway up the door, then all the way past the top. The attendants kept yelling, and still the lift kept rising, right on above the plane.

"I knew it had to stop sometime," Ma-Ma told me later. "I just wasn't sure when."

It did finally stop, and there she sat, high in the air, looking down at the plane and enjoying a bird's-eye view of the airport. All of the attendants seemed highly anxious. Several inside the plane leaned out of the door calling reassurances up to her.

"They kept telling me, 'You're going to be all right. Don't worry. You're going to be all right,'" Ma-Ma told me later. "I said, 'I know I'm going to be all right as soon as I get down from up here.' I was just afraid the plane might take off and leave me sitting up there."

While passengers with window seats craned to get a look at her, people on the ground were scurrying about frantically trying to get the jammed lift into reverse.

"I heard one of them say, 'Well, it was working all right yesterday,'" Ma-Ma said. "And another one said, 'We didn't use it yesterday.'"

Shortly after the plane's captain came to the door for a look, a maintenance truck screeched to a halt beside the plane, and men with tools got out. Ma-Ma said that it took about five minutes for them to figure out what was wrong and lower her back to the airplane door. The airline employees kept apologizing, but Ma-Ma assured them that she hadn't been scared or worried at all. Indeed, she said, she had enjoyed the ride.

When the flight attendant finally rolled her into the plane, the other passengers gave her an ovation. Ma-Ma said this probably was the only time gout had ever brought anybody so much attention.

Some of the attention her age brought to her, Ma-Ma would just as soon have done without, though.

We had all gathered at Ma-Ma's house a few days before her ninety-third birthday — children, grandchildren, great-grandchildren. One card was lying out in a particularly conspicuous place although she was careful not to mention it. We, of course, made much ado over it.

"From the President," somebody oohed.

"And Nancy, too," said another.

Ma-Ma laughed. "She can't half write, can she?" she said of the First Lady's shaky signature.

As we were getting ready to take her to her favorite restaurant for a birthday dinner, I lost track of where Ma-Ma had gotten to. I found her in the bedroom, trying to tie a bow in the sash on her pretty blue-and-lavender birthday dress.

"You don't ever want to be ninety-three," she told me disgustedly as she fumbled with the sash. "You can't do anything. I can't even put my clothes on right. I put 'em on inside-out, backwards, upside-down." She laughed her raucous laugh. "Can't hardly walk. I fall all the time. It's awful to be so old."

This wasn't exactly true. She was still living alone, still tending her little house, cooking for herself, keeping the flowers blooming on her porch. She was still adamant about "old-folks' homes" and nursing homes, still sure she'd rather be dead than live in one.

"Don't you dare ever let them put me in one of those awful places," she said to me many times. "Just go ahead and shoot me first."

She preferred the comforts and the freedoms of her home. She had given up hitchhiking by this time, but she still managed to get to church on most Sundays in a special van sent for elderly members. Her little house was arranged so that she had things to hold onto and to pull herself up on where she needed them. An aluminum walker and a sturdy cane also stood ready for her use.

I helped Ma-Ma tie the sash, and once we got to the restaurant, she cheered right up. We all sang "Happy Birthday," and the organist dedicated a tune to her: "The Old Gray Mare."

"She sure ain't what she used to be," Ma-Ma agreed.

As usual, humor proved to be her saving grace. The frustration of getting herself dressed vanished, and she turned into the Ma-Ma we all knew best—the consummate storyteller. That night she told one of the funniest stories of all on herself and the problems associated with trying to grow old gracefully and independently.

While visiting at my cousin's house not too long before her birthday dinner, Ma-Ma had needed to go to the bathroom and was seated there with her girdle around her ankles when she realized that she had no wall bars or other apparatus with which to pull herself up. She decided to raise herself by pushing on the toilet-paper dispenser. She was just beginning to rise when the dispenser broke loose from the wall, toppling her sideways, head-first, and bottom-up, into a cat-litter box.

"There I was in that mess," she said, "and I couldn't move."

My aunt heard her muffled cries for help and rushed to her aid, only to find her thoroughly stuck between the wall and the toilet. For a while it looked as if the rescue squad might have to be called, but Ma-Ma was adamant that she was not about to allow strangers, especially male strangers, to encounter her in such a predicament. After a difficult struggle, she managed to free herself with nothing injured but her dignity, although it did take a while to get the cat litter out of her hair.

Another story she told that night demonstrates both her humor and her independence, but it also speaks loudly of the limitations of aging. Ma-Ma got tired at the supermarket and decided that she simply couldn't go another step. She summoned the manager and told him that he'd have to fetch her a chair.

"A what, ma'am?"

"A chair. I've got to sit down," she said. "Go get me one."

He did, too, and there she sat in the aisle, the Queen of Produce, smiling and greeting quizzical shoppers as they wheeled their carts around her until she was rested enough to go on.

When she finished this story, I asked her when it had happened. I'd heard it before, of course, but I couldn't remember how long ago the episode had taken place.

"It was two or three months ago, wasn't it?" she said.

"More like two or three years, I think," I said.

"Months, years, they're all the same to me anymore. I'm telling you," she said with a laugh "it's terrible to be old."

My aunt Vivianne was Ma-Ma's total opposite. While Ma-Ma chose to stay put and flourished in her little house, Aunt Vivianne literally traveled the world. Ma-Ma's whereabouts were as predictable as the date of Christmas; where Aunt Vivianne was likely to be at any given moment was as hard to figure as the course of a storm in the days before high-tech weathermen. Staying put just wasn't in Aunt Vivianne's vocabulary, even when she pretended she was ready to settle down.

No one was surprised when she came rolling in from Florida, driving her little white station wagon, a '61 model, jam-packed with trunks and suitcases. We assumed she was home for another of her unannounced visits. We were surprised, however, when she announced her intention to stay. After a lifetime washed in stage-lights, wrapped in furs, traveling all over the country, indeed, the world, she had rented a house. Of course, renting wasn't buying, so she was, as always, keeping her options open.

At the outset of this experiment, she told me, "You can go everywhere and see everything, but then you want to be with your own people. My people are here."

Aunt Vivianne was a singer. She started singing in church on Schoolfield, Virginia, went on to radio at twelve, and eventually became a nightclub star. "Decorative Vivian [she later added the extra *ne* to her name] Hubbard, songbird of the Silver Fox Cocktail Club, smiles wistfully for the photographer," said the cutline beneath the picture in a yellowed edition of the *Washington Star*. She was a sultry, buxom redhead when that photo was taken, a real babe.

An "After Dark" column made note of her rendition of "Tango of Roses," which the columnist described as "sung ever so softly by vivacious Vivian Hubbard in the Hi Hat." Journalists in other cities mentioned that she sang in five languages other than English — French, Greek, Spanish, Russian, and Hawaiian. One wrote that her style was "decidedly churchlike." Later, the Danville newspaper headlined: "Schoolfield's Own Vivian Atkins [her maiden name] Reaches Top Billing Singing Popular Songs."

After eighteen years in show business, Vivianne sold real estate in Cleveland and took photographs in nightclubs, still singing occasionally, if the spirit so moved her.

"Here I am on a camel in Algiers," Aunt Vivianne said as we sat going through a suitcase filled with old photos and newspaper clippings. "See the silly things I save."

Her hands flailed dramatically as she talked. Her laugh was deep and throaty. Now and then, she would lapse, actress-like into put-on voices.

"Well, before I ever went anywhere, here I was in the Red Cross in Danville," she said, looking at another snapshot.

There were many pictures of Little Tony and Uncle Charlie. Aunt Vivianne was married more than a few times, but she had only one child. Little Tony, as he was always called, died of a rare form of meningitis when he was three. It had been many, many years ago when we sat going through her photo albums, but the hurt was obviously still as real as ever for her.

At the time we were reminiscing, Uncle Charlie was her last husband. Two more would come later, but at the time he was the one. "The only man on the face of this earth who was really good to me," she said. They met in a nightclub in Florida. Uncle Charlie was Russian-born, Jewish, a singer of light opera. He was an unassuming little man, short, chunky, bald, toothy. He seemed shy to me, just the opposite of Aunt Vivianne. He had been a singing waiter in a Bavarian restaurant.

After their marriage, Aunt Vivianne gave up singing. "I let Charlie go on and be the singer," she explained. "See, he thought my type of singing wasn't anything much." When I think of Ma-Ma splitting with Pa-Pa over her right to independence, it seems odd that Aunt Vivianne was the one to capitulate to a man's ego or opinion. But she did.

She and Uncle Charlie traveled back and forth between Chicago and Miami, the two cities where he worked regularly. The Internal Revenue Service got after Uncle Charlie about unreported tips, and, according to Aunt Vivianne, their agents hounded him into a heart attack. The day he was released from the hospital, the agents were waiting at his door. Fiery mad, Aunt Vivianne, having succeeded in several fights with less formidable foes, took on the IRS. The federal agency was soon begging for a settlement.

Uncle Charlie never quit singing. He finally keeled over in mid-song at a nightspot in Florida and died on an Easter Sunday. Aunt Vivianne was left alone, a babe no more, and she was uncertain about her future. She was frightened.

She took up crafts and joined a church. The way she figured it she had started out there, and it was the perfect refuge at such a lonely time in her life. Even after Uncle Charlie's death, she didn't consider singing professionally again. She said, "I don't care about it at all unless it can help in a religious way. If it can help somebody, I'll do it. Otherwise, I don't give a hoot."

So, it seemed, after years of wandering, Aunt Vivianne, home and active in her church, would become more and more like Ma-Ma. She was winding down. She had the wanderlust out of her system, once and for all. Or so it seemed.

But only a few months after announcing that she was home to stay, Aunt Vivianne had to return to Florida to wrap up some business there. She left with every intention of returning to her widow's quarters and sinking back into the comforts of the memorabilia she had surrounded herself with. So, when we didn't hear from her for several weeks, we began to worry.

Then came the surprise, which shouldn't have been a surprise at all, if we had thought for just a minute about exactly who it was we were dealing with. One evening the phone rang. It was Aunt Vivianne, bubbling with excitement, telling us about a wedding — her wedding. In our minds we were all thinking, "Let's see now. This will be number . . . ," but we were, without exception, eager to look him over, this Uncle Walter we were acquiring so unexpectedly.

My grandmother talked to him over the phone. "Humph!" Ma-Ma said. "He called me Mama. Old man, seventy-one years old, calling me Mama. Why, he's not much younger than I am. Calling me Mama. How do you like that?"

About all that we knew about Uncle Walter was his age and that he was English, a builder by trade. He had been good friends with Aunt Vivianne and Uncle Charlie for several years. His wife had died the year before he and Aunt Vivianne made their announcement.

Nobody who had ever known Aunt Vivianne would have believed their eyes when the happy couple arrived for their promised get-acquainted visit. Who would ever imagine Aunt Vivianne coming from Florida spending her nights in an Arctic sleeping bag in the back of a pickup truck? That simply was not her style. The very idea would have been . . . well, laughable. But, ah, for love . . . anything, it seemed.

Uncle Walter turned out to be short and wiry with wispy white hair and leathery sun-browned skin. He spoke with a Scottish brogue. I thought he would wrench my arm out of the socket when we shook hands for the first time. He was plainly an individualist. He liked to rough it, and it was his policy never to stay in motels or eat in restaurants. He had built his own camper to go on the back of a half-ton truck, in which he had traveled most of the country.

So when he and Aunt Vivianne got ready to make their visit to her family, he got out the gas lantern, the camp stove, and sleeping bags. They stopped along the way, and Uncle Walter cooked all of their meals. His specialty, he announced, was stew. And, of course, Uncle Walter being English, they also stopped to prepare morning and afternoon tea on the camp stove. Aunt Vivianne thought it was nice, but she did have her reservations about spending the night in a sleeping bag in the back of a truck.

"I thought I'd freeze to death in that thing," she said with her usual hearty laugh, "but, you know, I got in there and I was perspiring."

When Uncle Charlie was married to Aunt Vivianne, he always referred to her as the "General," but Uncle Walter announced that he had demoted her to Pfc. That was our first clue that things might not be all moonlight and roses for these unconventional newlyweds.

Sure enough, Uncle Charlie's successor was not to be Aunt Vivianne's "last" husband. Her marriage to Uncle Walter was followed by another brief and finally annulled marriage before she came to rest for what truly did appear to be the last time in a high-rise for the elderly in High Point, North Carolina, about twenty miles from where I live. But settled never meant what it usually does if you were talking about Aunt Vivianne. She wasn't even really elderly, but she had taken to describing herself as "a little old lady with heart trouble."

Despite her real or imagined infirmities, she managed to sing in five languages for the mayor and other dignitaries at an affair at the high-rise. She did say that she was embarrassed by her voice, which had been too long out of practice.

Despite her reduced sense of life's possibilities, Aunt Vivianne was incapable of going for very long without something totally surprising and miraculous happening to her. When she called to say that she had a story for me, I hadn't heard such excitement since the last time she got married. She kept saying that this story was "one for Ripley," as if her entire experience didn't fit that description. She assured me that what she had to tell me was different. "It's strange," she said. "It's weird. It's just not normal." It's Aunt Vivianne, I thought.

It seems that she had walked uptown to meet my sister-in-law, Janet, for lunch. She didn't know exactly how to find the restaurant where they had arranged to eat, so she stopped a woman on the street to ask for directions. When the woman told her how to find the place she was looking for, Aunt Vivianne noticed a strong accent.

"Are you Greek?" she asked her, in Greek.

"Ah, yes," the woman replied, looking quite understandably surprised to have encountered a fluent speaker of Greek on the streets of High Point.

"Long years ago I lived on the island of Cyprus," Aunt Vivianne told her, still speaking in Greek. "That's where my baby was baptized."

Aunt Vivianne's first husband, Tony James, was a Greek immigrant. The birth of their son, Tony, Jr., had been a very difficult one, and not long after the child arrived both the baby and Aunt Vivianne had fallen seriously ill. In his prayers, Tony, Sr., promised that if his wife and child recovered, he would take his son back to his home village in Cyprus to be christened. They arrived on the island in June 1935 and stayed for nine months. Tony, Jr., was christened on August 15, his first birthday.

Two-and-one-half years later, Tony, Jr., died: Aunt Vivianne's life shattered; her marriage ended. Tony eventually moved back to Greece and became a minister before his death. Aunt Vivianne disguised her sorrows and went on to enjoy her singing career and to survive a string of marriages, some good, some not so good. But she never had another child.

"Oh, where in Cyprus?" the woman asked.

"A village called Komayailou."

The woman suddenly grabbed Aunt Vivianne, kissed her, and with much excitement said, "Please, please, come and meet my husband. He's from Komayailou."

It turns out that the husband operated another restaurant, the Golden Nugget, not the one Aunt Vivianne was on her way to. She told the woman that she didn't have time then, that she had an appointment, but that she would return the next day. They exchanged names, and Aunt Vivianne went on to her luncheon with Janet.

When she went to the Golden Nugget the next day, as anyone familiar with Aunt Vivianne would have known she was bound to do, a smiling Pete Davis greeted her.

"Are you really Vivianne?" he asked. "You don't remember me, do you?"

Aunt Vivianne had no idea who he was.

"Ah, I remember you so well," Pete said. "You dance so well, sing so well. I'm Getou's son."

Aunt Vivianne was flabbergasted. She couldn't believe it. Getou was Tony James's first cousin. And Getou had tended Tony, Jr., while they were in Komayailou. Later Aunt Vivianne told me that Getou had loved little Tony almost as much as she had.

Instantly, the scene in the restaurant became a homecoming, complete with hugs and kisses and a flurry of excited talk as memory after memory came flooding back to the "old lady with heart trouble" and her long-lost family from Greece. Aunt Vivianne was amazed, after the fact, at how much she had forgotten about those years of her life.

But, she told me, she had never forgotten the reception the family in Komayailou had given her when she arrived there, a young mother from the Deep South of the United States. "There were roses strewn for us to walk on," she recalled, "and a big dinner, eight courses. But I couldn't eat much because they had left the eyes in the lamb."

Pete Davis, who had been only ten when Aunt Vivianne went to Komayailou, told her how he had come to this country, met his wife, Roxanne, and settled in High Point, how he had named his three sons for Tony and his two brothers. And, yes, he said, his mother, Vivianne's beloved Getou, was still alive, still in Cyprus.

Aunt Vivianne had not seen or heard from Getou or any of the people of Komayailou since 1935, but she had always loved them and kept them in her heart and mind, she told me. After their first meeting at the Golden Nugget, Aunt Vivianne kept in touch with Pete and Roxanne Davis. Tony Davis, namesake of her first husband, came to take her to the Greek Orthodox church. Pete showed up at her apartment with a huge Thanksgiving dinner.

"They act just like I had never been away, and it's forty-three years later," she told me. "I tell you, Greek people are kind of clannish, but once they accept you, there is nothing on earth they won't do for you.

"I keep thinking this couldn't have happened in a million years. It just couldn't have happened. There's a purpose. I don't know what that purpose is yet, but I really believe God put me right there on that corner at that moment for this to happen.

"These people have been so good to me. I want to do something for them, yet what can I do? I'm an old lady with heart trouble."

Yet . . . a few years earlier, as a hobby, Aunt Vivianne had taken up making artificial flowers that looked and smelled like the real thing. She decided to make roses for Getou.

I think back to the rhododendrons and other plants I carried out of my father's piece of his past. The old house was a symbol of decay, destruction, neglect. Yet all around it were signs of life, of stubborn resistance to the very forces the house itself had come to embody. And I was able, with my father's help, not only to carry away some of that life, some of the essence of where I come from, but also to imagine that place, that world, as it must have been for him, when he was young and full of hope about what lay ahead.

Now those plants flourish in my yard, far removed in time and place from their origins, but firmly rooted in the present, clear reminders of both the past and our hopes for the future, signs of both change and continuity.

Whatever pain springs from our sense of loss as we wander back through time and remember the world we come from, the places and the people that define us, that pain is far outweighed by the miraculous joy of discovery and rediscovery that Aunt Vivianne's Ripley-like encounter with her past on a street corner in High Point makes entirely valid.

The Main Street School and Noah's store and the young boy throwing papers from his worn-out J. C. Higgins bike from Sears may be long gone. I may worship only once a year at New Home Church of Christ. Bledsoes I love and depend upon may decline and suffer and finally disappear as surely as the house on my father's homeplace has. But the sights and sounds and smells of it all will last forever in my mind, just like Aunt Vivianne's roses, sent across time and space, to another woman, so different yet so like her, too, a woman who had loved what she loved. I can almost smell them now, can almost see and hear it all.

Seasons I
Move
Through

$\mathcal{B}$efore there were buildings old enough now to be decaying, even before there were the people to create them, there was nature. One of the biggest advantages of country living is that it puts you so directly in touch with the natural world. Drought and rain, heat and cold, water and the soil—all of these and much more are intensely present in the country. They insist upon your attention and, once they have it, remind in a thousand ways that we are as connected to earth, its waters and air, as we are to one another.

For country dwellers seasons are perhaps the primary measure of time. The continuous cycle of change regulates what we do in our spare time, wrestled from the demands of our city selves and what passes for work behind a desk. The seasons tell us when to plant, when to gather wood, when to keep ourselves safe indoors, isolated from icy cold or parching sun, when to rush outside to embrace spring's hopeful promise, autumn's melancholy beauties.

Gradually, since I've lived in the country, I have come to know myself and my moods better. I can now calculate with an accuracy that impresses me at least how I'll feel, how much energy I'll have, what task I'm likely to undertake by reading nature's messages to me. Nature provides challenges, real work—the hardest I've ever done—insights. As I've learned her rhythms, I have also discovered my own.

For days my patience had been tested. The sun shone. Warm breezes blew. Each day I walked to the garden to check, but the soil remained too wet to work. After last summer's disastrous drought, I had sworn that I would have nothing to do with a garden again. How many times have I made that vow? A hundred? A thousand? Every time I've known it wasn't so.

Having suffered through all of my sad gardening experiences, a person with half a brain surely would come to the logical conclusion that growing a successful garden is impossible, that all those beautiful gardens other people have are optical illusions. But this is beyond logic, a deeper need that wells up each year as surely as spring comes. Instinct. I can no more control it than a cutworm can keep from chomping down my fragile vegetable plants as soon as I set them out.

A spell of bad weather always makes it seem unlikely that warm, sunshiny days can continue even when they arrive. But they eventually do, and the ground finally seems dry enough to plant. I roll the tiller down the hill, check the oil, and crank the machine for the first time since the previous summer. While the engine idles, I go to the house, get out the onion sets, cabbage and broccoli plants, and seeds of lettuce, carrots, spinach, radishes, green peas. I lug fifty-pound sacks of fertilizer down the hill, fetch a bucket, a hoe, a row setter from the barn.

The tiller handles easily, cuts deeply, leaves dark, damp trails. After only a few passes, my boots leave deep imprints in the soft soil.

And I attract an audience.

At first, I notice only a few. Then others arrive. Soon there must be forty or fifty robins in the field with me. They scramble to the edge of the garden at my approach then rush in behind me as I pass, pecking at the freshly turned earth. My tiller provides a feast of lively red wigglers and sluggish fat grubs. I feel bad about the wigglers being devoured; every garden needs them to keep the soil aerated. But the robins are acting on instinct in plucking them from their havens and swallowing them like strands of stray spaghetti, a perfectly natural thing. The worms have to accept it. About the grubs, my feelings aren't quite so charitable. Whenever I spot one, I pick it up and toss it in the direction of the robins: one less summer beetle to strip my plants of foliage.

I till a section big enough for a large spring garden, pull the tiller out of the way, and start to pick up stakes to lay out my rows. But a commotion erupts behind me. I turn to see not thirty feet away a hawk swooping down on an unwary robin. The hawk must have been watching from one of the big trees near the edge of the garden all along. The strike had been quick and silent, the approach unnoticed not only by me, but also by the other robins, now fleeing in panic.

The hapless robin in the hawk's grasp struggles frantically, shrieking in terror. Feathers fly from the scuffle. Surprised and startled, I'm not sure what to do. "Hey," I shout, not really knowing why.

I take a tentative step toward the struggling birds, but without loosening its grip on the squirming robin, the hawk turns its head and gives me such a fierce look that I halt in my tracks. Confident that I present no further threat, the hawk patiently secures the smaller bird in one claw and makes a slow takeoff, like a heavy cargo plane lumbering into the air, flying low through the orchard to the woods up the hill. Even after it disappears, I can still hear the robin's feeble cries.

There is nothing to do but go on about the work at hand. I feel bad but have to remind myself that the hawk, like the robin and me, is only obeying instinct. Two hours later, my seeds are all planted. My garden is in, as we country people say. To some degree, it is already a success. It has fed the robins. It has fed the hawk. Even now it is feeding the surviving worms with the fresh organic matter I turned under for them. It may eventually feed me and mine.

At least we're sure it's spring.

Spring rains can seem unending, coming in torrents. Our hillside, already saturated from a big snow, once became a bog in such a storm. At the back door, where the brick wall takes a slight dip, water stood to the door sill. Periodically, I had to go out in my rubber boots and push it away with a broom and a shovel to keep it from creeping into the kitchen.

Between rounds of that outdoor duty, I was busy inside emptying and rearranging pots, pans, bowls, buckets, and trash baskets that were spread about the dining room. There water poured through the ceiling in at least a dozen spots in spite of my best roof-top efforts with buckets of tar. I tried not to take it as a sign from above when the biggest hole of all presented itself directly above the spot where I usually sit to write. More sensitive souls might have read this as literary criticism, but I just moved my chair.

I remembered the cellar too late.

Dug under one corner of the house years ago, our cellar was obviously designed for the express purpose of collecting water in the event of drought. When we came to this house, the cellar was filled with muddy water, and it has since been something of a hobby for me to pump it out. I'm on my second pump already.

But all my efforts to keep my little cellar dry were to no avail, so I finally spent the better part of two weeks in that damp hole building rustic walls and shelves to create a place for storing the wine I was planning to make from my anemic, weed-choked vineyard. I made accommodations for the water, building my shelves three feet off the floor, figuring I surely should be able to keep the water from reaching that high. The wine itself I stored upright in tall, five-gallon carboys.

During this particular monster of a spring storm, we had been wet for two full days before the cellar crossed my mind. I rushed to check it and found the sturdy carboys submerged. My wine had drowned.

The worst was still to come. Darkness descended suddenly and unexpectedly. Thunder rumbled and news of a tornado watch came from the TV. The rain came so hard that for a while I thought the house had been set asail. When it slackened, I went outside to discover that the big creek in the bottom across the road had become a lake, wandering aimlessly through the trees.

But my own little creek concerned me more, for it had gone wild. At the road, where it was trying to squeeze through a culvert too small to accommodate it, the creek had climbed a five-foot embankment, spilled into the field where Tracy Saunders plants his garden, and was threatening to flood the road.

Once that creek was my joy. It was the most beautiful part of our place. It flowed through heavy woods, over several small falls, around boulders. Ferns, moss, wild lilies, violets, wild azaleas, May

apples, and muscadines grew along its banks. Here and there were
sand bars where smooth pebbles collected in a myriad of colors.
Small fish and crawdads played in the pools, withdrawing to the
shelter of overhanging roots and banks at even the quietest
approach. The water was so clear and lively that when I first
tramped the place with surveyors they stooped and drank from it.

Then, a couple of years ago, developers bought a large tract of
forest adjoining our place. They raped it for the timber before
sending bulldozers, in spring, as if they wished to emphasize the
irony of their destruction. The big machines gouged broad roads
with wide banks and shoulders all through the hilly land before
they departed, leaving roads unpaved, shoulders and banks
unseeded to erode into our fragile creek.

Once when Erik and I were prowling along the creek searching
for its source, I spotted an old chimney through the trees. I pointed
it out to Erik. The discovery surprised me because I'd thought I
knew the area well from previous prowling and from conversations
with old-timers. But I'd never heard about a house in these woods,
or in what was once woods, before the developers wreaked their
particular brand of havoc.

Our search for the creek's source was in part a search for signs of
hope that it might someday recover. What had been my tranquilizer,
a wondrous thing to soothe my soul with its calm beauty, had
become a raw gash in the land and within me as well. Its source was
also the source of my best solace. But we weren't having much luck.

We had just found the two cattail bogs where springs rise alongside one of the roads to create our creek when I spied the old
chimney. When we got closer, we found that wild growth had
overtaken the house before it was reduced to a pile of splintered
boards and rubble. Only the chimney remained intact. It was built
of flat fieldstones, chinked with clay, and the fireplace was now
home to a colony of mud daubers. The dwelling appeared to have
been a one-room cabin, added onto at some time or another. The
floor had been built of logs laid on piles of flat stones. I pointed out
the hand-hewn logs to Erik.

We stepped gingerly through the wreckage, keeping a wary eye
out for snakes. Erik picked up an old can and tried to read the label.

It is the nature of abandoned houses to possess eerie auras, and this one was no different. I sensed other presences, and Erik must have, too, for we both began wondering aloud about the people whose home this had been.

Traces of an old wagon road passed near the house, and we followed it through the wild growth, batting away spider webs, until it disappeared into the trees at the foot of our own little mountain.

Later, I stopped to see Ector Bonkemeyer, whose land also adjoined the tract where the old house had been. Oh, yes, he said, he knew about the house. It had been a one-room log house with a sleeping loft, and it had been standing until recently when marauders ripped it apart and made off with the logs.

According to Ector, a fellow named Beane used to live there. Ector understood that Beane had built the house as a young man and reared his family in it. Ector, who was seventy-eight at the time, remembered Beane as a very old man during his childhood. He figured the house had been built about the time of the Civil War, maybe before. He could remember when the fields around it had still been tended. But after the old man died, the farm had changed hands, and woods eventually reclaimed the fields.

So many years had passed since anybody lived in the house that even the road that once led to it had disappeared. Until the new roads had been cut, the only way to get to it was by tramping through the woods, and few people knew that there was anything to tramp toward. But just as surely as the developers had destroyed the woods and my creek, they had destroyed the house by exposing its presence and inviting the vandals who carried it away piece by piece. It wasn't my house, of course, and it wasn't Ector's. But he finished his story with a note of disgust in his voice.

He said, "It's never going to be the same around here again."

Thinking about my creek, I had to nod my agreement. "I know," I said. "I know."

The developers' invasion, my discovery of what remained of the old house, and my conversation with Ector all happened nearly a year before the monster storm. But the storm served to make clear that we would be measuring the impact of what the developers had wrought for quite some time to come. The little creek had to carry many times the run-off it did before, and with all that water came tons of red mud. The creek never flows clearly anymore, but during this storm wildflowers were ripped from the banks by the frenzied run-offs. Even big trees fell and blocked the stream's passage through the ravaged banks, adding to the buildup of potentially dangerous mud we would have to contend with during nature's next violent outburst. Our creek had been murdered.

With dread in my heart, I walked out to check after the worst of the storm had passed. I could hear the creek all the way from the house. Once so gentle and calm, it now roared in anger. Savagely, it ripped at its banks in a red fury. I didn't have to walk far to see that another big tree was down on its banks. Despairing and unwilling to see more, I squished back to the house in a fury of my own.

Fighting my dark mood, I made ready for a family gathering. Linda, Erik, and I climbed into the car and set out. It was late afternoon, and in the west a narrow yellow band appeared in the gray sky. It broadened rapidly, a break in the clouds, and soon a sliver of sun appeared. Everything took on an eerie yellow glow. A television transmission tower suddenly became a golden ladder into the clouds. Directly above us, the clouds were on two levels, the upper gray and turbulent, the lower fast-moving wisps of pink and gold—a spectacularly beautiful sunset that reached out to envelop and free rain-burdened spirits.

Surely this was a sign, perhaps a promise, of gentler and brighter days ahead. But it proved to be a false promise. Within an hour, rain was beating down again, pounding my spirit back into the bog.

Once I emerged from my spiritual bog, I realized that it wasn't nature I was mad at. It was the developers and what they had done to nature. Without their interference my creek would have continued to babble along, soothing and refreshing me as I had come to expect it to. The storm would have affected it, of course, but it wouldn't have transformed it into the monster it became that spring if men and machines hadn't entered into the equation. I'm a reasonable man. Give me enough time, and I'll figure these things out. That's one of the advantages of growing older. You get wiser, more philosophical. Things like temperamental springtime weather can be handled in stride.

When I was younger, for example, if we'd had two hard freezes in the first three weeks of spring and snow all day on April 8, I'd have been seething. My blood pressure would have been in the danger zone. I'd have been cursing the elements, raging at the fates. Now I am calm. These things don't bother me anymore. I've learned to live with the vagaries of nature, no matter how extreme or spiteful they may be.

Of course, I spent the first thirty years of my life largely unconcerned about such matters. I rarely noticed the violent thrashings of dying winter overlapping into spring. Not until I'd moved to the country and become consumed with the idea of growing things did I begin to pay it attention.

At first, in my ignorance and horticultural enthusiasm, I failed to heed spring's wild whims. Lulled by its gentleness and warmth, I overlooked its schizophrenia, tried to ignore the cold, vengeful, violent side of its personality that always lurked under the surface, waiting for the right moment to unleash its furies.

Oh, was I smug. When old-timers told me about May frosts that wiped out foot-high corn, I smiled tolerantly and went right on planting my corn in early April. I put out my tomato and pepper plants as soon as the warm days seemed to have a hold. Invariably, I'd find myself scrambling around frantically on some chilly, late April night, anxious and angry, covering plants with paper bags, burlap sacks, newspapers, and sheets of plastic, trying to protect them from coming frost.

I used to take that personally. I became convinced the weather was out to get me, and it enraged me. I would sit up all night fretting and feeling helpless when temperatures dipped into the twenties while the peach trees were in full bloom or the even more sensitive grape vines were sprouting. I'd be out early the next morning, checking for damage, drifting from anger into despondency that would last for days.

This went on for years, for I am a notoriously slow learner. But gradually slivers of wisdom began to penetrate the thick husk of my brain. I began to see that even in those rare years when a few peach blossoms managed to survive, the peaches were later claimed by insects or rot or some exotic happenstance. And cold was no big deal to the apple trees because it slowly became obvious that they never had any intention of bearing fruit in the first place. If any cherries escaped the clutches of spring freezes, it merely meant I'd have to face the stress of futile combat to wrest them from the birds. Any grape blossoms that successfully avoided April's frigid stings did so only to provide targets for hailstones and summer nectar for wasps and bees. It got to the point that I sort of hoped a frost would nip the pear blossoms so I wouldn't have to feel guilty about all those pears rotting on the ground in late summer with all of those jars of pear preserves from previous years' crops still uneaten on the pantry shelves.

I learned perspective. It was just as easy, after all, to see spring's lapses back to winter as a favor as it was to look at them as enemies bent on destroying me. So when a spring freeze wipes out any hope for peaches and pears for another year, I simply shrug it off. I've never had peaches before, so I won't miss them, and I don't want the pears anyway.

Admittedly, that freeze could also take out my radishes (something that almost never happens, for radishes are hardy indeed) and kill the broccoli plants in my tiny, unheated greenhouse. But radishes will grow from seed in thirty days, and maybe I can buy some broccoli plants. These freezes are no matter for grave concern.

So I'm not going to let it get me worked up. I couldn't do a thing about it if I wanted to. Forcing up my blood pressure while railing at the fates wouldn't do a lick of good. Thank goodness I have learned to control myself, to accept nature in all her mystery.

Among spring's unending mysteries is the way that the season manages to call particular attention to one of its glories. That one plant, one creature, one startling quality of light becomes our touchstone for that spring, marks it in our memory as distinct from the spring that precedes or follows it. One year it may be azaleas; another, jonquils or robins or dogwoods. Years from now I know that my memory will call forth one season of my life as the spring of the wisteria.

I don't recall that I even knew what wisteria was until I moved to the country. Oh, I'm sure that I had seen it. Probably I had even fleetingly appreciated it without knowing what it was. But if I recognized it on sight, I don't remember it, and I doubt seriously that I did.

Then we bought the overgrown, broken-down farmhouse that was to become our home, and I quickly came down with a massive case of wisteria tangle. At the base of a walnut tree near the side of the house was a wisteria the likes of which I've seen only a few times since, and those were in professional gardens. This wisteria had completely overtaken the walnut tree. Its trunk was a great twisted thing as thick as my leg. Its leaves formed a canopy over the tree.

I was trying to whack out a clearing around the house when an old fellow I had hired to help make the house livable examined the wisteria and said, "This ol' vine is strangling that walnut tree. If I was you, I'd try to get it out of there."

I didn't know what kind of vine it was or whether it had any value at all, but I knew that walnut trees were to be treasured, not only for their tasty nuts but also for the price their lumber will bring. If this vine was strangling a walnut tree, it had to go. I went at it with ax and saw and lugged it away to the trash fire in big chunks. But the outer branches of the tree remained entwined with ungrounded vine, and for years afterward decaying pieces rained down during windstorms.

I felt good about saving my walnut tree from this choking entanglement until a couple of years later when a neighbor asked me, "What happened to that magnificent old wisteria that used to be at your place? Did it die?"

I wasn't sure what he was talking about until he explained.

"That used to be just about the prettiest thing around here in the spring," he said. "I used to drive down there just to look at it."

Then I realized that I had probably made a mistake in cutting down that vine, and I was ashamed to admit to my neighbor that I had done such a thing. I told him that I had pulled out the old vine but left some sprigs that had rooted from runners. Indeed, that had happened. In fact, I had dug up one of the sprigs and set it out at the base of a persimmon tree not far from the walnut that had served as support for the mother vine. It is from these sprigs that I have learned all that I know about wisteria.

Wisteria is from the bean family, and surely it was the stalk that Jack climbed, for if any vine could reach through the clouds it would be wisteria. It rivals kudzu in its ability to grow, spreading in all directions in great leaps and bounds. Its ambition seems no less than to rule the world, and if ever there was an Armageddon of plant life, no doubt it will be fought by kudzu and wisteria.

I'm sure that the wisteria vines on our place must capture small animals that happen near because I've become so entangled in them a time or two that I thought they were going to claim me. I'm convinced that those vines reach out and snatch food off the picnic table that sits under them.

One of those sprigs that I left to grow has overtaken a high cedar-pole trellis I built for it and gone on to seize my little office and the power lines that lead to it. It has set its sights on the garage, already establishing a foothold. The other little sprig has overwhelmed the persimmon tree and spread to two other nearby trees, including the walnut under which the original vine grew.

Both vines send out ground runners for hundreds of feet, pushing their way under porches, buildings, patios. They are always grabbing my feet and tripping me or ensnarling my lawn mower blades and forcing them into impotence. In midsummer, when the wisteria is at its peak of growth, I fight it almost daily with limb snips to keep it from overwhelming the hillside. I haul away cartloads of leafy vines to feed the goat.

I would not tolerate these vines if goat food was their only produce. It's their flowers that I value, great clusters of fragrant lavender blossoms that hang like grape bunches. They come in early spring before the leaves develop and the vines spurt their wild growth. That is, they are supposed to come then. But every year, just as the buds begin to open, a late frost settles in our little hollow and kills them. We have never had more than a few scattered clusters of late blossoms.

I was certain that this spring of the wisteria would be no different, and I watched the vines with my usual anxiety. They had just begun to open their blossoms when a cold front moved through. I had to go out of town as the front was arriving, and I was certain that I would return to find my wisteria covered with brown, dead buds. Instead, I came home to a sight of rare and complete beauty. The blossom bunches hung from the trellis, the trees, the power line, the porch, my little office. And, as my neighbor said years ago, they were just about the prettiest things around. They easily made up for all the trouble and frustration that produced such bounteous beauty.

Of course, bounty of all kinds leaves its residue, apart from memory. There are always the realities of that residue to cope with, and putting the task off never makes it go away. My pile had been growing since fall. It was in the garden, by the edge of the vineyard, and it began, appropriately enough, with the garden debris — the tough okra stalks I chopped out of the weeds to signal the end of the year's horticultural follies. To the okra stalks, from time to time, I had added prunings, fallen limbs, lumber scraps. The pile burgeoned dramatically after the ice storms of winter downed big limbs and felled whole trees. More recently, it had received dead azaleas, camellias, and yuccas, victims of the winter's cold.

All in all, the pile grew to a respectable size, more than ten feet high, maybe twenty feet in diameter. I had intended to burn it early in the spring, before gardening time, but for whatever reasons I put it off. Then came the drought and with it wildfires and burning bans. When rains finally did fall, other matters kept me from attending to the pile, but circumstances eventually forced me to deal with it. I had planted seeds nearby, and I knew that if I didn't burn the pile before they sprouted, I'd have to leave it all summer, a haven for rodents and snakes, an eyesore.

So it was that on a drizzly May evening, after days of afternoon thunderstorms, I approached the pile as darkness was falling. I carried a flashlight, a can of kerosene, and what once was called a penny box of matches.

One corner of the pile I splattered liberally with kerosene. I tossed a match, which was deflected by the tangle of branches. A second match bounced downward like a steel ball in a pinball machine and fluttered out. The third I held to a kerosene-doused branch until it nearly burned my finger, but the branch showed no inclination to burn.

A fourth match fell through the branches and touched off a small flame on the ground. I grabbed the can, splashed some more kerosene on the pile, and the little flame blossomed and danced. With a woosh the fire spread, the oil flaring to life with a quickness that sent me retreating with my paraphernalia.

Within minutes, I had a roaring bonfire. It crackled and popped, the reports echoing through the hollow. The flames licked at the night, twenty feet high, twenty-five feet, even higher. Sparks soared a hundred feet or more. Now and then a big flaming chunk coursed into the air before realizing it was too heavy to fly and falling back to the fire's edge.

A whippoorwill that had been calling frantically from just up the hill suddenly fell silent. Awed at the spectacle? Only the frogs, crickets, and other tiny creatures that create the nighttime cacophony that passes for quietness in the country remained unimpressed.

I retreated further, to the corner of Erik's porch, where the dogs quietly joined me, the three of us entranced by the fierceness of my fire. Even there, I could feel the heat, and the orange glow was bright enough that I could have taken notes if I had been in a note-taking mood. I'm sure that the glow in the sky could be seen for miles. Could that be the reason that traffic seemed to increase on our road? Could these passing vehicles be occupied by curiosity seekers hoping to witness tragedy?

Sorry, no tragedy here. No burning barn. No house aflame. Only the showy passing of an impressive limb pile.

As the furor of the fire began to subside, I was drawn closer, carrying my shovel, hoping to refuel the blaze with branches that had fallen out of its reach. The heat drove me back after only a few seconds, my face radiant. For several minutes, I darted in and out of searing range like a jabbing fighter, flickering limb ends toward the fire with my shovel before staggering away, sweating and breathless, beaten by my own exertions.

Ten minutes later, the fire was a spectacle no longer, the flames barely waist-high. Only occasionally did a spark leap out in a fizzling attempt to escape. The dogs lost interest and went off to snooze. The whippoorwill began to call again, this time much closer, at the edge of the field. Another answered across the creek.

A horse whinnied in Bill Dulla's pasture across the road. On the other side of the hill, somebody turned up a stereo. An obnoxiously loud car tested every gear to its limit somewhere in the distance. A jet roared overhead, out of sight. A sliver of moon peeked through the clouds.

I swatted at a mosquito on my neck, leaned on my shovel, and stared at the flickering embers. My feet were muddy, my face hot, red, and beaded with sweat. I smelled of wood smoke. But the dying of the fire, I realized, had brought a deep sense of satisfaction, as if a primal hunger had been fed.

When Andy Warhol made his famous comment about fame and fifteen seconds, he was referring to people. But the things of nature appear, in this modern world at least, to have their own moments of glory in the public eye. Consider, for instance, the kiwi, a fruit few had ever heard of, much less eaten, until it suddenly became inescapable in restaurants and even began showing up in grocery stores. Or the raspberry, an altogether admirable berry, I think, but need it be the berry of the decade, serving as the basis for every dessert sauce and garnishment created in the eighties?

Along this same line, as surely as summer comes, we start to hear the praises of the peach sung by voices all across the land. Newspapers offer us peach pictures and peach recipes. TV crews rush to film heavily laden trees and maidens blushing over baskets of blushing fruit. Mounds of ripe peaches lure us into roadside stands. And if all else should fall silent on a Sunday afternoon, the grinding of ice cream freezers churning with fresh peach concoctions in backyards surely would be thunderous.

Peaches are a fine fruit. No question of that. Far be it from me to disparage them. They deserve all the attention lavished upon them. But early summer is also the time of another fruit that gets little notice amidst the yearly hubbub raised over peaches. I speak of June apples, for which I would like to offer a few words of much-deserved praise.

When we moved to our country place, we were blessed with two apple trees. One is an ancient, gnarled thing, its trunk riveted with woodpecker holes. It is a fall producer, but it is cranky and sporadic at its work. I'm still not sure just what variety of apple it bears — when it chooses to do so. Uncle Walt Saunders, who lives on the hillside across the hollow from us, calls them "ol' rusty apples," which is as good a name as any for them, I guess. But another local fellow who stopped by one day and examined them at my request said, "Why them's just them ol' horse apples." Which is okay, too, I suppose.

The other tree is younger, more energetic, less diseased. It stood alone when we arrived in a field of sedge and scrub pines that has since become our garden. It is a June bearer of little green apples, and of the two trees it has been by far the greater blessing. It has been a bountiful provider, giving us bumper crops every year except one, when a late freeze caught it in full blossom. Even then it struggled to give us enough for munching and to make a couple of pies.

Aromas come to our hillside in waves. First in spring is lilac. Then comes mock orange, followed by the enchantment of honeysuckle. These are heavy, sweet smells, fine for spring when the air is light and whimsical. But no aroma is more welcome than that of ripening June apples. It arrives with the summer, when the air has turned heavy and sultry and freshens the atmosphere with its pleasing sweet-and-sour tang.

That odor is very nearly mesmerizing. It often leads me to the apple tree, where I can whiff the scent in big gulps, storing it in memory for later use. I find myself being drawn especially in early mornings when the dewy grass beneath the tree is littered with the night's fall of fruit.

The box turtles and squirrels will have been gnawing at the prettiest and greenest apples. It is surprising how many they will have eaten, and I find myself wondering if they go away in daytime to nurse green-apple bellyaches. Usually I find myself searching for a pretty apple that the critters have missed so that I can start my day with a tangy crunch.

June apples are different from fall apples. They rot quickly, and they will not store, even under refrigeration, for very long. They lack the crispness of fall apples, and they are best eaten when still green (with a little salt, if you like). Once they begin to yellow, they become soft, almost mushy.

June apples are fair for pie-making, not much good for jelly, and absolutely hopeless for cider. Erik and I once spent two days chopping and squeezing, trying to transform a wheelbarrow load of them into cider. We got about a quart. And it turned to vinegar. But because they are not particularly juicy, June apples are excellent for drying to be used for wintertime fried pies or chewy snacks. They make a superb applesauce, too, with a good, tangy bite. But their primary purpose, I'm convinced, is to become apple butter.

A day after Linda makes the year's first batch — rich, creamy, dark — the house still smells spicy-sweet from it. Talk about aromas . . . now there is one of life's great ones. Surely heaven will smell like apple butter cooking. Linda's apple butter, spread over a hot biscuit, is the ennoblement of little green June apples. No peach, however transformed, can ever hope to compete.

June apples come from nature as a gift of sorts. We don't have to do any real work to produce them. The tree does it for us. When summer comes, we simply amble out to receive the reward. Even if much of it lies on the ground, victim to smaller creatures than ourselves and their seemingly voracious appetites for the fruit, there's enough for us. And it's no sweat off our brow, as some of the old-timers would say.

To lose plants that you have put into the ground and watched grow, that you have worked and tended almost like children, is an entirely different matter. Yes, you are older now, mature, and you've been doing this, this business of growing things from scratch, for a long time now. You should know better. You should remember that nature always has her surprises, her vagaries, and that you can't control her, no matter how hard you work. You should know all this, and you do. But when disaster strikes, it still hurts. Every time. No matter how old and wise you get.

The storm came fast and unexpectedly. Most of our storms blow in from the west, but this one sneaked in from the north. The sun was still shining when a thunderclap announced its presence and I first noticed the vicious-looking black clouds looming. At first I took it for one of our usual storms, just passing to the north. That happens in summer, storms passing north and south, watering gardens a mile away but leaving us dry. I complain. Remembering past drought, I worry about the garden, where the ground turns too hard to hoe.

But this time the wind was blowing from the north, the storm heading straight for us. Under the constantly rumbling thunder, I could hear an ominous roar, like the sound of high-flying jets. The first rain came in a wave that lashed the windows. The wind was unlike any I'd experienced since Army days when I'd sat through typhoons in Okinawa and Taiwan.

The house shuddered and creaked. Hail beat on the windows with such fierceness that I expected them to break. The lights flickered off. Water burst through the ceiling in the dining room. Linda wasn't at home, and Erik and I huddled on the living room floor. I thought the roof was about to go. Then, almost as fast as it had come, the storm was gone. The sun peaked out. I went to the backdoor and took a tentative step outside, only to be sent scurrying back by a warning shot of lightning from the fleeing marauder.

A couple of minutes later, I ventured out again to find that the countryside had been turned into a freezer locker with the door just opened. Fog rose eerily from the ice-covered ground. Against the north wall of the house, the ice was two inches deep. The brown wall was now green, plastered with battered leaves. Tree limbs littered the ground. I picked up six hail stones that filled my hand and would have iced a large drink. Erik and I were marveling over them when I noticed my corn patch.

Silver Queen corn is one of my favorite foods. It is available in its ideal form, fresh from the stalk, for only a few weeks each summer, and I crave it the rest of the year. The year before drought had claimed three different patches of Silver Queen, and I never got even a single ear. This year, the corn was doing beautifully: tall, full, darkly green, just beginning to tassle. I was only days from my first sweet offering. Now the patch was flattened. Just a few tattered stalks remained standing, bewildered stragglers among the fallen ranks.

I walked to the patch and stood looking silently at the devastation. The heart was gone from me, and Erik knew it.

"Maybe we can put 'em back up," he said, squatting and righting a stalk. He packed mud at its base, and although it leaned precariously, it remained standing.

I tried a couple, but they toppled slowly back to the ground. "It's hopeless," I said.

"We can try," Erik said. "It won't cost us anything but our time."

He was already moving along a row, setting up other stalks. I joined him, working from the other side of the patch. It was a big job, five rows, each eighty feet long. We worked feverishly, desperately, crawling in the mud, using bare hands to dig up the soggy red-clay soil and pack it around the exposed roots. Erik talked to the corn as he worked, pleading, "Come on, stand up. *Stand up!*"

An hour later, we were only half a row from finishing. Our hands were cut and raw. We had been stung by yellow flies, pricked by briers nestled in the rows. Our bodies itched from contact with the corn, and we were sweating heavily in the heat and humidity, the sweat streaking the mud that had smeared us head to toe. But we were exultant, laughing.

"A mud bath is supposed to make you beautiful," Erik said.

"It's not helping you any," I said with a grin.

"Well, at least now I know how a hog feels."

When we had finished, the corn patch looked a little like a fellowship of drunks leaning on one another for support. All but a few stalks were standing, however tenuously.

"I don't know whether it'll do any good or not," I said. "It may all be dead tomorrow."

"At least we tried," Erik said.

Our work in the corn patch had diverted my attention from the rest of our place, but a quick survey soon showed just how widespread the damage was. The big garden down the hill from the house, away from the Silver Queen corn, was a disaster area. Pepper plants were stripped of leaves, tomato plants broken and beaten into the mud, their green fruit cracked by the hail. A second, smaller corn patch — this one yellow corn — also was flattened. Wherever we looked was destruction. Green apples and peaches had been wrenched from the trees. Those that still clung to branches were wounded and bleeding.

The vineyard was hit hardest. After years of hard work and frustration, I had expected a full crop from my four hundred vines that summer. But the leaves that remained on the vines were shredded, the hard, green grapes cracked and bruised, already showing the sickly brown of damaged fruit. I couldn't find a single bunch untouched.

Defeated, I trudged wearily back to the garden and began trying to right the yellow corn. I was halfway through when thunder cracked close again. Another storm was approaching fast from the north, apparently intent on finishing whatever work the first had left undone. I hurried to the house just ahead of the rain and lightning. Hail again rattled the windows, and the wind seemed even angrier than before. When the second storm finally passed, I emerged to find both corn patches flattened again.

Dreams usually die slowly, tortured by disappointments and sorrows. Sometimes, though, they are blown away in a sudden fury.

Once in a while I am overcome by the notion that summer will always be a choice between the lesser of two evils: drought or the destructive fury of sudden, unrelenting storms. I struggle to remember that there are alternatives — sweet, gentle, soaking showers, for one. They do exist, come in the nick of time, and do their magic. Of course they do. How else would our gardens ever produce the first bite? How else would we reach mature wisdom without self-destructing from frustration at our inability to control or predict nature? Summer showers are her way of preventing us from giving up the struggle once and for all.

I was sitting down to supper when I heard the sound. At first I wasn't sure that I was actually hearing it. It was just a quiet hum that seemed to be building slowly. I went to the door to see if it was what I hoped it would be. Indeed it was.

Big drops of rain were splatting all about.

The dogs got up from their favorite snoozing spots on the deck and ambled under the eaves near the door to escape this rare substance falling from the sky. But I went out to welcome it, allowing the cold drops to splash my upturned face, while the dogs looked on as if I'd lost my senses.

It had been a spring when I could remember only one shower's having fallen on our place. That had been several weeks earlier, and it was so brief that it barely dampened the ground under the trees. With summer in only its second official week, the drought, the unrelenting sun, the extreme heat were extracting harsh payment. The garden was the first victim. Despite the spring drought, I couldn't help beating the hard ground to a dusty powder with my tiller and planting a late crop of Silver Queen corn, squash, cucumbers, tomatoes, and peppers.

I watered after planting and kept watering the tomato and pepper plants for a week, but they couldn't take the sun's daily tortures and quickly surrendered. The squash sprouted only to face an early and agonizing demise, the yellow promise of death assaulting the leaves from the outer edges and marching briskly to the heart. Realizing it was defenseless, the corn didn't bother to come out to fight.

The few blossoms on the June apple tree that escaped a late frost produced grotesque fruit, gnarled and warty and stunted, aborted by the tree in embarrassment. The grape vines, struggling to recover from the crippling frost, cruelly cast off the tiny hard berries that formed on runty stems—infanticide in the interest of survival. The wild blackberries at the edge of the fields ripened weeks early, miniature fruit, hard and bitter.

The whole hillside took on a somber and threatened cast.

Each morning, a fresh batch of leaves from the big willow beside the house was scattered over the deck, usually a nuisance common to late fall. Walking to the goat lot with my potful of feed one night, I realized that I was shuffling through fallen leaves as if it were October. The tall tulip poplars were already yellow and dropping leaves in wild abandon. The dogwood trees, shallow rooted, curled their leaves, cringing defensively. A few weaker ones simply gave up and succumbed, their brown leaves still clinging to the branches, as if caught by surprise and unwilling to acknowledge their fate. The cherry trees were nearly bare of leaves, but the walnuts, usually the first to shed their foliage in late summer, were holding their own. They had put out their own sunscreen; their leaves glistened with heavy coatings of oil secreted in self-preservation.

The grass had assumed the brown shades of winter (I never thought I'd see the day when I'd complain because it wasn't growing), and even the weeds had hurried to seed far short of their normal stature. Every car venturing up the driveway kicked up clouds of dust that settled in thickening layers on everything in sight, an ever-present reminder of the cleansing rain that wouldn't come.

In the air-conditioned sanctuary of the house, we worried with each turn of the faucet that this might be the last shower the well could stand and that we, too, might soon be as dustladen as the world outside, our spirits as dry as the ground beneath us. Is it any wonder then that I would welcome an evening shower so joyously?

I sought refuge inside the screened porch as the rain quickened, abandoning my supper and a TV movie for the more nourishing and uncommon spectacle of rain. It came in waves, drumming loudly on the tin roof, ebbing trickily, then picking up the beat again. It performed for about five minutes, then slipped away without encores, leaving the trees dripping with soft applause and me silently shouting, "More!"

It wasn't a drought-breaker, merely a dust-buster, a brief sustaining sip to a parched countryside. But it was genuine refreshment to brittle, dehydrated spirits.

In 1772, James Bruce wrote a description of summer that breaks its tortures down into categories that are useful if you feel the need to clarify precisely how bad you feel. Bruce says, "I call it hot, when a man sweats at rest, and excessively on moderate motion. I call it very hot, when a man, with thin or little clothing, sweats much, though at rest. I call it excessive hot when a man in his shirt, at rest, sweats excessively, when all motion is painful, and the knees feel feeble as if after a fever. I call it extreme hot, when the strength fails, a disposition to faint comes on, a straitness is found round the temples, as if a small cord was drawn round the head, the voice impaired, the skin dry, and the head seems more than ordinary large and light. This, I apprehend, denotes death at hand."

A friend of mine was in a sweat when he came across the above passage from the journal of Bruce, an early English explorer of the Nile. Thinking it appropriate to the summer that we were then enduring and having no other use for it ("The thing is just too long to work into conversation," he said), he sent it to me.

Using Bruce's definitions, I suppose I'd have to classify that summer in the excessive-hot to extreme-hot range. Even to a summer lover such as myself, it was surely an oppressive one, driving body and spirit to lethargy. For days on end it was hard to find strength for anything other than seeking an air-conditioned place in which to sip a cool drink.

But inevitably the day came when we awakened to change. I stepped outside and instantly realized that something was different, although it took a moment to register just what. Was that really a nip in the air?

A nip indeed. And, oh, how welcome.

The heat had broken, and I could sense in the air that it was gone for good, for this year at least. Sure, there would be hot days still, maybe even hot enough to build a sweat at rest. But I knew that the strength-sapping, mind-enfeebling, spirit-breaking heat would not return—until the next summer.

I shut off the air-conditioner, opened windows and doors, and, revived by fresh air, mind and body began to stir again. The coolness hinted at season change, and that reminded me that heat and drought had kept the fall garden from being planted. So out came tiller, row setter, stakes, and hoe, and into the dry, powdery soil went fertilizer and seeds. Lettuce for salads of October and November. Radishes to keep through the winter. Green beans, peas, squash, and cucumbers on the outside chance of getting some of their produce before first frost. Corn that will never have ears but will make food for the goat anyway. Onions and cabbages that will thrive into winter. And carrots to be dug, sweet and crisp, from beneath an insulating layer of hay in January and February, when the cold will be as merciless as the summer heat had been.

But this particular day was not the time to think of bitter days to come. It was a time to enjoy. The sun had become friend again, the breezes a balm. So invigorating were they that they led me from garden chores to mowing, long neglected because of the heat.

And when twilight came, and this rash of energy brought on by weather change had been spent, I found myself resting beneath a walnut tree, muscles trembling from strain, aches beginning to creep into abused joints, a touch of chill settling with the night.

Suddenly, a whippoorwill began to call from woods' edge. It was not the urgent call of spring, pleading for a mate, nor the joyous clamor of summer nights, ripe with satisfaction. It was a mournful cry of farewell, for when the heat goes, so go the whippoorwills, fleeing far southward. For a moment I was filled with rue for having so eagerly embraced the first signs of summer's death.

In fact, it wasn't long at all before I had to pay the price for my glee at summer's demise. It happens every year in early September. Just after Labor Day, depression settles in. I've never been able to do anything about it. Maybe it harks back to childhood and the start of the new school year. I always thought that a rather dismal way to end a summer. Surely it has something to do with the death of a season. Officially, of course, summer is still around, for a while at least. But everybody knows that Labor Day drains its last joy and marks its real end.

Like so many others, when Labor Day arrives, I find myself wondering what happened to summer. How could it be that I didn't make the fishing trips, camping expeditions, canoe journeys I'd mapped out in my head during the dreary and bitter days of winter? Why didn't I do any of the other summer things I'd dreamed about at such length? The trouble with summer is clear. There is too little of it and too much grass to mow.

Part of the depression that overcomes me each year at this time is caused, no doubt, because my failures become so obvious. To confirm that, I need only look at the big garden I worked so hard to prepare and plant with such high hopes in spring. As usual, it produced little, overwhelmed as it was by weeds, bugs, hailstorms, and my inability to devote to it the time and effort it needed to flourish. Morning glories now entwine the few spindly okra plants that have survived, the wildly flourishing flowers gloriously proclaiming in pink and purple each morning the victory of nature over feeble human effort. The sweet potatoes and peanuts that I should now be harvesting found life too hazardous to face in their earliest days and meekly submitted to the inevitable.

When I wade through the conquering weeds to the watermelon patch, I find dozens of watermelons grown only to fist size before withering on their neglect-shrouded vines. Strange bugs have made houses of the tiny, decaying melons. My vineyard is all but unapproachable. The vines have been struggling for weeks to keep their heads above the sea of Johnson grass, wild blackberry vines, and other odious growths that have engulfed them, but now I can see that they are tired and despondent, no longer hopeful of rescue.

Depressing.

Perhaps this depression wouldn't be so bad if it didn't seem that nature joins me in it. The air is heavy and torpid. The days seem to have no particular purpose. Some trees have already begun shedding their leaves in anticipation of winter sleep (the walnut trees around my house are almost bare). Flowers, particularly the zinnias and marigolds, annuals, seem listless, as if they have sensed the end is near and all is hopeless.

And yet . . .

Outside my window, the crape myrtles blossom brilliantly, as they do each year at this time, and every day the hummingbirds come. The tiny birds dart nervously over the trees, their wings a blur, sipping nectar from the pink blossoms. I never see hummingbirds except at this time of year when the crape myrtles are in bloom. For all I know, this may be the high point of the year for hummingbirds, the time they look forward to through all the other months. They at least seem to be utterly without post-Labor-Day depression.

Watching them, I find myself wondering why I can't simply be like them, seeking out the nectar to be found in these late summer days. But something prevents me. I sense clearer destruction to come.

I noticed the flowers first. By mid-morning the zinnias — so brightly red, pink, yellow, and orange the day before — were a uniform brown, their leaves blackening by the hour. The morning glories that had taken the garden, coloring it each morning with pink, lavender, and white, were now only dark, shriveled lines twining over the high grass and dead cornstalks.

In my busyness, I had not heard a weather forecast. I guess I should have known by the chill in the night air that seasonal ritual was imminent, but my mind was on other things, so it took me by surprise. First frost. It sometimes comes a little later than it usually does, but it always affects me the same way, leaving me morose. Maybe because it's the day the flowers die. Or maybe it's just because first frost is such a stark reminder of what is to come. Such cold, hard evidence that I've been caught short again.

I had meant to get into the garden before frost to collect its final offerings. But I had too many things to do, and then I had been away. By the time I got there, the damage had been done. The tender okra pods, reaching like fingers into the cold air had turned translucent in the grip of the frigid night. Tomatoes were turning dark green where their flesh had been seared by the frost. Peppers were already limp where the frost had touched them.

It wasn't only in the garden that I was caught by this harsh announcement of coming winter. The ashes from the last fire of spring were still in the wood stove. Since August I had intended to get up on the roof and clean the chimney of creosote. But that's such a hard, dirty job, and when the days are still hot, there seems to be plenty of time, and . . . well, you know how it is. I dared not start a fire until the chimney was cleaned. Last winter a neighbor had his explode from creosote buildup. He was lucky his house didn't burn down.

I suppose it really didn't matter that the chimney wasn't yet clean. There wasn't a stick of wood in the woodbox. In two winters of heating with wood, I had never been quite able to keep it filled. I cut wood almost every day, but I was never able to get more than a two- or three-day supply ahead. I cut wood in rain and sleet and snow and on days when it was so cold I thought my fingers would splinter like kindling. And every day I swore that the next winter I would not be caught short. I would cut trees in spring and leave them to season through the summer. And by first frost I would have the trees sawed into firelogs and stacked high, a visual snub to winter.

But now the frost had come: the flowers were dead; garden produce hung rotting in the sunshine; and I sat wondering how it had all slipped up on me again. What had I been doing all those spring days when I should have been cutting trees? And where was I when the firelogs should have been piling up around me?

Soon I would have to get up on the roof and clean that chimney and begin again my ritual cold-weather search of the hillside for dead wood. But first I had to find a way past the overwhelming sense of despair created by my own procrastination and nature's efficient progress along her prescribed path.

I realize that I put myself into these situations. One miraculous October I managed to have the barn stacked high with wood, enough to carry us at least into February. It was a sight that offered a warm, secure feeling as cold weather approached, and you'd think that would be enough to teach a smart man his lesson.

Alas, human nature doesn't always work so logically. The next fall rolled around without my having had much time for woodcutting. Only a few sticks graced my barn, cut from the limbs of an oak that had died and begun to lean precipitously toward the house. Even with a ready wood source so nearby, I had managed to leave the oak's trunk lying on the ground waiting to be sliced into chunks and split.

Even if I had finished the oak, that wouldn't have added much to the sparse store, enough to warm us for a week or two at most. So I found myself on a late October Saturday doing what I should have learned not to be doing so late: searching for a new supply of wood.

I cut only dead wood, preferably from trees that have already fallen, thus sparing me the labor and danger of bringing them down myself. It's amazing how many trees have accommodated me by toppling themselves in years past, but always there are some that I must fell, and it's easier to spot the dead ones while their neighbors still sport leaves.

I headed downhill to the creek to begin because that's where I've cut most of my wood in recent years, thanks to the creek's unrelenting efforts to clear its banks of adornment.

Nothing new. Part of the trunk of a massive oak I cut two years ago, so thick that it successfully resisted the best efforts of my puny chain saw, still lay where it fell. But there were no trees newly downed and none recently dead either. A big poplar that the creek pushed over last year had sprouted new growth, miniature trees, up and down the length of its trunk, and an ancient dogwood forced to the ground when the big poplar fell still struggled for new life, too.

Nearby, I stopped to ponder again a monstrous twin oak — two huge trees from the same trunk. I began contemplating this tree three years ago when its first side died. The other died last year, and I continued to ponder. The wood in this tree would no doubt keep us warm for a good part of the winter, but I have never been able to figure a safe or easy way to bring it down.

It stands at a high point on the creek bank, a spot too steep for acceptable footing, and the way it leans makes for difficulty in figuring how it would fall. There seems no way to cut it safely — not for an amateur lumberjack, at any rate — and after a considerable period of fresh contemplation, during which I found an old five-cent Pepsi bottle wrapped in one of the tree's roots, I passed on up the creek looking for better prospects.

Beyond the old stone dam, washed out by a long-ago freshet, I came across two more big poplars recently upended at a spot where the creek descends a series of wide stone steps. The trees were still alive, although their intricate root systems, studded with big stones, stood exposed, higher than my head. The craters they had left formed new pools in the creek, virgin territory already being explored by adventurous minnows.

Why couldn't these have been oaks? I thought, as I climbed onto one of the trunks and walked to the upper branches, balancing carefully. Poplar, as experienced wood-burners know, is not good firewood. It burns too fast and is far too lively. It pops, spraying showers of sparks and cinders that could eliminate the need for firewood when they eliminate the house.

I knew there was no need to venture beyond this point because anything I found would be too far from the house, through growth so thick as to make it inaccessible, but I went on anyway, just looking. I wanted to check a big oak that fell in a far corner of our property two years ago. I've longed to cut it, but it would be impractical to try to get the wood back to the house, requiring far more work than it is worth. The tree had already shed much of its bark and its soft outer wood — haven for giant black beetles and other bugs — was decaying, but the core was still sound, as I knew it would be. Last year I cut an oak like this that had obviously been downed years before we came to this place, and it was still solid, so solid that I nearly wore out a chain saw blade cutting it.

I continued my search, crossing the creek, climbing the steepest part of our little mountain, then descending toward the back of the house, looking for more accessible dead trees, fallen or not, but there were none, surprising in view of the summer drought that preceded my search. This clearly called for reassessment of the firewood situation for the coming winter. Considering the options and the lateness of the season, I called a wood dealer and ordered a pickup load just to get started.

Woodcutting is a ritual of autumn, but it is also a reality. If you depend entirely on wood to heat your home, there is a very real physical danger involved in not having the wood you need on hand. Thus, you learn to compromise at times. You use modern tactics, telephone, and buy what you need. You acquiesce, pay someone else to do the labor you should have done, perform the task that was to have been a part of your chosen way of life.

But the season has other rituals, more spiritual in nature, and to avoid performing them can be every bit as threatening as to skimp on the wood supply. Somehow, I managed to find myself in the position of ignoring one of autumn's most pleasing and most important rituals. I had not paid homage to the season's beauty.

We had missed our annual leaf-viewing trip to the mountains, and I can't say that I regretted it after reading news reports of traffic jams on the Blue Ridge Parkway and high-school gyms opened to accommodate the crush of tourists. We hadn't even been to an apple stand or a pumpkin patch, nor had we plucked a single plump persimmon from the tree behind the house. I was feeling almost sacrilegious.

So on a sparkling Indian summer afternoon I set out to rectify as best I could. If I could not drink the grand color-splashed panoramas of the mountains, I could at least sip the smaller but no less satisfying vistas of my Randolph County hillside. Erik came along.

And the dogs. We leaf-crunched through the woods as the dogs raced around, sniffing and scratching after small creatures, throwing up sprays of dry leaves.

The late afternoon sun, slanting through the trees, gave the woods a golden aura—proper, it seemed, to our pilgrimage. We stepped carefully over the big rock outcroppings halfway up the hill, talking of snakes. Once, in late November, I came across a snake here. It had yellow stripes, and I had never seen one like it, nor have I since. Fat and sluggish, it seemed resigned to doom, irritated at my intrusion into its private agonies, and I left feeling sorry for it.

Only here and there did we find patches of brilliant color, mostly on lower leaves. It had been a drab fall around our place, the trees dressing from green to brown without the spectacular preening that usually accompanies the change.

We stopped now and then to examine leaves. I had brought along my copy of *Common Forest Trees of North Carolina, How to Know Them,* a pocket manual produced by the North Carolina Department of Natural Resources. Erik and I had talked of learning more about our trees for a long time. My ignorance is immense, and it bothers me that I don't know the things that live so close around me. I can't identify half the trees that grow on our place. And I know far fewer of the weeds and wildflowers, birds and insects. Somehow we had just never gotten around to identifying things.

And we weren't having an easy time of it now. The leaves of too many trees look too much alike. We found, for example, several types of oak, but none with leaves exactly like any of the fifteen oaks pictured in the book. We made positive identification only of a white oak, and that only because of its shaggy bark.

Near the top of the hill, we came to the big spreading beech, one of my favorite trees on the place. I had suspected it was a beech but hadn't been certain until now. It is a regal tree, and other trees stand back from it, as if in obeisance, giving it room to grow. Winter's ice storms had devastated its massive limbs, but its nobility, although wounded, remained intact.

Until I read it in my pocket manual, I didn't know that beeches bear edible nuts, much favored by wildlife. We searched until we found some of the small, prickly husks in which the nuts are wrapped, but other creatures had already made off with the treasures inside. We will have to be quicker in coming years if we are to sample them.

On the backside of our property, as we were going down the steep hill toward the creek, we came upon a large tree that had fallen, apparently toppled by a storm. It had not been down the last time I walked in the woods. I tentatively identified it as a scarlet oak. Strangely, it had fallen uphill, ripping up a huge slab of earth with big rocks entangled in its roots. The root slab towered over my head. The trunk was more than two feet thick at the base. I climbed onto it and, balancing precariously, began pacing it off, putting one foot carefully in front of the other.

"Thirty-seven feet to the first limb," I called to Erik.

"Are you sure?"

"My foot's a foot," I said

"Mine is too," he said, grinning, "but it's only nine inches long."

I stepped off another thirty feet to the crown.

When the tree fell, it had uprooted a fair-sized hickory and a gnarled old dogwood. One of its huge limbs snapped in half another dogwood with a trunk ten inches thick. Here was enough wood to keep my stove burning all winter, and I knew that soon I would have to return with my chainsaw and pay a more physical homage to autumn with sweat and aching back. Even so, our afternoon walk provided nourishment I sorely needed despite its failure to take me completely away from the season's most pressing demands.

Of all the seasons, winter is the one that seems purposefully designed to test our faith. Hal Borland reports an exchange that makes clear the connection between winter and faith: "A wise old countryman once said to me, 'Every winter I have to renew my belief.' And when I asked, 'Belief in what?' he said, 'My belief in believing.'"

Like most spiritual things, renewed belief comes quietly, without big news stories to laud it. But nevertheless it is a wondrous, no, a miraculous, thing when winter manages to give us hope. For me, the winter solstice is a sign of hope.

The sun, bless its heart, halts in its long trek southward, away from us, turns on its heel, and starts slogging wearily back toward us. I don't know exactly what happens astronomically, but metaphorically this image will suffice. The sad part is that this milestone of our calendar year so often goes by unnoticed and unnoted. Yes, it does fall right in the midst of Christmas's hubbub, but I do sometimes wonder how long it would take us to miss this yearly miracle if one year the sun changed its mind and kept going.

The winter solstice is a promise of rebirth. The gradually lengthening days assure us that although the worst of winter lies ahead, spring is just beyond, and once again the soggy, drab, forlorn earth will stir with life. That is why since humans have existed this season has been holy. Each year the winter solstice forces me to admit that I am not really the cynic, the abject pessimist, I think I am. Only optimists pore over seed catalogs. And only the most optimistic of optimists continue to reach for seed catalogs knowing all the sorrows of gardens past.

It is no accident that the seed catalogs arrive at this time of year. I doubt that any of the seed companies had to hire corporate psychologists to tell them that it is in the darkest days of December that people most need to dream of warmth and light and greenness, to believe that once again flowers and vegetables and fruits will come, that life will be renewed.

Seed catalogs are the best of dream books, far superior to the fatter catalogs of Sears and J. C. Penney. They come to my mailbox by the sackful—more than a dozen the week after Christmas alone. I welcome them all. I could no more turn away a seed catalog than I could reject spring itself. They are, for one thing, so full of wonders. Red okra. Purple cauliflower. Golden beets. Yellow watermelons. Are there people who refuse to eat fruits and vegetables in natural colors who cry out for such things?

And speaking of wonders, it was through seed catalogs that I first was introduced to kohlrabi, a plant that proves from all appearances that we are not alone in space. Something that looks so strange surely must have been brought to this planet by visitors from another galaxy.

Just when I become convinced that I know every vegetable that will grow in our part of North Carolina, even the exotic ones from places like India and China, not to mention other galaxies, along comes a seed catalog with pictures of something I've never seen before.

Celtuce, for example. I'd never even heard of it. A combination of celery and lettuce with four times the vitamin C, I was assured, of head lettuce. And oyster plant. It looks like a hairy carrot although its flesh is creamy white, and it has a flavor, so the catalog tells me, "not unlike oysters." Must be for the person who craves the taste of oysters but gags at the sight of the slimy creatures; otherwise, why not just eat oysters?

The same company that brings us celtuce and oyster plant, Burpee, is also introducing the very first bush butternut winter squash. It looks so good and sounds so promising that I'm tempted to order a packet of seeds although I don't particularly like winter squash and the only ones I ever grew proved to be worm-infested when I tried to cook them.

But I don't mean to get carried away with the latest wonders from the seed catalogs. I mean only to point out what welcome visitors they are at this time of year. In his book *Homeland*, Borland, who writes beautifully of rural life and seasons, has this to say of the winter solstice: "Winter has begun to pen us in, but eventually we will walk the pastures again, the quickening soil beneath our feet, root and seed alive reaching for rain and sunlight. This we know. We have no option, no choice except belief."

Seed catalogs are canons of that faith.

On the bleakest occasions of winter, when not only the weather but also your own mind seem to conspire against you, a seed catalog alone may not be enough to restore lapsed faith in nature and self. On those occasions, action is required although it sometimes takes a while to figure out exactly what action.

In the midst of a cold winter drizzle, I sat looking out the window, hoping for words to come. They didn't. I really hadn't expected any. Winter gloom was descending, wrapping me in melancholy as securely as the gray clouds enveloped the hills out-side. In the darkness of my mood, both bonds seemed eternal.

I squirmed uncomfortably, but I knew there was nothing I could do. It happens every year in January and February, and every year it seems to grow worse. Bears know how to deal with these months. Trees and plants blot out the whole thing and emerge in the warm months with renewed vigor. People, pathetic creatures, charge right on, business as usual, trying to pretend these vicious months aren't savaging them physically and mentally.

I turned to my typewriter, and the blank sheet of paper taunted me. I pushed myself away, walked through the house, and stood at another window, looking out at yet another view of dead fields, barren trees, and hills hiding in fog. A flock of crows flew away through the valley along the creek, and I could hear them cawing in what sounded like displeasure. Were they miserable, too?

I went into the living room, stoked the fire, and sat for a while watching the embers flicker. They only reminded me that I needed to fetch a load of wood from the barn. Pulling on a jacket, I headed outside, ducking my head into the gray drizzle, trudged to the barn, loaded the cart with logs, and pulled them back to the house, pausing to run my fingers through the water drops collecting on a low-hanging branch of our walnut tree. They weren't freezing. Not yet.

I shook the water off my jacket, scraped mud from my shoes, loaded the wood box, and threw three more logs onto the fire before returning to the typewriter. The paper was still there, still blank. It hadn't accomplished a single thing all day, and I was disgusted. I glared at the paper, but it only mocked me, so I picked up a three-day-old newspaper and reread it. Finally, after fidgeting for a while and trying not to look out the window, I turned to the only thing I knew that offered hope.

I'd been trying to avoid them, hoping to save them for worse days, when the winter doldrums reach their most despondent depths: the seed catalogs. I grabbed the top one and thumbed through it hungrily, lingering particularly over the green peas and lettuces. After the third one, I could stand it no longer.

I pulled on my jacket again and drove uptown to an old brick store where hoe handles and washtubs hang in the front window. The owner was alone. He greeted me with a big smile.

"Seeds come in yet?" I asked

"Just the other day," he said. "I think the boys got 'em put out. Yeah, they're over there."

It was beautiful, a virgin rack, resplendent in spring and summer colors.

"Anything I can help you find?" the owner asked.

"No, I think I'll just browse for a while."

Finally, I chose a single pack of tomato seeds and picked up six of those little compressed peat tablets, the kind that swell into sprouting pots when soaked in water.

"Getting an early start, aren't you?" the owner said.

"Just thought I'd like to have a few tomato plants blooming when time comes to set them out," I said.

Back at home, I tossed the peat tablets into an aluminum pie pan, filled the pan with water, and watched the tablets balloon miraculously. Just to be safe, I put three seeds into each peat pot then set the pan on the shelf beneath the window beside my typewriter.

When I sat back down at the typewriter, a word finally emerged. I typed it hurriedly ... APRIL.

No matter how deep and pervasive my lust for April, no matter how longingly I fondle my seed catalogs during winter's gloom, snow gets me every time. No matter that I dislike almost everything about it: hate being trapped, cut off from normal activities; abhor attempting to drive, spinning and skidding in fear for my life; despise digging out of it with eyes watery and stinging, nose rosy and running, fingers and toes cold and tingling. Snow still enthralls me. Its beauty enchants me and exerts a mysterious pull that I can't quite explain.

When snow is falling, I keep going to windows to watch it magically transforming all that it touches. Before my eyes, it makes the empty seed pods of the bare rose of Sharon bushes outside my bedroom window blossom as beautifully as in summer. From an old pile of rotting lumber next to the garage, it creates a layered, sugar-frosted confection fit for a giant.

When snow comes at night, I find myself being drawn outside to watch the flakes swirl out of the blackness, and I am instantly transported back to specific moments of childhood when I did the same thing, tense with excitement, welcoming every flake, rejoicing in the prospect of no school, of snowball fights, snow-fort building, and sliding down steep hillsides on flattened cardboard boxes.

After the storm has passed and the new day comes with clear skies and dazzling brilliance, nothing short of serious illness can keep me inside. I bundle up and tramp all over our part of this little mountain where we live, marveling at how the snow has made it such a different place.

A rusty wire fence, sagging in the woods, has become a long strand of fragile white lace. The rain that came between the snows has left every tree bejeweled and winking in the sunlight. Every tree, too, is alive as the ice on the fragile upper branches yields to the warming sun, loses its grip, and crashes groundward, leaving the branches dancing with relief.

Near the peak of the hill, I look back toward the house and see smoke swirling around the eaves of the little A-frame cabin that I use as an office. Gripped by fear, I race toward it, my feet heavy, slipping, falling, knocking snow from the undergrowth as I brush rudely past, certain that the building is afire although it has been shut tight all winter, unused, unheated, no lights left on.

I arrive, breathing heavily, to discover that the steep roof on the south side has dumped its heavy load of snow in a long, straight pile, burying the rose bushes growing there. The gray cedar shingles are merely steaming themselves dry.

Relieved, I head back up the hill with Shiska, our lion of a dog, at my heel. She nips playfully at the snow-coated cuffs of my jeans. In the upper field, the snow has bent the sedge into arches and flattened the honeysuckle thickets, but the blackberry vines remain erect, every thorn accented in white. A hawk soars low over the field, casting a graceful blue shadow on the snow. Shiska pounces wildly after the shadow, barking ferociously. Then while I laugh, she circles, confused, the shadow vanishing magically as the hawk glides over the trees down by the creek.

Not even a heavy snow can completely hide the big junk pile that accumulated near the creek long before I came to call this place home. Old washing machines, bottomless washtubs, crumbling metal drums, rusting bedsprings protrude from the blanket of whiteness, all decorated by snow but still not beautified. A broken glass milk jug, filled with snow, looks as if it has resumed old duties.

I make my way across the fences of the old pig lot to the remains of the stone dam that had its heart broken by a spring freshet decades ago, giving freedom once again to the creek. Almost frozen over, its twisting course defined only by its steep banks, that creek is now upholstered in immaculate white. But its clear waters break free as they flow with a contented murmur over the white-tufted rocks of the old dam.

I stand admiring the scene, listening to the creek and the crashing of snow and ice falling in big clumps from the tall trees until my cold feet and a near-miss by an unloading pine tell me that I've enjoyed all the enchantment I need for a while. I call to Shiska, who has been sniffing for squirrels at the base of trees, and trudge back to the house, feeling somehow ennobled.

Snow may ennoble, but ice is a different matter entirely. It always sets me on edge.

"Are you going to pace all day again today?" Linda asked as I took my morning coffee and went to the window to look down the hill toward the road for the third or fourth time. Even from the distance of a hundred yards I could see that the road was still icy. I'd seen only a couple of vehicles pass, moving slowly.

The newspaper carrier's car wasn't one of them. I don't blame the carrier. I wouldn't risk my neck so some guy could sit in his house, warm and cozy, reading about foolish people having wrecks on icy roads. But my day and disposition are thrown completely out of kilter when I don't get daily newspaper fixes in morning and late afternoon. I feel shut off. I don't know what to do with myself. This was my second day weatherbound and newspaperless. Already I was suffering severe pangs of newspaper withdrawal. I tried writing, but I couldn't concentrate. Instead, I paced.

"I'll sure be glad when it warms up," Linda said. "You're driving me crazy."

She doesn't pace when she's trapped by weather. It's hard to pace when you're stretched out in a recliner with your feet practically propped atop a wood stove. In record cold, most people complain of frozen pipes. Linda claims that her feet freeze, even in thick socks and a warm house.

Frozen pipes, miraculously, we did not have. We've had them every other cold snap. When we had an awful Christmas Eve freeze once, even my well froze. But last fall I took a week's vacation and built myself a little subterranean well house. Maybe that had something to do with our good fortune. Also we'd left the faucets dripping at night.

Anyway, we had water. We could make coffee and hot chocolate and soup. I could shave, bathe, brush my teeth, and, most importantly, not have to go outside to attend to other personal matters and face the possibility of frostbite to areas not normally susceptible. In the past, all these activities have been cold-weather luxuries at our house.

I almost wished for frozen pipes, though. At least they cause me to concentrate my attention and efforts. A few hours trying to thaw pipes with a hair dryer and a propane torch might provoke cussing or set fire to the house, but at least the task would prevent pacing.

I tried writing again, but no thoughts came. I read a little from a book about surgery but quickly gave it up when I began coming down with symptoms. Besides, so early in the day a book doesn't feel comfortable in hands longing for a newspaper.

Erik, caught at home by the snow and unable to get back to his college, was reading too, trying to study, mixing Chaucer with *Gomer Pyle* on TV. Gomer and Sergeant Carter seemed to be winning the battle for his attention. Chaucer should never challenge the Marines.

After another jaunt around the windows, I bundled into my down jacket, tied the hood tight, and went out to get wood for the stove. The cold nearly took my breath. The dogs, having spent the coldest night of their lives in unaccustomed quarters, locked inside Erik's bathroom, were frisky and playful, jumping all over me, obviously happy to be freed, apparently enjoying the cold. I could identify with their joy at freedom, but from the cold I could take no pleasure at all.

Since I was already bundled, I got a set of long-handled clippers and trudged up the hillside, slipping in the snow, to cut pine boughs and honeysuckle vines for the goat to eat. The pine boughs snapped at the bite of the blade. The still green honeysuckle leaves, curled and hardened by the cold, cascaded from the vines like beads from a broken strand when I tried to carry them to the goat's lot.

Numbed fingers and feet and a shiny red nose brought me back to the wood stove where my fingers slowly and painfully recovered. I craved milk although I normally drink no more than two or three glasses a week. We had run out of it, you see, and I was convinced that if I had to go another day without milk, I probably wouldn't make it. I opted for hot spiced apple juice instead — and carried it with me as I resumed my pacing.

"Can't you sit down for even a minute?" Linda asked.

By midafternoon, I had: done twenty-three pushups and sixty-five situps; made three trips to the road to see if the ice was melting; made six awkward starts at writing; thumbed through at least a dozen books; read in a supermarket magazine why women have affairs; warmed and eaten a bowl of canned chili; and looked out the window exactly forty-six times.

Finally, I announced that I was going to risk taking the car out to see just how bad the roads were and maybe even try to make it to the Y for a workout and the supermarket for milk.

"Good," Linda said. "If you don't get out of here soon, we're going to have to buy new carpet."

All my life I've been told that we can find humor in almost any situation if we try, and generally I believe that to be true. But a severe cold spell makes a doubter of me. I had spent two days searching diligently for something funny in all the misery of winter's bite, but so far I hadn't come up with even a mild chuckle.

For example, I almost came down with a hernia straining to get a laugh out of the water pipes' freezing at noon Sunday while the water was running, a phenomenon I had not thought possible.

Fortunately, I was wise enough to give up the effort before I'd done serious injury to myself.

When the pipes in the most inaccessible reaches of the house began to split with reports like rifle shots, I was so certain that there had to be something funny in it that I lapsed into a depressive sulk because of my inability to find it. I know that Erma Bombeck or Andy Rooney would find something absolutely hilarious about living several days without water for bathing, washing dishes, and flushing the toilet, but I'm sad to report that I have struck a dry well, so to speak.

I've discovered that body odor is funny only in the abstract. And, try though I may, I can't remember the last time that I was able to uncover a belly laugh in a sinkful of hopelessly dirty dishes. To some, I'm sure, having to go to the woods when nature calls, if I may be delicate, is worth at least a grin, if not a giggle. I can remember my dad's grinning when he told about growing up on a hardscrabble tobacco farm without benefit of an outhouse, not to mention the undreamed-of luxury of indoor plumbing. I wish now that I'd asked him how he managed when temperatures dipped to levels that not even a polar bear would risk. Very quickly, I imagine.

Maybe I could get a chuckle or two out of watching some loony movie in which a desperate man with a frozen john rushes out of his house into a frigid morning, hurrying toward the blessed sanctuary of a warm and functioning restroom at a friendly Biscuit-ville, only to discover that his cars are too cold to start. And if this frantic fellow finally got one of them going and made it several miles to Biscuitville without calamity, only to discover it flooded from a burst water pipe and the restroom out of order, I might be able to work up a guffaw with a little effort.

But let me tell you, if you happen to be the desperate and frantic character in question, you look at things from a different perspective.

While I am at it, let me warn you that there is little likelihood of finding jocularity in a depleted woodpile if you are dependent on wood for heat and it is only eight degrees at midafternoon with the sun shining brightly. And whatever comedy is to be found in learning that fingers go numb after only three licks with the ax while attempting to chop wood in such weather is hardly worth discovering.

I admit that dressing for the severest cold offers comic potential for some people. There seems to be something inherently funny about long underwear, for instance, particularly to members of my family. Linda and Erik break into laughter every time they see me in mine. But as far as I'm concerned, long underwear is about as funny as itching powder, the major difference in the two being that long underwear does provide some warmth.

Some people also find it amusing that I refuse to go outside in temperatures below twenty without wearing at least two pairs of pants, two shirts, a bulky sweater, and a down parka over my long underwear, plus three pairs of socks, insulated boots, lined leather gloves, and a toboggan. Of course, most of these people do not know what it is to face unreasonably cold weather with a body chemistry designed for spending winters lolling in the tropics.

Then, just when I have decided I'll never smile again, nature throws me another curve. Groundhog Day, and what should awaken me but birdsong. Just outside my bedroom, a spring-like rhapsody was being performed, and when I stepped onto the deck, I felt like joining in. The sun was shining brightly. Balmy breezes were blowing from the south. Bluebirds were frolicking in the walnut tree that shades the patio, and I looked around to see if robins might not be plucking worms from the lawn. It wouldn't have surprised me.

The night before, in shirtsleeves, I had barbecued ribs outside, and as hickory smoke wafted deliciously around me, I stood listening to a remarkable sound for the first day of February — a summer-time cacophony rising from the creek across the road. It was almost loud enough to drown out the roar of a jet passing far above. Hard to imagine that just three weeks earlier the creek had been shrouded in winter silence, ice encrusted, and I, snowbound on my hillside for six straight days, was complaining that this had surely been the worst winter ever.

Now the winter that began so cruelly had munificently handed us this end-of-January gift, a four-day foretaste of spring that altered my whole attitude. Why, it was almost like a free trip to Florida.

And as I sat writing on my deck, sipping from a glass of fresh orange juice, enjoying balmy breezes, basking under a midday sun that was suspiciously low in the southern sky to be providing such warmth, I was able to close my eyes and imagine myself in Palm Beach.

Well, okay, maybe Daytona.

Four miracle days rejuvenated not only my winter-weary soul but my sluggish body as well. I rode my bike for the first time in nearly three months. At four miles I had to stop to catch my breath on a hill; at six, halfway through the ride, I found myself resting on a curb for five minutes. Unable to suppress urges to stir the soil, I finally got around to planting our Christmas tree, a white pine that sat for a month on the patio while the ground remained frozen so hard that only a jackhammer could have penetrated it.

With my ever-optimistic instincts again suppressing sad experience, what I really wanted to plant was a spring garden, but the ground was far too wet for that. I settled for harvesting the winter crop of fallen limbs from the yard, collecting them into a huge pile in the garden for a calmer-day bonfire. I even cranked a push mower and happily cut some of the high grass that I had ignored so happily in the fall.

To show just how invigorating a few days of false spring can be, after only two days' recovery time from my first ride, fueled by nothing more than a glass of juice and a cup of coffee, I rode my bike for twenty-three miles with no stops for breathers. I didn't even stop when, two miles from the finish, a bug flew into my eye leaving it red and burning. As the bug in my eye attests, I was, of course, far from alone in my midwinter rejuvenation by sunny skies and balmy breezes. All about me winter shackles were being cast aside in celebration.

A red convertible whizzed by on the road, top down, the young people inside obviously playing hooky from school and whooping to rock music that was loud enough to cause the wind to tremble. Twice, wasps dive-bombed my head, a phenomenon I don't recall ever having experienced in winter.

Jonquils grew at least an inch a day during this flukish warm spell. In a search for the first crocus blossoms, I discovered an assortment of tiny wildflowers abloom, white and blue and lavender. A stroll across the pasture revealed half a dozen dandelion blossoms shining sunny smiles through the winter-brown grass. So joyous were the creek's creatures they continued their nighttime chirping throughout the day. Perhaps that was because they sensed that this weather was too good to last, that the time for celebration was short. It was, after all, Groundhog Day, and I had been casting a long shadow across my deck. Winter was not done with us. There was no doubt that it would come roaring back with its usual fierceness. The wildflowers would withdraw, the wasps retreat. Birds would huddle sullenly in the sanctuary of cedar limbs, fluffing their feathers against the merciless cold, and the creek would once again fall into chilly silence.

Smoke would drift from my chimney, as it had not done for three days, and my woodpile would dwindle drastically, as it had through all but the last two days of January. And my bike would remain locked in the garage once again for days, maybe weeks, on end. But for those few precious days, although clouds were approaching from the west, the balmy breezes beckoned me to enjoy.

In many ways spring is an embarrassment of riches. There are sometimes too many pleasures, too many beauties, to absorb, so I find myself focusing on those things that have become touchstones of the season for me: the wisteria, the first show of green in my garden, our redbud tree. But just when you think winter's done with you, there's one more message to let you know just how powerful that season is.

I don't know how I missed seeing it. Each night I flipped on the outdoor spotlights and walked right past it on my way to feed the goat. Not once did I sense anything amiss. Not until days later, when I was coming down our little mountain with a wheelbarrow loaded with wood, did I notice that something was out of place. At first, I didn't realize what it was. Something just wasn't right. A vacancy. Then it hit me. The redbud tree was gone.

I parked my wheelbarrow and hurried to investigate. The tree had simply snapped at the roots and toppled from the little embankment on which it stood, no doubt a victim of an ice storm. I stood looking at the tangle of limbs and trunk with dismay and a deep sense of loss. This was my favorite tree.

Redbud trees are common on our place, as they are throughout North Carolina. They are trees that bring the first blush of spring to the state's woodlands, their clusters of tiny pinkish-lavender blossoms usually appearing in March before buds begin to show. Later, when hot weather comes, their big, heart-shaped leaves and long, graceful, low-hanging branches offer comforting nooks of shade and coolness.

Redbuds never get very tall, twenty to twenty-five feet being about average for full-grown trees. Their trunks are squat and rarely straight. They are sociable trees. They seldom spring up alone in empty fields, preferring instead to nestle along wood's edge, seeking the comfort of bigger, stronger trees, bending their backs a little more each year as they reach out for sunlight. They are not strong. Their red-hearted wood is light and of little practical use. Their weakness and horizontal growth make them highly susceptible to ice storms.

Once, when two big ice storms hit within days of each other, we lost the biggest redbud on our place, the one that guarded the cherry trees. I sawed it up and hauled it away except for a fat section of trunk that was too difficult to move. It didn't bother me so much to loose that tree, except for the work of removing it. We had lots of other redbuds. Besides, its loss made room for the cherry trees to grow.

Redbuds peek out of the treeline that screens our land from the church that sits a few hundred feet from the back of our house, and quite a few mark the beginning of the big woods up the little mountain. Several more, including the biggest and oldest, are near the house. They add a delicate and beautiful touch each spring, but with each ice storm a little more of that beauty is lost.

Now a storm had brought a big limb crashing down from the sprawling redbud at the side of the house. That particular tree helps shade the brick patio I built a couple of years ago, and it was this loss I was concerned about without being aware of the far greater one on the other side of the house.

When I eventually found this big tree down, I was heartbroken, for it was like no other tree I've ever seen. It was a dedicated performer, a real trouper. It put its whole heart into springtime. It was an old tree when we first saw it, its trunk gnarled and ugly. As if to compensate for that, or perhaps to hide it, it put on a display unequalled in all of redbuddom.

Every spring, the entire trunk and all of the big limbs blanketed themselves with blossom, hugh pink clusters masking the imperfections of age. But this was not a wrinkled crone shamelessly smearing herself with lipstick and rouge. This was a graceful beauty swelling from within.

I loved for visitors to come in redbud time. I always showed off this tree. Sometimes I would go out with a flashlight at night just to play the beam over the blossoms, which glowed against the darkness with a special brilliance and intensity — my own little light show.

Maybe this tree performed with such vigor and enthusiasm because it sensed its end was near, that it was only a matter of waiting for the predestined ice storm to come and claim it. Maybe it decided that while it was alive and standing, it would shine as brightly as it could, despite its flaws and deficiencies. Maybe. Whatever the case, spring surely will never be the same here.

Winter's power can seem relentless. His attack is so various and so unpredictable that you suddenly realize that you've been living for months without knowing what to expect from nature. Such insecurity begins to drain all hope and optimism even from nature's staunchest fans. Winter's trickery makes you punchy, like a man who hasn't slept for a while, and just when you think you might be able to lie down and rest a bit, old winter winds himself up for the final assault.

The day arrived with warm drizzle and an uneasy sense of impending violence. A shower came at coffee time, and afterwards the sun broke through briefly then disappeared again. I was in the little A-frame cabin where I work when I heard a distant roaring. For a few moments I puzzled over the sound. By the time I figured out that it must be the wind, it had arrived with a jolt. The cabin shuddered. I could feel the little building trembling through the floor boards.

At first, I was fearful that the cabin might tip over. It perches on big rocks, with no real hold on the earth. On the front side, facing north, the door is shaded by an open-sided spire, with no obvious purpose other than to catch the wind and test its strength. I heard something clatter loudly down the side of the roof and thought perhaps the cedar shakes were ripping loose.

I opened the door, only to have it thrown back on me by an unseen force. I had to pull hard to slam the door shut behind me after I stepped outside. I saw immediately that the clatter on the roof had been a dead limb the wind had snapped from the big willow tree. The cedar shakes were holding fine.

The wind was coming in mighty gusts, driven from the north. Beyond our hill to the north and west the rolling sky was almost ebony—a frightful sight. These ominous clouds were tumbling along at such a pace that they were too disoriented to loose their torrents.

Each great gust was preceded by a roar and violent swaying of the tall trees atop the little mountain on which our house nestled halfway up, facing the morning sun. From somewhere on the hillside, I heard the crash of a tree or giant limb as it fell. Gosh, our goat, baaed with fright and ran in frantic circles in his pen.

One gust caused a sheet of metal roofing, which was shielding a lumber pile near the cabin, to pitch off two concrete blocks holding it in place and soar into the air and across a fence. A five-gallon bucket danced down the driveway, twirling like a ballerina. Barn doors broke loose from the ropes holding them shut and began banging loudly. A whirlwind of leaves skipped across the pasture, reaching for the tops of the tallest poplar trees. One gust picked up the rabbit's cage and flipped it on its back. I raced to assist the rabbit and found him huddled, trembling but unhurt, inside the mailbox that he uses for winter warmth.

As I headed for the barn to secure the doors, a piece of asphalt shingle tore from the roof of the house and went sailing across the yard. A ladder that had been left standing against the side of the house since a chimney fire a while back came crashing down on my feeble azaleas, stripping branches from the healthiest bushes. At the barn, I discovered the screws holding the hinges on one of the doors had been pulled from the wood.

When I finally got everything battened down, I went back to the cabin to work. The wind blew fiercely all day. The cabin quivered periodically. I could look out the window and see the power lines and telephone lines twirling like jump ropes. A couple of times, the lights flickered. Small limbs continued to rain down on the yard that Erik and I had just cleared of tree debris the day before.

By late afternoon, the angry wind had cleansed the sky of every trace of cloud and pollutant and ushered in a brilliant red sunset. With nightfall the wind departed as suddenly as it had come, leaving bitter cold as a reminder of its visit. Winter had mounted a quick and vicious counterattack, recapturing the premature foothold won by that brash but capricious usurper spring. March was up to old tricks.

Spring can be like a high-school girl taught to play hard-to-get. She tempts with her prettiness, puts on just enough of a show to fill your heart with longing, to convince you that nothing, nothing on earth, except this will do. Then she turns and runs, leaving you alone and wondering how you managed to fall for these old stunts yet again. You are supposed to have gotten smarter. You're no high-school boy waiting to be fooled. But, ah, spring—she manages to get me every time.

Restlessness builds daily. There is nothing I can do about it. Nothing anybody can do. You can't force a reluctant spring, and it always seems that the one I am waiting for approaches so cautiously that it has to be the most reluctant ever. Usually it only seems that way, of course; they can't *all* be the most reluctant.

Still, winter can be an old man whose house stands in the middle of a proposed freeway. He sits on his porch, a shotgun in his lap, unwilling to listen to reason, determined not to leave without making a fight of it. An ornery cuss, winter. Always has been. I've scrapped with him for years and always managed to hold my own somehow, even though I've often emerged bruised and battered, well aware that I've been in a hell of a fight.

Maybe it's that I'm older now. Maybe winter is getting tougher — and longer. I don't know. But I feel like I've been crying "uncle" for weeks sometimes, yet winter yields no mercy. He keeps twisting my arm behind my back and rubbing my nose in mud and slush while somewhere, off in the distance, I can swear I hear spring, that coy and timid creature, tittering about my predicament. I have begun to wonder why I've always been so attracted to her in the first place.

That attraction is based on yellow crocuses abloom under the walnut tree in my front yard — in the second week of February. Now, well into March, nary a crocus will show its hopeful face. Daffodils, too, seem to have become wisely reticent, but, even so, they are likely to find themselves buried by snow the moment they rear their heads.

The spring I love would not let us slide deep into March without gracing us with her presence. My spring would have forsythia about to burst into bloom when I need it. Her quince would sport bright red buttons of blossom. Her grass would be green, and tiny blue wildflowers would be twinkling in the garden long before March was in double digits. The big willow next to the house would be putting forth its faint, pleasing aura, and the redbuds' dark blossom clusters would be brightening to pink all over our hillside. Goodness knows I don't demand perfection — if spring were what I want when I want it, I know I would have slapped my first mosquito, too.

But I look out at March and see an earth still barren and brown, snow still lying in patches in the woods. The willow trees remain in shock, seriously wounded by one of winter's most deadly assaults. Cherry and redbud trees, including my favorite of all redbuds, will blossom no more because of icy savagery. The corn patch has yet to yield a single mess of creecy greens when, if spring were what I expect her to be, we would have dined on at least two messes by the time March begins to ebb. Should I chance to see a sign of spring, say a robin, he would probably be hopping on one foot through snow, cursing his travel agent.

I'm used to onions three or four inches high in the garden by now; lettuce should be coming along; my peas and carrots should be fragile lines of pastel green in orange-brown soil. Instead, snow still falls; cold winds blow; my garden remains a frozen bog. It will take weeks for the soil to dry enough for tilling. Even so, the tiller has been repaired, serviced, and stands ready. My seeds have been bought, and I can feel their impatience. They are ready to burst into life, and my restlessness mirrors theirs.

Then they come, at last, the first twinges, on a morning when I step out to get the paper. Warm breezes and a symphony of bird-song greet me. I suppress the urges long enough to get ready and leave for work. But they well up again as I drive past farm fields, plowed last fall, that are clearly dry enough for planting.

The vision of those fields seals it. I need to smell fresh earth again, to pinch it between my fingers and feel its promise of renewal. Somehow I will manage to slip away from work early enough to get back home and plant a little spring garden. It is getting late for spring gardens, after all, and with the forecast calling for rain, this day could be my last chance.

By four P.M. I am back at home in old blue jeans and clodhopper shoes. No need for a shirt — spring's belated answer to my longings. My body hungers for sunshine; the radio tempts me with its report of the temperature: seventy-five. I'll have to rush. Daylight hours are still short. I open the garage door, make my way through the winter clutter that has collected behind it, and pull out the tiller. It's supposed to be ready. I've seen to that as a way of dealing with my anticipation.

I roll the tiller outside, check the oil, add gas, and make my first mighty tug on the starter rope.

Nothing. Not a sputter. Not even a cough.

Pull, pull, pull.

Still no response.

I continue pulling till I break a sweat and have to stop for a breather. Now and then the engine hiccups a little puff of white smoke, but it is clearly more content with its long repose than I am.

Pull, pull, pull.

Mutter. Curse. Rest.

Tinker.

Pull again.

The dogs gather to watch the showdown. Man against machine. A battle of wills. The beauty of the hastily departing day and my primitive needs won't allow me to back down. I am ready to pull until I drop. Or until darkness comes. I am more likely to drop first.

The machine must have needs of its own stronger than thwarting mine (its purpose, after all, is to stir the soil), for after robbing me of twenty precious minutes, it finally rises to the occasion.

My choice of garden spots is severely limited by the ruins of the previous summer's garden, stark in the spindly dried weeds and high dead grass that have claimed that area. Brown corn stalks sprawl in clumsy array. Tomato vines hang brittle on their wire supports. Okra pods, gray and cracked fingers of death, point in all directions. The one clear patch of ground is in the hardest clay, and the first pass of the tiller leaves only a trail of earth chips. The second pass spits up clumps of the hardy green plants that thrive in winter by snuggling close to earth.

Back and forth. Pass after pass. Until gradually hard clay becomes a cushion beneath my feet.

I fetch my anxious seeds and begin the old ritual. I lay off the rows, set them with the hand plow, spread the fertilizer, drop and cover the seed: lettuce, spinach, radishes, June peas, and snow peas. I race against the darkness. I hurry but am satisfied, as always.

The dogs come again to see if I have finished the job, the older two flopping contentedly on the soft edges of my garden patch, the youngest—the puppy, we still call her, unnamed after almost a year—nosing curiously about. As twilight falls, I look up from my hose and catch the puppy dragging off a bag of onion sets, strewing the tiny bulbs as she goes. At my startling shout, she drops the bag, but she makes off with the almanac I'd stuck inside.

No matter. The only signs I use for planting are the urges that hit on balmy mornings, long awaited. Their power is enough to release all that has lain dormant in me through the dreary winter. I go forth to meet spring on her terms, surrendering, as always, to nature's power and wisdom, grateful that she allows me to be her partner in the season's traditional dance.

Fish, Fowl,
and Other
Creatures

We can call them dumb animals, and technically that is true. But I know from long experience that animals do understand us and communicate with us. Especially since moving to the country, I have been aware of how connected we are — humans and animals. There are the obvious relationships we have with our pets; there are also equally strong connections to those creatures that happen to share the world with us. We may not engage in extended exchanges with most of them, but they come into our lives, almost by chance, touch us in some way that is very hard to explain logically, and move on to pursue their own paths through time and place. But the memory of them lingers, rises up at the smallest suggestion, and reminds us that we are not alone on the planet, even on the small postage stamp of earth that we call home.

If most of us sat down to name our favorite animals, our lists would probably get pretty long before we got to the whippoorwill, yet few of nature's creatures occupy so clear a space in the memory of anyone who has experienced its haunting and beautiful night-song. Henry David Thoreau said of the bird, "The note of the whip-poor-will, borne over the fields, is the voice with which the woods and moonlight woo me," and I think he puts into words a feeling many of us would share, if we took the time to stop and think about it.

I have learned to take that time where the whippoorwill is concerned. Every year I make a note of the date and time of the bird's first call, and for me that is the official beginning of spring. Nevermind what calendars say, or weather forecasters; I measure spring by the whippoorwill's call. On our place the call usually comes from the hollow down by the creek.

I stand in the yard and listen with satisfaction. The call has always had a strange, magnetic effect on me, almost hynotic at times. I'm not sure why. Perhaps it is because they begin to call at twilight, my favorite time of day in the warm months, the time when work is finished and calm has come, a time of contemplation, when hope is most real and magic seems almost possible.

I am irresistibly drawn to whippoorwills, and I wonder why their calls are often so different, at times plaintive and mournful, shrill and angry, jubilant and joyous. Why do they cry against the calm, and why in so many moods?

Many times have I searched for them when they called from nearby trees or hedgerows, but they have always eluded me. I had never caught so much as a glimpse of one. But that changed, sorrowfully.

I was returning home one spring night from a trip to the coast. As I neared my driveway, I saw a blur, a flash of white at the edge of my headlight beam, and something slammed — *ka-whap* — into the driver's door of my pickup truck. A bird, I figured, perhaps an owl or nighthawk. I stopped at the driveway but didn't see or hear anything. Whatever it was, I wanted to think that it had been only stunned and would recover. When I got out of the truck at the top of the driveway, I paused to listen and could hear a single whippoor-will calling from across the creek.

The next morning when I went down to fetch the newspaper, I checked along the road banks and found a dead bird lying in the ditch, its feathers crumpled and bloodied. A whippoorwill, the first I had ever seen. Later, with the help of a bird book, I determined that it was female.

I felt terrible, but I told myself that it wasn't my fault. The bird had flown into the truck. I could have done nothing to prevent it. I tried to put it out of mind. But a few days afterward, as I was walking through the orchard at twilight, a whippoorwill broke from a tall tulip poplar near the old chickenhouse and came swoop-ing at me, whippoorwilling angrily. I thought that it meant to attack me and actually ducked before it veered suddenly to the left at head height, banked under the big willow limbs, and disappeared across the vineyard, still calling out in shrill tones.

Had it indeed intended to attack me? Could so unusual an event have been provoked by the other bird's death? The thought was unsettling, but reason told me to dismiss the timing of the two incidents as mere coincidence. Surely the bird was just chasing insects, and I happened to walk into its path.

But after that night, I began noticing a strange thing. Always before, whippoorwills had kept their distance from the house. We would hear them calling from down by the creek or from up the hill at the edge of the woods, but they were never close by. Now night by night, indisputably, the calls were getting closer. One night Linda and I were sleeping peacefully when we were startled awake about two o'clock by whippoorwill calls. They were so loud that it sounded as if the bird were actually in the bedroom. I sat bolt upright and saw a whippoorwill staring through the screen of the open bedroom window from a quince bush at the side of the house, its face distorted as it cried out in cold fury. It didn't scramble away until I started climbing groggily from bed.

Could this be the mate of the bird that I had killed with my truck? Did it want me to know its agony? I couldn't help wondering. We had no more incidents after that, but I couldn't go out at night without feeling that eyes were watching me from the darkness, eyes filled with pain and bitterness.

All of this comes flooding back each spring as I stand in the yard listening to the first whippoorwill. The sound grows ever sadder and lonelier. I hear no answering calls.

One night, Linda and I were in the kitchen cooking supper when I heard a whippoorwill start up close by. I thought that it might be in the big walnut tree by the kitchen door, and I stepped outside to see. As I did, I realized that the calls were even closer than I thought. I turned to see the whippoorwill perched on the edge of the roof, directly over the kitchen door. We looked at each other for a long moment before it fluttered to the peak of the roof at the far corner of the house, still calling forlornly. When I walked around the house for another look, it flew off towards the creek.

I came back inside to tell Linda about it, but she interrupted. "Do you hear the song they're playing?"

A country music show was on TV, and some singer was wailing that old Hank Williams tune "I'm So Lonesome I Could Cry." He'd just reached that sad line about the "lonesome whippoorwill." I felt a strange chill and turned toward Linda. I started to ask her if she thought this whippoorwill could be the same one, the mate of the bird that flew into my truck all those months ago. But I stopped myself before I asked, thinking surely, surely, such a thing couldn't be true. And if it were true, surely we were better off not knowing for certain that loss can be so devastating and enduring.

We think of birds, when they cross our minds, most often as small, frail, pretty creatures. Certainly there is a frailty about the whippoorwill, but there is also enormous strength inherent in the bird, as I observed after the female whippoorwill flew into my truck. That strength was largely emotional and spiritual, I suppose, if we can use "human" terms to describe a bird's behavior. But there is great physical strength in these creatures as well.

I first noticed the hawk on a hot summer day. He was perched atop a power pole on a high bank overlooking the highway, a majestic presence is an unexpected setting. I paid him no more attention than I normally pay a beautiful creature encountered unexpectedly and fleetingly on the roadside, and he might have made no lasting impression if I hadn't seen him again a few days later in the same spot. It wasn't until I'd noticed him several more times in the area, though, that I began to look for him.

After that, I saw him almost every day. Sometimes he would be soaring on the currents high above the highway, sometimes staring down from the power lines or nearby treetops. His domain was an intersection on a four-lane U.S. highway only a few miles from my house, a place I pass almost every day. I wondered why he'd chosen this particular busy spot when there is so much wild and open land in Randolph County, so many places that would seem to offer more appealing surroundings, more promising hunting. Somehow, I couldn't picture the highway providing a home for the numbers of little creatures he needed to survive. But he obviously got along well enough.

I even saw him make a catch one day. He startled me, in fact, swooping low over my little Datsun as I was exiting the highway. His wing span appeared to reach nearly four feet, and I confirmed that he was a red-tailed hawk. He alighted briefly in the grass near the exit ramp then rose with powerful wing flaps, clutching a tiny, furry creature in one claw.

I remember well the day a few months after I began watching for him that I began to see the hawk in a different light. I was approaching the intersection on my way home when I saw him standing on the railing of the overpass, looking down on the traffic. I expected him to fly away when I made my exit and drove across the bridge past him, but he didn't. Indeed, he appeared hardly to notice me as I passed slowly by, only a few feet away. His attention was riveted on the traffic beneath him. That was when I began to wonder if the traffic was the real reason he had claimed this stretch of highway as his own, the thing he'd had his eye on all the time.

Does a hawk dream? Can a hawk be afflicted with ambition? Could this hawk be looking down at those unending streams of vehicles day after day and seeing challenge? Could he be picturing himself swooping down, snagging a Mercedes or a Buick Special, and making for the treetops with it squirming in his clutches?

A silly thought, I knew, but I couldn't shake it from my mind. And the image was only reinforced when on several subsequent occasions I saw the hawk dive toward the highway and pull up short of some speeding car or truck. One day, he swooped within inches of my own windshield. Test runs?

On a winter day, eight months after I began watching the hawk, I approached the intersection searching the sky for him. But he was not to be seen. Instead, I spotted something lying in the highway ahead. Surely just another squashed dog, I thought, but as I drew closer, I saw white feathers flutter in the wind from a passing car. Must be a chicken fallen from one of those jammed cages on those grotesque poultry-house trucks that pass this way so often, I told myself. Then I saw a big wing rise grotesquely from the pavement, stirred by the wake of a truck ahead of me, and I knew it was the hawk.

I'm sure his luck finally ran out, that he simply allowed himself to get too accustomed to the traffic and got killed in a careless moment. But I'd rather think that he went down trying to snag one of those big critters, maybe an eighteen-wheeler.

Certainly one of the lessons we learn from observing other creatures is that life is fragile, even for the strongest among us. We see the lessons of life and death all around us on the shortest drive we make. The red-tailed hawk reminded me of death in a single vivid image, one that inspired me to hope that the manner of his passing had been worthy of his stature. During the summer that I remember as the summer of the wasps, nature provided hundreds upon hundreds of daily reminders that our stay here on earth is short.

That summer the body count mounted daily. The dead were the unlucky ones, those that slipped inside with devious intentions, became trapped, and expired in the extreme heat. Their carcasses numbered half a dozen, maybe more, spread along the dashboard of my car, every day. They represented several species, all vicious, and I left them there as examples, hoping that the already gone would scare off others. It didn't work. Nothing worked. The bodies kept piling up.

That summer our little hillside was beseiged with wasps. There is no other word for it. But this phenomenon was not confined to our property, I should point out. News reports told of large numbers of wasps, particularly yellow jackets, in other areas as well. The experts blamed a mild, dry winter.

With such extraordinary numbers of wasps about, equally extraordinary numbers of people were inevitably stung by them, a phenomenon that has something to do with drought, I learned. Wasps, like all living creatures, require water. When they can't find it readily, they take it where they can—even from the sweat on human bodies.

We are supposed to stand still for this, according to the experts. When a wasp alights upon your body for a drink, if you don't erupt into a St. Vitus dance of fear, if you don't swat at the insect or flee in panic, screaming, the wasp will simply drink its fill and take its leave, grateful for your patience and sweat glands.

That's what the experts say.

I ask this of the experts: When yellow jackets are swarming around my body, how am I to know which ones are merely thirsty and which are out to cause me great pain and misery? But the wasps, I know the experts will say, are without malevolent intent. They sting only to feed or in protection of themselves or their nests. This, I'm sure, is true as far as it goes.

But how am I to know if some ambitious wasp isn't eyeing me as a tasty morsel? And how, in heaven's name, am I supposed to know what makes a wasp feel threatened?

Actually, I do know a few things that threaten wasps. Lawn mowers, for one. This is particularly true for yellow jackets, which build elaborate nests underground. If you by chance run a lawn mower over one of their nests, they will pour out in an angry cloud looking for something to sting. But do they sting the offending mower? No. They go straight for the innocent operator. When you consider that a single nest can house several thousand yellow jackets, you get some idea of the immensity of such a situation. People have been stung to death by disturbing yellow jacket nests in such fashion.

During the summer of the wasps I disturbed three this way myself on a single day. The result was luckily only three stings, which I scratched for days, a reminder of my narrow escape. I have come away with more than a dozen stings from running a mower over a single nest. I got a faster mower.

Another thing that apparently makes wasps feel threatened is turning a steak. I wouldn't have believed this until I experienced it first-hand. The summer of the wasps severely restricted outside activities of all kinds, even cooking out. But the weekend came when I could resist the appeal of a charcoal-broiled steak no longer, no matter what the risk involved. I waited until almost dark to fire up the grill, thinking the wasps might have retired to their nests for the night by then. But just as I was flipping the steaks for the first time, a wasp zoomed down and stung me on the thumb, causing me to flip my steak right into the fire. Explain the provocation of that.

One other thing that will seriously provoke a wasp is driving away its breakfast. This proved to be our most serious problem during the summer of the wasps. Our house is surrounded by walnut trees that spend the summer emitting some kind of resin, which covers our cars. The wasps consider this stuff the delicacy of delicacies, apparently. They feed on it from sunup to sundown. Every morning we would walk outside, hoping to use our cars, only to find them crawling with wasps of what seemed like a dozen varieties. Hundreds of them. They got riled up if I walked close to my car. Sometimes I couldn't even open the door because the handle was coated with a dozen or more wasps. When I did finally manage to get the door open, several of the creatures inevitably buzzed their way inside with me.

With them, I had to fight to the death before I could leave my driveway. Usually, I prevailed. After all, I am bigger and stronger and smarter than a wasp, than several wasps. Now and then, though, one would hide for a while, then strike me as I went down the highway in perfect innocence. These surprise attacks caused my driving to be dangerously erratic. I wasn't content to think that the attacker was merely in search of a soothing drink.

In addition to those that deceived their way into the car to share my ride, many of the wasps who were dining when I departed refused to give up their table, so to speak, and remained on the outside of the car, munching away as I drove. You might be interested to know that a wasp can cling to a windshield at speeds up to sixty miles per hour.

If you go fast enough, the insect will eventually lose its grip. I spent that summer hauling loads of wasps around, dropping them off wherever I could for others to deal with them, but when I'd get home, we would still have more than enough to cover my car the minute it was standing still. One or two would almost always dart in as I got out of the vehicle, and I found myself taking greater and greater pleasure in slamming the door quickly to trap them. Many of the ones I trapped added to the daily body count I was forced to make each morning, an activity that inevitably led me to question my glee at having trapped them.

Yes, they were wasps, beastly, mean-spirited creatures, and they had ruined my summer. But what if the experts were right? What if they were merely creatures seeking water, staying alive the best way they knew how? If that were the case, shouldn't I at least be willing to sacrifice my glee at their demise? Was I learning the right lesson from the summer of the wasps or missing the point entirely?

We tend to long for nature's abundance, but we always want to make our stipulations as to what kind of abundance we seek. Not too many wasps, please. More tomatoes and whippoorwills instead. Fewer snakes, more red-tailed hawks. We have our preferences, and the lowliest creatures don't rank very high on our list. Take slugs, for instance. Is there a lowlier creature in the universe? Yet nature can see fit to grant us an abundance of slugs.

A fellow who likes to chat about gardening experiences called one summer to ask if I had noticed an excessive number of slugs. He said that he was suffering from a veritable plague of the slimy, omnivorous creatures and that all of his efforts to deal with them had come to naught.

I told him that I was indeed enduring the same problem and that it was so bad that slugs were even eating my radishes, something that never had happened before. Some nights, I said, I had entertained myself by sitting on the porch listening to the chorus of slugs burping in the garden.

Why, there were so many slugs around our place that summer, I went on, that you could almost skate on the slime trails, if you were the kind who goes for cheap entertainment. And you dared not walk outside at night with bare feet.

Erik learned that lesson. One pleasant summer evening he came hopping into the living room holding his foot and groaning.

"What's the matter?" Linda asked.

"I stepped on a slug."

"Ooh," Linda said. "Don't get close to me."

That's the way it is with slugs. It would be hard to find anybody who liked them even if they didn't devour gardens. Slugs have a bad image. And not even the best PR man could do much to improve it. For one thing, slugs leave slime wherever they go, and it is a rare person who finds slime attractive. Beyond that, slugs are just plain ugly, all in all, detestable.

Some people simply can't abide them. We had a cookout to bid farewell to some friends who were moving to Florida. While we were eating, one of the guests placed her plate on the patio next to her chair and went to fetch a fresh beverage. When she returned and reached for her food, she let out a yelp and dashed to the far side of the patio. Two slugs had crawled onto her plate and were feasting greedily.

This obviously distressed her deeply, for she paled and made faces and shuddered for some minutes. "I'm sorry," she said, "but I just have a thing about slugs."

I didn't have the heart to tell her that the section of the patio to which she had fled was practically Slug City. A couple of days earlier I had overturned the landscape timber behind the chair where she had taken refuge and discovered at least two dozen slugs clinging to the bottom, hiding from the sunlight.

People haven't always shied away from slugs. In reading about them, I discovered that the sultans of slime have been considered a remedy for various ailments. People once ate live slugs as well as slugs boiled in milk in hopes of curing tuberculosis. The ashes of cremated slugs have been taken to cure ulcers and dysentery. The little shell that every slug carries inside its body was once dried and crushed as a toothache remedy. Some people still believe that slugs cure warts. They say you just rub the slug on the wart and afterward impale the creature on a thorn. As the slug dies and withers away, so will the wart. Or so folklore has it.

Impaling slugs on thorns might be one way to get rid of them although I doubt that there are enough good, sturdy thorns around to accomplish that Herculean task. I have a friend who loves to put salt on slugs and watch them as they writhe in agony. She is a little strange, this friend, although I guess that goes without saying.

The fellow who called to ask me about slugs said that he had bought some commercial slug bait in a garden shop, but he was afraid to use it because a warning on the box said that pets and wild creatures could be harmed by it. I had bought some of that stuff myself once and never used it for the same reason, I told him.

I have tried only one effective remedy for slugs. That is to put little jar caps filled with beer around the garden and other places where slugs hang out. Slugs love beer. They will crawl into the jar top and drink themselves to death. Or maybe they just drink until they pass out and drown. Whichever, the result is the same: a jar lid filled with dead slugs and some awfully slimy beer.

My caller said that he'd tried this and it worked the first time, but after that it didn't seem to attract the slugs anymore although he was still seeing plenty of the creatures about. He thought that the slugs might have gotten wise to that little trick.

I wasn't sure that slugs could be so smart, I told him. My research hadn't turned up anything about their mental capacities although it had provided an elaborate and graphic description of their mating habits, which might be considered erotic if so much slime weren't involved.

Perhaps he should get himself some ducks, I suggested. I'd read that they eat slugs and can be quite effective in controlling them. But he said that he thought he'd just keep looking for other solutions. He wasn't sure, he said, that he wanted anything around him that would find slugs appealing.

Even the most repellent of creatures can be fascinating as long as you are able to keep an adequate distance between you and nature's less than desirable manifestations. The wasps that chose to spend a summer with us were inescapable, and, therefore, I couldn't get too enthused about observing their habits and learning from and about them. Slugs are interesting enough to read about, even to discuss with a neighbor, but the idea of watching slugs doesn't really inspire. Bees are a different story. If they keep their distance (or you keep yours), they can fascinate. Even anthropologists argue that the highly organized structure of bee societies can be instructive.

I first heard the noise while I was inside the house: a high humming sound, almost electrical; maybe an electric motor malfunctioning, I thought, or a transformer going bad. Because it was coming from outside, it didn't really concern me, and I paid it little attention. I was getting ready for a bike ride, and my mind was on other things.

Not until I had gone outside and bounded off the deck toward the garage did I realize that I had stepped right into the sound. Still it didn't immediately dawn on me what it was because my mind was trying to deal with all the small objects flying at me, bumping into my head, arms, back, chest, shoulders. Bees, my mind registered, just as a spurt of adrenalin shot through my body, sending me fleeing back toward the house, waving my arms in an instinctive and frantic effort to fend off the unexpected and unintentional assault.

Safe on my deck, unstung, breathing hard as relief surged through me, I turned to see that I had innocently bounded into a virtual tornado of bees. Thousands and thousands of honeybees in a great funnel-shaped swarm were sweeping across my yard. The base of the bee cloud, where the creatures were swirling at dizzying speed, measured only a couple of feet across, but the apex, which was treetop high, spread out to twenty feet or more.

Never had I seen, or heard, anything like it, and I watched with fascination as the swarm stopped its forward progress next to the huge weeping willow beside the house. For several minutes the cloud just hung there in a buzzing swirl. Then the bottom of the funnel made a sudden swing to the left, alighting on the fat, squat trunk of the old willow. The rest of the bees, caught in the vortex, plunged swiftly downward, searching for landing spots.

Within minutes, the gnarled trunk sported a big, squirming, pulsating beard of bees. I ventured as close as I dared for a better look and realized that I might have a problem on my hands. Once, a colony of yellow jackets built a nest in the wall of a house I lived in, and I climbed into my bed one night to find it crawling with vicious little wasps. Before I could jump back out, I was stung half a dozen times. A few years after we moved to the country, I noticed honeybees entering and leaving through small holes in the kitchen wall, but I plugged the holes and the problem disappeared. I do not want anything that stings living by the hundreds or thousands in the house with me, and I was fearful that this bee swarm was just resting while scouts searched for the best place to take up residence in my house.

What should I do?

Not having the slightest idea, I went bike riding as I had planned, hoping all the time that when I returned the bees and my problem might be gone with the wind. I pedaled back up the driveway a couple of hours later and went straight to the tree. Even from a distance, I could see that the bee beard had disappeared. Moving closer, though, I saw bees hovering near the trunk. Abandoning my bike, I edged close enough to the tree to see that a small group of bees was hovering over a crack in the trunk that I'd never noticed. Other bees were crawling in and out.

So the venerable old willow was hollow inside. No wonder it had been surrendering so many of its monstrous limbs in ice and wind storms of late. Clearly, it had been the intended destination of the swarm. The scouts that had found its inviting empty innards must also have taken note of the profusion of blossoms around the house. What better location? Already the bees were busy making the tree their home.

I went inside and got out my wildlife encyclopedia to read about honeybees. Apparently a nearby bee colony had become over-crowded. A second queen was created, and she had left the hive to start a new colony, taking with her thousands of workers and a few drones who soon would be sacrificed so that the queen could lay the thousands of eggs necessary for the new group to thrive.

In short, the bees had had a problem, and they had worked together to find a solution. Now settled in their new location, they would continue to work together, to follow the organizing princi-ples of their society, in order to survive. Sort of the bees' version of the American Revolution, it occurred to me. And if I was as smart as the bees had been, I'd find a way to feel comfortable with their presence — as long as they kept their distance.

Those animals and other creatures that live closest around us we sometimes take for granted. They are so much a part of our daily experience that we forget to notice them, to understand their wonders. We are much more likely to observe closely and appreciate adequately those living things foreign to our environment. This explains, I guess, our fondness for zoos, and I know it explains my feelings about creatures of the sea. Living landlocked, as I do, I find that the riches of the sea exert a strange, almost hypnotic power over me.

I was awake at first light, well before the alarm, and I pulled back the curtain to a scene of eerie beauty. The river was shrouded in fog. A flight of coots emerged from mist and alighted, splashing near the marina outside my window, squabbling with morning crankiness. A rubber-necked anhinga — snake bird, some call it, because it dives and reappears, snake-like, with only its head and long neck above the surface — materialized briefly in the low-hanging fog, winging toward the coast.

I had slept little, despite a late arrival and long trip the day before, perhaps because the prospect of seeing the manatees always stirs me. Long ago I learned that if you want to see manatees, you have to be an early riser. But not necessarily this early.

Not wanting to disturb my friends still sleeping in the next room, I got up quietly, donned my swimsuit, fetched a glass of orange juice, and sat watching the river greet the morning. The sun's first rays struck the top of a tall, spindly palm standing regally above the fog on a nearby island, creating a crown of gold over the unseen river. An inspirational sight and an omen, I was sure.

With the sun up, gently coaxing away the fog, I began to make noises to rouse my companions, who soon appeared, bleary-eyed, staring at the stirring scene beyond the window. With little conversation, we set about our work, tugging at contrary wetsuits, struggling with balky zippers. Soon, without benefit of breakfast, or even coffee, we were out in the morning chill, launching an inflatable boat.

As the fog lifted, a huge, open-mouthed machine appeared unexpectedly, a noisy avenger in the quietness, voraciously chewing up the garlands of undesirable weeds that clog the clear river, irritating boaters, swimmers, and fishermen. It disappeared around a bend, growling and belching, as we paddled quickly and quietly the short distance to the spring. King Spring, it is named, a big hole in the river, closeby the small, palm-crowned island. From a cavern sixty-five feet below, it pours millions of gallons of seventy-two degree water into the river daily, making it a favorite year-round spot for divers, fish (both fresh and saltwater), and, in cool months, manatees.

They are strange creatures, manatees — huge, ugly, and genial — water-bound mammals that cannot survive cold temperatures, not even Florida's in winter. So they seek the warmth of springs and power-plant discharges. Perhaps more congregate at this spring in Chrystal River than at any other spot, sometimes a herd of forty or more of the few hundred still clinging to existence in the U.S. Manatees must come to the surface to breathe, and the main threat to their well-being is boats. I've never seen one without ugly scars on its back from propeller gashes. Many, less fortunate, don't survive their encounters with boats.

Sea cows, some call them, but they are actually related to elephants and have many of their characteristics: thick gray hide, coarse hair, small eyes. Instead of a trunk, they have a broad snub nose, and they propel themselves with two small flippers and a wide, rounded tail that likely made them the source of mermaid legends.

A lone snorkeler, kicking slowly over the hole, had beat us to the spring. A big mullet jumped a few feet away as we tied up in the shallows. I scrambled from the boat, tumbling awkwardly into the water, feeling its coolness seeping through my wetsuit but beginning to warm almost instantly.

"I'm going to do a little scouting," I said, hurriedly donning mask and fins. "I think I saw one breaking surface over there."

One of my friends had never snorkeled. I knew the others would be slow because of it, and I couldn't contain my eagerness.

All around us in the shallows lay a huge school of mullet, unexpectedly large, mostly motionless, some stirring lazily out of my way as I swam through, disturbing their rest. I skirted the hole, getting a good view of other fish, mostly grunts and snappers, hanging in big schools by the deeper ledges. Away from the spring, large sheepshead and small pinfish scavenged the bottom. Stray bream peered curiously into my mask. A patrol of big amberjacks, roaming predators, cruised past, their quick eyes signaling wariness at the sight of me.

Suddenly a manatee loomed. No matter how many times I've seen them before, the first sight of one always sends a thrill through me. This was a young female with broad scars on her back and a chunk missing from her tail. I approached slowly, extending my hand. She closed her eyes at my touch and rolled over in friendly greeting as I said good morning, rubbing her belly.

Others approached from the murky distance, including one that looked to weigh a ton. As they came closer, I saw that one was shepherding a baby, the first I'd ever seen. The mother cautiously kept her distance, but the others came close enough to be petted. As mother and baby veered off toward a protected area, the big one turned and followed, nuzzling the mother as he caught up, stroking the baby with a flipper.

I swam back to report to my friends, spotting other manatees along the way. "There must be at least a dozen today," I said excitedly, removing my mask. "A mother and baby and the biggest manatee I've ever seen. I think it's the daddy."

For more than an hour we swam and played among these monstrous, gentle creatures, as more boats and divers arrived. Finally, nudged by hunger and cold, we reluctantly climbed back into our bobbing boat and rowed back into a more mundane and less genial world, taking with us memories of the best manatee morning ever.

So often man takes advantage of his fellow creatures. We get along fine with manatees, they like us, until we factor in boats with powerful engines. Then it's no longer an even exchange. The manatees lose first; we lose in the long run. I'm an enthusiastic fisherman, but I'm not willing to tame nature when she's working with a handicap. I've learned enough to know that I'm no victor at all under such circumstances. This lesson hit home again on a fishing trip to the beach with friends.

McAllister and I were on Springmaid Pier at Myrtle Beach when we saw some fishermen taking a big net out through the surf in two small boats. They were several hundred yards up the beach from us.

We had fished from the pier the day before. After a few hours, I had given it up as hopeless and gone to the fish market. McAllister, more persistent and patient, had stayed on the pier for seven hours.

The only thing he had to show for it was a face burned red by the sun. He didn't get a single bite. Not even a nibble.

This day promised to be no better. The pier was lined with people, as it always is on beautiful October weekends, but nobody was catching anything. I had begun to believe that the ocean had been mysteriously emptied of fish. Up and down the pier, people kept saying that if the temperature would just drop or if the wind would just shift, the fish surely would come in. Optimists kept repeating that maybe they would arrive on the next tide.

I had become discouraged that they would ever come again when I saw that the professional fishermen up the beach were pulling in their net. There were fish in it. Many fish. I could see the sun flashing off their silvery sides.

"They've got something up there," I told McAllister. "Let's go see what it is."

A lot of people had the same idea. By the time we got there a big crowd had gathered, many of them having seen the netters at work from the multistoried hotels along the beach. There were men in coats and ties; women in snug, warm jackets; hardy Yankee tourists wearing swimsuits in the chill wind. Some were snapping photographs.

"Mullet," I said to McAllister, as we walked along the great stretch of net that had already been pulled onto the beach. "There's not a fish of any other kind in there. Not even a blue. We can forget fishing, man."

When the surf produces only mullet, the ocean might as well be empty for pier fisherman. Mullet will not take their baits. Mullet are bottom grazers, largely vegetarian, and their mouths are very small. I've never seen one take a hook.

In this school were some very large mullet, and the bulk of them were still in the water, fighting to free themselves from the net. The fishermen, all older men, were struggling in the waves to save their catch. One of them kept dancing back and forth in the churning water, pleading with bystanders for help in getting the huge and cumbersome fish-filled net onto the beach.

"Come on, fellas," he kept calling. "Give us a hand. Get on that rope down yonder! Catch this net up here!"

A lot of people were responding. Men shucked off their suit coats, kicked off their shoes, rolled their pants legs, and high-stepped gleefully into the water. Others plunged in fully clothed, grappling with the net, catching escaping fish with their hands and tossing them onto the beach. It was as if some primitive instinct had seized them.

McAllister and I fell onto the big rope with a long line of men engaged in a great tug of war. We would gain a few inches as each wave crashed in then go stumbling forward in the backwash, straining and stumbling over one another's feet, yelling, "Whoa! Hold it! Pull!"

The net must have held two tons of fish. I could feel blisters beginning to form on my hands. Behind me, a man suddenly dropped the rope, looked at his red hands, and said, "Hell, what am I doing this for? I ain't going to get nothing out of it." He walked away, disgusted with himself.

We almost had the net on the beach when I saw the boy. He looked to be about ten. He was wearing a Cub Scout uniform, and his hair was black and curly. With dark, sad eyes he stood staring silently at the fish struggling in the net.

Slowly, the boy edged along the net, away from the crowd. Looking nervously about, he suddenly stooped and began scooping flopping fish out of the net and tossing them back into the waves. He had freed four or five when his mother spotted him.

"Michael!" she cried. "What are you doing?"

He turned, startled at being caught, but he was defiant in his guilt.

"Well, they have a right to live, too," he said.

That was when I dropped the rope and asked myself what *I* was doing.

Perhaps two tons of fish is too much for our minds to comprehend. That young Cub Scout was not going to change anything much through his quiet defiance. Most of the two tons of mullet were going to die. No doubt about it. It took us only a decade to pretty well decimate a buffalo population of about seventy million. What's a couple of tons of mullet? Still, I think if we listen well, nature speaks volumes in her sheer munificence. Take, for example, the monarch butterfly. Listen.

At first I didn't realize what was happening. I saw one. Then another. A mile or so down the road I noticed a few more. Then I realized they were all around. Some were flying high, near the treetops. Some were only fender level, and I was afraid they would be sucked into my radiator and stuck there until they became as dry and brittle as collectors' trophies pinned to a board. The monarchs were migrating, and I had driven into the midst of a swarm.

Somehow swarm doesn't seem the appropriate word. This was too disorganized to be a swarm. Nothing like a swarm of grackles that can blacken a late evening sky. These regal butterflies with wings of black and orange, spotted in white, seemed independent in their determined struggle southward. Rarely were two seen close together. Although I saw hundreds, they were spread over a distance of several miles along U.S. Highway 220, a few miles from our place.

But I knew that at night they would all come together on one or two trees to rest until morning when they would strike out southward again, each setting its own pace, flapping doggedly on the air currents. It seems improbable that a creature so delicate as a monarch can make a journey of thousands of miles, but that's exactly what the monarchs do each fall and spring. Some fly all the way from Canada to Florida, Texas, Southern California, or Mexico and make the return trip in the spring.

These are the young, summer newborns, and they go south to the same places their forebears came from, often to the very same trees. There they hang in clusters in semi-hibernation until time to fly northward and begin the life cycle again. In Mexico, the trees the monarchs choose are national treasures, tourist attractions.

These monarchs, no doubt, were headed for Florida, for researchers have found that is where the East Coast monarchs spend their winters. They had chosen the same route I'd pick if I were going. But it seemed particularly dangerous for butterflies, with its big, roaring trucks and steady streams of cars. If strength should flag or a downdraft intervene, a beautiful monarch could become just another splat on a windshield. Was this path set for them by instinct? Had the highway builders put their road along an ancient monarch route? Or had the monarchs simply found the wide, unobstructed highway a convenient trail to follow?

This was only the second time I had seen monarchs migrating. The first had been a few years earlier when I was fishing at the coast. After that, I'd read about them in wildlife books. I'd learned that in the butterfly kingdom, they are truly monarchs. Although they aren't the only migratory butterflies, they are the most celebrated, perhaps the most recognized butterfly of all. As butterflies go, they are anything but fragile. Indeed, they are tough, with leathery bodies, hard to hurt. Their bright colors and distinctive wing patterns are actually protective devices, fair warning to birds to keep away. And all but the most inexperienced birds do, for the monarch is deadly poisonous. The ingestion of a single monarch is enough to kill some birds.

With their toughness and few enemies, the monarchs have no trouble surviving so long as they can find the fields of poisonous milkweeds where they feed and lay their eggs, where in their caterpillar stage — striped in black and brilliant yellow — they make their cocoons and emerge as butterflies.

Surely, though, many of them are lost in their long migrations, and it is difficult to encounter such a spectacle and not wonder how many will make it. Where do they get the strength for such a strenuous journey? And how do they know where to go when they have never been there before? Another of nature's mysteries to ponder.

A multitude of monarchs, unerring in their travels along an unknown course, is almost incomprehensible to us. It overwhelms. To penetrate nature's mysteries, we sometimes need to narrow our focus, to ponder something closer to home, less numerous, more like us, perhaps. One year, back before Christmas, Linda saw a chipmunk and reported its having taken up residence in our barn.

This puzzled me because I had never before seen a chipmunk on our place. I'd begun to believe there weren't any. But Linda responded to my challenge by informing me that she knew a chipmunk when she saw one. When I asked her what the chipmunk had been doing, she said it was running along the top of the wall in the loft. I speculated that it was probably a rat or a squirrel. Linda assured me it was a chipmunk and ended the conversation abruptly. Later, I slipped out to the barn to see if I could spot the creature and prove myself right, but nothing was stirring.

Then one night in January I went to the barn in search of some piece of junk or another (our barn's primary purpose is to house such treasures), switched on the light in the loft, and there before me, frozen in terror on a stud brace of the front wall, was the chipmunk. It seemed to be staring straight at me, but I realized it was probably only blinded by the sudden light. As soon as I made a step in its direction, the chipmunk dashed a couple of feet along the wall and disappeared into the canvas bag of a seed sower that I had hung on a nail. That was the first time I'd noticed leaves sprouting from the sower.

"I saw your chipmunk," I said to Linda when I got back to the house. "It's made a nest in that seed sower hanging on the wall.

"I told you I saw a chipmunk," she said.

I saw the creature only once more during winter because during cold weather I usually venture to the barn only to fetch firewood and rarely climb into its upper reaches. But one afternoon I slipped quietly up the steps just to see if I could spot the chipmunk. It was peeking over the sower bag top, eyeing me warily, and I left it to its privacy, reassured that it was still there.

I wasn't even thinking of the chipmunk when I went to the barn on an evening in early spring. I was in quest of some ancient and lost newspaper clippings. I blundered around the loft, muttering to myself, tossing things aside, lifting heavy boxes, grunting. I was shuffling through papers in one big box when I touched something alien. A snake skin. Fortunately, it was no longer attached to the snake but had been abandoned, like the old garments we had shed and stored in nearby boxes. Instantly, I remembered the fat king snake that had made the loft its home the previous summer. I had seen it several times, usually dozing on top of the wall or one of the stud braces.

Only then, with a sense of foreboding, did I think of the chipmunk. I looked toward its nest and there it sat, tense and alert, watching me from the same stud brace where I first had seen it. On another brace, to one side and slightly higher, sat three more chipmunks, all smaller, all sitting upright, tails erect, as still as targets in an arcade.

"Well, well," I said to the mother, "haven't you been busy? Congratulations."

Hoping for a better look, I inched slowly toward the wall, talking soothingly as I went. "Is it okay if I look at your babies? They're beautiful." I stopped about eight feet away. The mother remained wary and alert, but one of the young relaxed and began preening its white belly.

"I tell you what," I said. "I'm going to get you a little present."

I picked up an empty shoebox, went to the house, scooped up three gummy handfuls of molasses-coated grain—Cracker Jacks for our goat—and took the full box to the barn. I was planning to leave the grain near the chipmunks' nest, but when I got back, all four were sitting in the spots where I'd left them, and I decided to see if I could get them to eat while I held the box in my hand.

I was only a couple of feet away when the mother dashed up the wall and, hanging upside down, skittered along the center roof beam inches above my head, an obvious attempt to divert me from her young.

"Hey," I said, backing away, "I'm not going to hurt your babies."

She reached the other side of the barn, started back along the beam, changed her mind halfway, and raced back. She was working her way along the eaves back toward her nest when, not wanting to scare her more, I pulled the string on the light and made my way down the steps, leaving the grain on the floor near the nest as a gesture of goodwill.

"Your chipmunk had babies," I told Linda when she got home later than night.

"She did? How many?"

"I saw three. They're really pretty, but I doubt they'll be there long. As soon as the weather gets warmer, that king snake that lives up there will be out, and I'm sure he'll head straight for that nest. He'll get every one. I found a skin he shed in a box up there tonight."

"Well, we may just have to do something about that old snake," Linda said, thinking just like a mother.

Sometimes animals gradually cross the lines we have drawn between ourselves and their kind. They become human to us, or almost human. That feeling is almost as impossible to explain as it is to escape. When you live in the country, as we do, the creatures likely to make such a transition are more numerous. Practically anybody can have a dog or a cat that gets treated like family. But few have a goat take over space in the heart that previously you couldn't have imagined a goat's occupying.

A sound invaded my dream and confused it: the clippity-clip of hooved feet on the deck outside the bedroom. A nudge brought the dream to an end, and I realized the sound as a reality.

"Jerry, Gosh is out," Linda said.

Dawn. I'd been asleep all of four hours and had been dreaming pleasantly enough to desire no intrusions. I muttered something that I won't repeat, a succinct and clear expression of my sentiments.

Despite my grogginess, I leaped from bed and hurriedly pulled on pants and shoes. I knew I had to move quickly. It wasn't just to save the geraniums that adorn the deck in barrel halves. I knew that when he finished those off, he was apt to see his reflection in the sliding glass doors. Gosh is a butter, you see, although that word sounds much too soft for him. I knew he couldn't resist the temptation of what would look to him like a butting contest, and I didn't want a spray of glass and a goat in my bed.

"Why do you have a goat in the first place?" I am sometimes asked by people who have encountered this goat or heard tales about him. There is a one-word answer to that: ignorance.

For many years I lived under the delusion that a goat was a creature that ate weeds, briers, tough grasses, an occasional newspaper or tin can, and various other forms of undesirable vegetation and debris. Our place has an excess of the above-mentioned nuisances, and I thought that a goat would be of great assistance in controlling them. I happened to mention this once to a friend, and not long afterwards he showed up bearing a gift goat into whose mouth I did not look.

Actually, I was glad to get him, this goat. We put him in a big lot that I'd built for our dogs and named him for the first thing a young friend said upon seeing him. Not until I'd chained him several times in weed patches and had him escape several times from the lot did the truth about goats begin to dawn upon me. It is this: a goat will eat nothing that you want him to eat and everything that you don't want him near.

A carefully nurtured azalea? Gosh will polish it off in the flicker of an eye.

The geraniums in the deck barrels are the quickest of snacks. A garden patch of Silver Queen corn barely whets his appetite. Give him an hour, and he will devour every leaf on an apple tree fifteen years in the growing. Then he'll strip it naked of bark for dessert.

Keeping a goat penned up becomes paramount, and with Gosh that proved difficult, especially in the early days. He was rambunctious, eternally restless, and living as he did without the company of other goats, especially of the female gender, he seemed to suffer an uncertainty about exactly what he was looking for.

Once, he simply disappeared, and we thought he was gone for good. A week or two later, Erik spotted him chained in the back yard of a house up the road. The folks who lived there said he strolled into the kitchen one night as they were having supper, and they didn't know what to do except chain him until somebody showed up to claim him.

Surgery brought an end to this period of anxiety, not to mention certain aromas, and for a long time afterward Gosh seemed spiritless, his desire to roam and plunder momentarily quelled. He mellowed into an amiable middle age, seemingly content to feast on grain drenched with molasses, and rarely did he escape his lot. When he did, I'd round him up, find how he got out, and patch the fence.

Then a change came over Gosh, why I'm not sure. Perhaps he started thinking that he was supposed to live in the house with us, for several times he'd tried to force his way inside. Whatever the reason, he began escaping his lot with regularity. He discovered low places in the fence that he could go over, weak spots he could go through. The fence became a real patchwork as I struggled to prevent the escapes, at times propping ladders, loading platforms, and tree trunks against it to hold it in place. Still, he found a way out.

His early morning intrusion upon my sleep brought a moment of decision and a renewed determination on my part. No more patching. I devoted a full day to rebuilding and reinforcing the lot. I dug post holes, strung barbed wire. I sweated, fought green-head flies and ticks—and for my efforts got butted in an appropriate place. I finished at twilight, exhausted, dirty, sore, bruised, cut, and scratched, but satisfied that I had constructed a fortress that would hold so formidable a goat.

All of which brings me to another question I am sometimes asked: "Why don't you sell that goat or give it away or, better yet, eat it?"

The answer is simple. That goat has been with us since Erik was in grammar school. He is family. Would you sell your grandmother just because she got a little rambunctious? Would you barbecue her and invite friends over to feed? Of course not. You'd just build a stronger pen to keep her in.

Dead wasps, drowned slugs, trapped mullet, even endangered manatees—these you get over, sometimes quickly, as with the wasps or slugs. Other times, like the ones with the mullet or the manatees, you feel a general sorrow that rises up every time you remember the fates these creatures have suffered and will continue to suffer. But it isn't the sort of sorrow that is ever present, inescapable, the kind that is specific and personal because one of your own is gone forever.

We arrived home from the beach during a rare and welcome shower. Two of our dogs, Tasha and Fuji, wandered out from their dry havens under the porch to welcome us with lackadaisical wags of their tails.

"Where's Shiska?" I said, looking around for the missing one, our enthusiastic greeter, the one who's always jumping on us, often to our irritation.

"She doesn't come out in the rain for anybody," Linda said. "She's probably on Erik's porch. Look and see if she isn't."

I didn't look. Instead, I hurried on in out of the rain. In the kitchen, I found a note on the counter.

"Erik says to call him at work as soon as we get in," I called to Linda.

"Oh, Lord," she said, heading for the phone. "I wonder what's wrong."

I could hear only bits of the conversation from the living room, where I was thumbing through the mail.

When Linda came into the room, she was crying.

"Shiska's dead," she said.

We had been worried about her. A few weeks earlier, on a routine visit, the vet had discovered that she had heartworms, but she had been responding well to the dangerous treatment. When we had called home two days earlier, Erik had said that she was fine. But he had found her dead on his porch the morning of our arrival, her mouth and chest bloodied. At first we thought that her big heart, weakened by parasites and poison, simply had burst. Later, I learned that she had been shot by a neighbor while uncharacteristically prowling away from home and had made her way more than half a mile back to Erik's door to die.

It was fitting that her life should end there. Although she loved us all, she clearly favored Erik. We got her when he was just entering his teens, and they became great pals. Shiska was highly protective of Erik. Nobody dared bother him when she was around.

When Erik outgrew his tiny room, we built a garage separate from the house and put a one-room apartment in it that gave him more room and more privacy. Shiska took up residency on his porch to look out for him.

One day when Erik was in school, Shiska came to the door of the house barking excitedly. Linda, who was home alone, went to see what was wrong. Shiska ran to Erik's apartment then returned for Linda, as if she wanted her to follow. When Linda followed her around to the porch of Erik's apartment, an intruder stepped from the sliding glass door, a knife in each hand.

"What do you think you're doing?" Linda demanded of the young man, as Shiska lunged for him.

He jumped back inside. When he went to a side door, Shiska was waiting for him, growling. She held him inside while Linda ran to the house and called a neighbor, who quickly arrived with a gun, then the sheriff, who showed up later.

That's just one example of what made Shiska the best by far of the dozen or so dogs that we've had in the past twenty years. She was the offspring of a chow mother and a mysterious father who could foil fences. From her coloration, the shape of her face, her disposition, I believed her father to be a golden retriever. Whatever her parentage, the result was a fine combination, a gentle and loving dog who could be ferocious when necessary—and who was smart enough to know when that was.

Her mane, her narrow hips, and upraised tail gave her the look of a chow. Golden orange, she had the grace and regal bearing of a lion and often looked like one when at rest. Yet she was more beautiful than any lion I've ever seen.

Her face was narrower and more pointed than those of most chows, and her nose bore the scars of a snake bite that laid her low a few years ago, the fang marks a full inch apart. Her eyes were her most striking feature. They were among the most knowing eyes I've ever seen, warm and perceptive, human eyes trapped in the body of a dog.

Those eyes betrayed her intelligence. Shiska was the only animal who ever made me feel that she understood when I talked to her, and sometimes we found ourselves in elaborate one-way conversations. This usually happened when she kept me company as I worked in the garden, cut firewood, or walked along the creek. Whenever I found a chance to sit on the deck and contemplate the calmness of the evening twilight, she would flop down beside me to offer the opportunity to tickle her ears and unload any troubles that might be bothering me.

When I took up running, she thought that she should run with me, but after I made it clear that she couldn't because the traffic was too dangerous, she settled for waiting for me near the end of the driveway. It really excited her to see that I'd somehow survived another run. She'd leap on me and race around in a frenzy and nip at Tasha and Fuji, who always waited with her. I'd shout, "No!" and

"Don't jump!" and "Shiska, calm down!" and it was the only time that she refused to listen to me.

The full impact of her death didn't hit me until I finished my run a couple of hours after hearing the news and returned to an empty driveway. I trudged up the hill alone, feeling lonely, and went to the spot by the old apple tree where earlier that day Erik had buried Shiska near the graves of our other dogs. For a long time I stood looking at the fresh red mound, wet from the afternoon shower, and while I pretended the salty streaks on my face were just the sweat from my run, I found myself wishing that Shiska was leaping on me again.

The faithfulness and intelligence inherent in Shiska's defense of our property and her loyal patience as she made herself a part of my jogging are the qualities that cause those special bonds between humans and animals to form. My neighbor Ector Bonkemeyer didn't have a special dog; nor was he the proud owner of a goat. Ector had a turtle, and what a turtle it turned out to be. Ector and his turtle made believers out of me.

I paused in my morning run to pluck a box turtle from the road. Before fetching it to safety in the grass well off the roadway, I turned it over, as I always do when plucking turtles from the road, and checked its belly. That's a habit I got from Ector.

I met Ector not long after I moved to the country in 1972. He wasn't a neighbor in the strict sense of the word. He lived a mile away on one of the most immaculately kept places in the whole countryside. I drove by his tin-roofed white house every day, and I usually saw him outside mowing, working in his garden, or helping his wife tend her elaborate flower beds.

My tractor led me to meet Ector. It was a cantankerous twenty-year-old Farmall Cub that I bought from a farmer in an adjoining county. I was always having trouble keeping it running and hitching implements to it so that they would work properly. Ector had a Cub, too. I'd seen him riding and tinkering with it many times. One day when I was befuddled by my own machine, I went to Ector's house and asked if I could look at his to try to figure out what I was doing wrong.

He was in his seventies then, a white-haired little man with a gentle disposition who'd been retired from his carpentry trade for quite a few years. He received me warmly, showed me his tractor, and offered to help in any way that he could. We had a long talk about gardening and about the area I'd recently made my own, his home since birth.

Before I left, he took me into his locked garage and showed me his most prized possession, a '56 blue-and-white Chevrolet that he'd bought new and driven only a few thousand miles. Only rarely did he still drive it to town. Even in the dim light of the garage, the car shone, looking as new as if it had just been driven from the showroom.

I didn't visit with Ector for a long time after that. I gave up on my tractor and sold it at a considerable loss. Ector's wife, Janie, died in 1974, and for a while I didn't see him out working anymore. The flower beds disappeared. A couple of years later, Ector called me. He had a story to tell. I went to his house and found him sitting outside his back door beaming at a box turtle in a cardboard box. The turtle was munching on a fat tomato from Ector's garden.

As a boy, Ector said, he'd loved to play with turtles. Sometimes he'd carve marks into their shells so that he could recognize them later. His fondness for turtles continued into manhood. He was always snatching turtles out of the road to keep them from being smashed by cars.

One Sunday morning, not long after Ector bought his forty-eight acres and the old farmhouse that he fixed up for a home, he walked out into his corn field when the corn was about calf-high and came upon a turtle. An old urge hit him. He took out his pocket knife, carved his initials — EFB — and the year — 1931 — into the shell of the turtle's belly and set it free.

For years after that, Ector picked up every turtle that he saw, hoping to find that particular turtle again. Thirty years passed before he found a turtle in his tomato patch one summer day, turned it over, and saw his initials. He could hardly believe it. He took the turtle to the house and kept it several days, showing it off to friends and neighbors, feeding it the best produce from his garden. Then he let it go. Two years later, he came upon it again.

Thirteen more years passed before it turned up in his watermelon patch and he called to tell me about it.

A few years later, one of Ector's daughters (all three lived within shouting distance of their father, clustered around the family home) called to tell me that the turtle was back, and I went to marvel over it once more.

"I expect that old turtle might outlive me by a long shot," Ector said then, "but I might just see him again."

That must have been the last time I talked at length with Ector. Sometimes I'd see him out in the yard, stop to say howdy, and ask if he'd seen the turtle again. Usually, I'd just toot and wave in passing. I kept meaning to stop and visit because I liked Ector, admired him, and enjoyed talking with him, but it's a busy life, and there's little time for sitting and chatting with old men. Every time I saw him, it seemed as if I was in a hurry to get somewhere — and every time I told myself that I really should stop because he kept looking frailer and frailer.

A time came when he could no longer do the work that he loved in his yard and garden. Family stepped in. Daughters, sons-in-law, grandchildren always seemed to be there doing something, and Ector's place remained as immaculate and well-tended as ever. His beloved Chevrolet stayed inside the garage all the time, only now and then dusted by loving hands. Eventually, Ector moved out of his house and into the home of his daughter Alice across the road.

I'd still see Ector standing out in the yard once in a while, a shriveled wisp of his former self. Sometimes he would be wandering about as if he were looking for something. He no longer responded to my toot and wave, and I kept intending to stop and inquire about his health and his turtle. When I came upon the "Slow — Funeral" signs along the road near his house, I knew I'd waited too late.

I called his daughter. She said Ector had died without seeing his turtle again. That's why my heart quickened when I came upon the turtle in the road near his house on the morning of his funeral. I was hoping his turtle had come back. It hadn't, but I'll keep looking. I'm a believer.

Escaping Seaward

*T*hat gray period before dawn is the best time to be on the beach in mid-summer. The breeze is cool. No oiled bodies glisten on the sand. No hardy souls test the waves on plastic air cushions. No dogs romp. No sand castles rise. No transistor radios blare. No Frisbees fly. Only another lone fisherman, a hundred yards down the beach, disturbs the solitude.

Few creatures are astir. Coquina clams and mole crabs are engaged in their frantic and incessant struggle to survive, perpetually washed into the surf, perpetually racing to rebury themselves in the sand. I feel mole crabs squirm under my bare feet as the fleeing tide rips away my foothold.

The black-winged skimmers are up, working the waves for breakfast. They don't seem to be doing very well. Blackbirds prowling the beach, investigating the night's offerings, fare better. Somewhere out there under the waves, the small, silver-gray fish known as spots are prowling. I am sure of this because I have already caught more than enough for my lunch, and they continue to take the half-rotted shrimp I continue to cast to them.

The paunch-bellied fisherman down the beach, standing high out of the water in Bermuda shorts and sneakers, hasn't caught a single fish, and I suspect he envies my success. Maybe the black-winged skimmers do, too.

When the spots aren't biting, I stand in awe of the overwhelming gray: the slate-gray sea broken only by the surf's white froth; the sky still too gray to reveal whether it holds clouds; in the distance, beach, sea, and sky a blur, murky gray. A distant fishing pier, its lights aglow, draws the only horizon.

From the haze up the beach, I see a figure emerge, tiny in the distance, walking at water's edge. As it moves closer, I watch it pause to stoop occasionally. Eventually the figure becomes a young man wearing cut-off jeans and t-shirt, carrying a crab net. He has a red mustache and, on his sunburned left bicep, a tattoo. We nod in greeting. I watch as he walks on down the beach, past the paunch-bellied fisherman, pausing and stooping still, raking his net in the surf, until once again he becomes a tiny black figure, disappearing into the haze.

Turning my attention back to sea, I see the first color come magically to the sky, a wisp of pink reflecting off a cloud high enough to peek over the still invisible horizon. And up the beach, I can see other figures, small groups, beginning to appear here and there.

Another spot jangles my line, and by the time it is safely in my bucket, the sky has changed dramatically: pink hues in several places and just a flash of gold. More people, too, emerge, filing over the high dunes onto the beach. Perhaps they are responding to a primitive urge to worship the sun, buried deep in their genes, perhaps to nothing more than the beauty of sunrise on the beach.

The sun sneaks into the sky. I had expected it to rise dripping from the water, forgetting that the beach at Salter Path on the Bogue Banks, low on North Carolina's jutting coast, faces southward. So I am startled to catch my first glimpse of the sun slipping up over the dune behind my left shoulder. I watch it rise out of a trailer top, a gigantic red-pink balloon drifting lazily upward, changing color, glowing as it gets higher.

Other fishermen begin to take stations near me. A darkly tanned young man races into the water and dives into a breaking wave, a jolting way to greet the day. The first plastic air cushion appears under the arm of a pale fat boy, who timidly tests the water with his toe. Two boys, sleep still in their faces, race across the beach and begin to scoop handfuls of sand from the edge of the surf near me. The evening before Erik and his friend Michael taught one of the boys how to scoop mole crabs and have them race in circles drawn in the wet sand. Now, flush with the excitement of new knowledge, the boy wants to show his friend. He was probably barely able to wait for daybreak.

When I begin to feel the sun's heat on my shoulders, I realize that the grayness is gone. I hadn't really noticed its leaving. I do notice that the beach is already getting crowded. So I reel in my line, and with fishing rod and bucket in hand I trudge back across the beach and begin to climb a dune. Breakfast beckons, and there are fish to be cleaned.

The stereotype of country dwellers suggests that we don't travel much, that we are homebodies, content to live out our lives on a small stage. This image is, to some extent, accurate, but today's country residents often find themselves sharing with their urban peers the need to stay on the move to earn a living. It's practically impossible to find more than a handful of people able to sustain themselves and their families on a small farm, the life that was the norm in rural America less than a century ago. Now, we country folk are more likely to spend hours on the highway each week in our efforts to earn the money that allows us to sustain our way of life. In that sense, rural life is a luxury item, an expensive habit—at least in terms of the time and energy required to make it work.

Thus, country people are far from immune to another of modern life's standard features: stress. And where there is stress, there is need for periodic escape. For me, the best escape has always been a trip to the beach. Yes, it involves a long, tedious car trip. Yes, it's hard to get away. Yes, there are all those tourists covered with oil that Jimmy Buffet sings about. But there is still some magic that transcends all the negatives for me. There is the sea itself. There are sand dunes, sunrises, fishing, and night skies unlike night skies anywhere else.

I wouldn't trade my inland home, my small piece of our little mountain, for anything in the world. But I also cannot give up the chance to head east when the need overwhelms me, the car crammed full of luggage and fishing gear, in search of the sea and its special brand of peace.

Beach memories tend to fall into two categories: solitary experiences and group activities. Each has its rewards. After a morning of solitary pre-dawn fishing, there is the quiet pleasure of feeling closer to the natural world, of having communed with the sea and its riches in a highly personal way. When you experience the beach with good friends, the pleasure is different but equally rich. You still take away something from the connection to nature, of course, and there's the added bonus of strengthening the bonds of friendship. That happens even if the fish aren't biting.

Fishermen huddled glumly in the café, drinking cups of steaming coffee as dawn began to pink the sky across the sound. Like us, they wore flannel shirts, boots, and heavy jackets, and they talked of the weather and the prospects, none of them good.

For three days a gale had blown. Wind had come from the northwest, driving sheets of rain, and it had pushed the water right out of Currituck Sound, the wide and shallow body of brackish water that lies behind North Carolina's northernmost barrier island, a longtime haven for fishermen and duck hunters. Just the day before, the portion of the sound outside the restaurant windows had been muddy bottom. Fish, trapped there in beds of milfoil, an alien water grass that clogs the sound, died struggling in the mud.

Now the rain had stopped, the sky had cleared, and the water had begun to return. But the wind still blew from the northwest, stiff and cold for October. Beyond the restaurant windows, a flight of ducks fighting the wind in the lightening sky seemed almost motionless.

My friend Buck Paysour wasn't optimistic. He sat drinking coffee and muttering about the weather. Everything was wrong, he said. The wind was plainly too rough for us to fish the sound; we'd have to try the North River nearby. He had organized this trip, and he kept apologizing as he drank more coffee.

"This is the worst time we could have picked to come," he said.

The trip had been planned for months, the weekend chosen because under normal conditions it would have been one of the best of the year for our purposes. We had come in pursuit of largemouth bass, the freshwater fish for which Currituck Sound is famous. Buck is an expert on bass fishing, the author of a book on the subject, a purist who scorns fancy, high-powered bass boats, professional bass-fishing tournaments, and members of the Bass Anglers

Sportsmen Society, who, he claims, aren't sportsmen at all. He regards the bass as one of nature's noblest and wiliest creatures and accords it great respect. His greatest delight is to catch a bass with a fly rod, using as bait an artificial "popping" bug (so called because it makes a popping sound when a skilled fisherman moves it on the water) that he has made himself.

"Did you hear that?" Buck asked.

I did. The professional fishing guide at the table with the glum fishermen, all Virginia businessmen, was gently preparing his party for not catching fish.

"We're not going to catch anything," Buck said.

A few minutes later, as we were paying for our breakfasts, my friend Hubert Breeze encountered another professional guide, whom he knew, and asked how the fishing was likely to be.

"Not worth a damn," said the guide with a snort of contempt for such weather on prime fishing days.

"We were thinking about fishing the North River," Hubert told him.

"You won't catch nothin'," he said.

If not for Currituck Sound, Buck maintains, the North River would be the best bass fishing spot in North Carolina. It is a blessing to Currituck Sound fishermen because it is so close, and it can usually be fished when the wind is too high on the sound.

We put our boats into a narrow canal behind a small hunting and fishing lodge on the main highway. The canal was shallow and clear; its water, black with tannic acid. It cuts through deep woods and always makes me think of the Okefenokee Swamp. A short distance into the canal, we had to clear a fallen tree from the water so our boats could pass.

Buck saw the nutria first. There were several — large, otter-like rodents brought to this country from South America for their fur. They have since spread through many southern waters. These were playing at the mouth of the canal. They seemed undisturbed by our intrusion and in no hurry to get out of the way. One swam so close to the boat I could have reached out and petted it.

"I love it," Buck said, watching the playful animals. "I come for this as much as for the fishing. I love it."

In open water, the cold wind hit. I was wearing a t-shirt, long johns, long-sleeved shirt, sweater, flannel shirt, denim jacket, and windbreaker. Still the wind cut through to chill my bones. My eyes watered; my nose ran. I pulled one of Buck's oversized fishing hats hard over my ears and hunkered in my seat.

Soon, however, we were in more protected waters and began to fish. Over the next several hours, we dropped lures next to every cypress knee in sight, into every dark hole where a big bass might lurk. We crawled lures over thousands of lily pads and fished into creeks barely wide enough for the boat. We saw coots, cormorants, red-winged blackbirds, ducks by the hundreds, Canadian geese honking their way southward in great V-formations, and many other wondrous and beautiful sights.

"I love it," Buck kept saying. "I love it."

But we saw no bass.

Just as we were getting ready to stop for lunch, I caught a fish. A chain pickerel, sometimes called a jack, a creature with vicious teeth and a nasty disposition. But it heartened the whole expedition. We tied our boats together in the middle of the creek and ravenously consumed a lunch of sardines, Vienna sausages, and pork and beans, everybody agreeing that it was a magnificent meal. As we ate, we talked about how poor the fishing was, but nobody suggested giving up.

Hours later, as dusk approached, we were still at it. And nobody had yet seen a bass. My arm was numb from casting, but Buck kept wanting to work one more grass bed, one more bank, persistent in his belief that the bass would start hitting any minute now.

We quit with reluctance and headed to shore, two boats, four men, a dozen rods, a plethora of tantalizing lures—and one ugly chain pickerel to show for nine hours of hard fishing. Buck kept apologizing. It was, he said, the worst fishing he'd ever experienced in these parts. We'd have to come back when the weather was better.

As Buck eased our boat through the narrow canal to the landing, I saw something swimming ahead of us. At first, I thought it was another nutria. Then I realized that it was a snake, swimming with its head high out of the water—a huge cottonmouth moccasin, thicker than my arm. It slithered onto the bank, coiled only a few feet away as we passed, and showed us its white mouth and frightening fangs.

"Isn't it beautiful?" Buck said.

Indeed it was.

"I don't care if we didn't catch any fish," said Buck. "I love it. I love it."

It's strange how the things I remember most from fishing trips have so little to do with catching fish. I remember sights and sounds, weather, conversations and silences with my buddies, food, and laughter—all more significant than any fish I ever caught. The old definition of a fishing pole as something with a fool at one end and nothing at the other applies only if your primary goal in fishing is to catch fish. If you're after the other joys inherent in that activity, you aren't such a fool after all, no matter what's at the opposite end of the pole. Sometimes, in fact, it isn't joy at the other end. It's knowledge, or recognition, a reminder, maybe, of nature's complexity and our own.

We hunched our shoulders into the wind and started up a barren dune. The wind was colder than I had anticipated, blowing from the northeast at gale force. It rippled the dune, picking up sand to sting our faces.

"Sands of Kalahari," McAllister said.

Ernie said nothing.

"I wish I'd brought my jacket," I said.

Determined, we tucked our chins into our chests and climbed on, scouting for a place to fish. The dune was high and magnificent, and when we reached the top, the wind almost pushed me back. It took my breath. If it hadn't, the view surely would have. I immediately regretted not bringing my camera. I wanted to say something but felt terribly inadequate.

"Look at that," I found myself saying. It was all I could come up with. "God, isn't it beautiful?"

Before us was a scene of incredible natural violence. The wind had whipped the ocean to froth. Great breakers crashed onto the beach. Above the tideline, the sand raced and swirled on the wind, and sea oats bowed in homage. We had come to land's end, and at the point where the beach began its turn to follow the inlet, a jetty of huge gray rocks reached into the ocean for hundreds of yards. But the jetty had been breached in the middle, leaving a wide gap through which a swift current flowed. Waves beat against the length of the jetty, sending clouds of spray into the air, here and there creating tiny rainbows.

Beyond the gap in the jetty, on the leeward side, small boats worked dangerously close to the rocks, wallowing in the choppy protected water. At the point where the gap began, a small group of fishermen clustered on the rocks. All around them, birds had gathered, mostly pelicans and gulls, hundreds of them. Some circled just above the fishermen's heads. Others rode the foamy swells in the protected water.

"There are fish out there," I said.

The jetty was a magnet. We headed for it without speaking, bending into the wind, hurrying, for we all felt a certain excitement. We started across the jumbled rocks, walking the top of the jetty. The going was difficult, the footing always uncertain. Several times the wind caused me to lose balance, and I grabbed for the rocks to keep from falling. Some of them were pointed and a fall could prove dangerous indeed.

To the right, close to the beach, where the water was calmest, a man in chest-high waders stood thigh-deep in the green water below us, guarded from the wind by the jetty, which was more than head-high. The man stood heron-like, motionless, watching the water, a nylon cast net poised in his hands and teeth. Suddenly he let the net fly. It caught on the wind, circled, and settled like a parachute onto the water. He gave the rope a hard tug and strained against it. When he lifted the net from the water, it wriggled with small silver fish.

A little further along, where the sea solidly pounded the jetty, the rocks were wet and slippery, and we were frequently splashed by cold spray. The six fishermen who had clustered at the gap wore hooded water-repellent jackets. They were on the low rocks on the leeward side, casting with long rods into the turbulent water amongst the gulls and pelicans. They were using artificial lures, spoons, and jigs. It didn't matter what. The fish were hitting anything that moved and glittered. As soon as the lures struck the water, the fishermen were setting the hooks and struggling to reel in their catches. These were bluefish, strong fighters, and each appeared to weigh two to three pounds.

A huge school had gathered in the protected water, and they were in a feeding frenzy. They churned the surface. Occasionally small fish leaped from the swells in panic. Pelicans scooped up the fleeing fish, and the gulls hovered, waiting for scraps to surface.

The fishermen were in a frenzy of their own. They worked silently and swiftly. After swinging the desperately flopping fish over the rocks from the water, they grabbed them with towels, held them to the rocks, and quickly sliced off their heads with sharp knives. Blues are bloody fish and must be bled quickly to keep their flesh white and tasty. The fishermen kicked the heads back into the sea and tossed the bodies into big buckets of crimson water. The rocks around them were so bloody from their efforts that they sometimes slipped and nearly lost their footing.

Talking wasn't easy over the roar of the wind and crashing waves. "If we're going to fish, this is the place," I shouted to McAllister. "You want to go get the rods?" he yelled back.

As we turned to leave, one of the fishermen cast, and I saw his silver lure hit a pelican that had just taken flight. The fisherman's rod suddenly bent. The pelican stopped in midair and, with its wings flapping awkwardly, plunged backward into the water. The man cursed and whipped his rod, trying to break the lure free, but the pelican was solidly hooked. Incapable of comprehending its obstruction, it kept struggling to get back into the air. At first, I thought the man was going to cut the line and leave the hook in the bird, but he apparently didn't want to lose the lure. He started reeling in, but the going was slow. The pelican moved backward and fought all the way. The man was clearly growing impatient at the loss of good fishing time. He cursed and yanked the line.

I couldn't watch. I turned and climbed back across the rocks toward the beach. It hadn't bothered me to see bluefish struggling and dying, but a hooked pelican, strangely, was another matter. When I reached the beach, I climbed off the jetty and onto the sand, out of the wind. McAllister was behind me, rubbing his backside.

"I took a fall," he said. "It's dangerous out there."

"Where's Ernie?" I asked.

"I don't know. I thought he was behind me."

I looked back and saw him with the fishermen at the jetty's breach. We sat on the rocks to wait for him.

"I had to check on that pelican," Ernie said when he climbed down to join us. "I couldn't leave that pelican hooked. They got it loose. It was hooked in the neck, but I don't think it was hurt bad."

The wind was at our backs as we climbed back over the dune, saying nothing of the violent spectacle we had just witnessed. Instead of getting out the rods, we climbed into the warm haven of the car and, bucking the wind, headed north toward home. Somehow we had no more heart for fishing.

The bond created by the sea is such that prior acquaintance isn't always necessary for its benefits to fall into your lap. A fisherman can wander into a seaside village, unknown to anyone there, sit down for breakfast in a café, and get up to leave richer for having talked to one of his fellows. The connection can spring up from almost anything, can overcome initial reserve, even distrust. It's as if there's something in the salt-air atmosphere that draws us closer, if not entirely together.

He had finished his grits and was sopping egg yolks with a remnant of toast when I slid onto a stool beside him.

"Boy, it's rough out there," I said. I had been drenched during the short dash from car to café door.

"Coffee?" asked the waitress.

I nodded.

Through the windows we could see the masts of sailboats bobbing violently at the dock. The rain was coming hard, driven by wind. He looked out as if he had just noticed and acknowledged that it was a little blow. It was obvious that he considered it a trifle.

I was curious about him. He was dressed in worn denim and sported a full beard, mostly gray. His hair was pulled into a ponytail. The laugh crinkles at his eyes made him look perpetually amused. We began to chat.

When he learned that I write for a newspaper, he said, "I've had experience with journalists." The tone of his voice told me that he hadn't been amused by it. "They write personal things about you," he said. "And they always want to take your picture. I don't like to have my picture taken."

A shame, I thought, as he told me he'd decided against granting any more interviews. Besides, he said, he entertained notions of writing himself, and he didn't see the point in giving away any of his good stuff. He smiled. "It's fantasy number three thousand."

"Did you ever write anything?" I asked.

"A few little things."

A woman he had once sailed with had taken most of his writings, promising to do something with them, he said. He'd never heard from her again.

"I was planning to write something else. Maybe a poverty-stricken sailor's guide to coffee shops on the Atlantic Coast."

We laughed, and he told me that he'd been sailing for ten years, wandering up and down the Atlantic Coast, over to Bermuda, throughout the Caribbean. "But I like to get in some little old port and just hunker down," he said. He'd been hunkering here in Beaufort, one of North Carolina's earliest ports, for five months. But he planned to be sailing northward with summer, a month away. First, he had a job to finish. He was helping a man fix a boat.

He didn't appear to be a man of means, and I, with my journalist's heart, could not resist a personal question. "How do you manage?" I asked. "How do you get by?"

"Well, Thoreau lived two years on twenty-six dollars. Of course, you'd know that."

He'd simply taken Thoreau's advice, he said, and simplified his life. His boat has no motor. He sails only under the wind. On land, he transports himself by bicycle.

"I don't need much. I tell anybody who wants to crew with me that we're not going to have a high-carbohydrate diet, it's a *total* carbohydrate diet. We have grits in the morning and macaroni at night, and at lunch we have cold grits and at midnight we have cold macaroni."

"More coffee?" asked the waitress, filling our cups without awaiting an answer.

I asked about his past, but he was vague. He'd lived around Washington, he said, the Chesapeake Bay area.

"What caused you to make the break?" I asked. "Why did you leave everything and go sailing?"

He smiled. "I was useless," he said, "and I got a headache. Every time I'd go into town, I'd get a headache. And people told me, or I told myself, 'Eb, you're useless. You're useless. You're a detriment. Go do something you can do. Go sailing.' So I did."

We talked about some of his longer voyages, about interesting people who'd sailed with him, about the time he rode out a hurricane in the North Atlantic ("Lost the mast, but that was all, never really felt in danger"), and I kept telling him that he ought to write about it all, ought to start keeping a journal. He said that he planned to.

The door opened with a blast of wind, and in came a man shaking rain from his slicker. It was the man on whose boat Eb had been working. He took the stool on Eb's other side, and they began to talk about the boat, to plan their day.

I got up to leave, distracting him from his conversation. We shook hands, wished each other well.

"Don't forget to write," I said.

He smiled.

I am certain after all these years that the sea provides many forms of nourishment, literal and spiritual, and that we are able somehow to find in the waters what we need. Eb is but one example of how this works. Defeated by land, scorned even, some might say, he turned to the sea and found the solace and the sustenance he needed to shape his life. Who is to say that his is a less fortunate existence than the ones most of us live out? Who is to say we are any richer in the ways that really matter? Meeting a man such as Eb, learning the outlines of his story, can only deepen and enrich our own memories of what the sea renders up to those who are patient with her temperament.

I snuggled deeper into my down jacket and pulled my Farmers' Exchange cap tighter around my ears in anticipation of the wind. It had been blowing all day, cold and steady at thirty miles per hour and more, sometimes gusting above forty. It was coming mostly out of the north and northwest although at times the direction gauge had swung in wild confusion.

The wind had come with the full moon and the year's most extreme tides, and from up and down the coast came reports of serious beach erosion. The ocean had been roiling with whitecaps all day. The party fishing boats that had gone out with the dawn were all back well before noon, hours early, disembarking pale, queasy, relieved passengers. We had been prudent and stayed in the channel behind the island, fighting the chop, fishing for winter trout with minnows and big red floats on our lines, an exercise in futility. Not one of us had known the pleasure of a certain strike.

After lunch, despairing of fishing, my companions had donned rubber boots and waders, loaded a small boat with crab traps, buckets, and rakes, and headed off into the maze of narrow creeks winding through the marsh grass between the island where we were staying and the South Carolina mainland. I had work to do and stayed behind. By the time I was done, my companions were back carrying a bucketful of clams and a tubful of oysters, which they had scrubbed clean of mud at the dock before I had a chance to help. I was, of course, guilt-ridden.

Hours later, our bellies bloated with heavy seafood dinners from a nearby restaurant, I joined Hubert Breeze and Neal Cadieu to retrieve the crab traps they had set earlier. Left overnight, the traps might be carried heaven-knows-where by the tide and never found. It was well after ten P.M. as our boat edged slowly out of the canal into the channel, its bow rising into the wind as Neal increased speed and swung southward toward the inlet. The wind had calmed considerably, but its bite was still cold enough to make my nose run and my eyes water. Leaking around my collar, it shimmied down my back, causing me to shiver.

The moon was high, its round reflection dancing on the surface before us. Neal swept the water and marsh grasses with a powerful spotlight, searching for obstacles in our path, making certain we steered clear of shallows and sandbars.

Past a big dredging barge moored in the channel, he swung the boat to the right into a wide creek, then right again into a narrower one. He cut the engine to a slower speed, and the bow settled back into the water.

"Right here's where we put them in," he said, flashing his light all around, but there was no sign of the traps.

"This tide has really come in," Hubert said.

"Sometimes it'll just carry them right away," Neal said.

We eased up the creek, searching with the spotlight.

"There they are," Hubert called from the bow.

I saw the white one-gallon milk jugs then, bobbing side by side near the edge of the high grass. Neal pulled the boat alongside them, and Hubert snared one with his hand and began pulling on the rope that was attached to it. When the wire cage broke the surface, I grabbed one side of it and helped heft it aboard.

"Hey!" Hubert said.

"Look at that!" I said.

"Boy!" said Neal.

The trap was filled with crabs, most of them skittering frantically about in the unexpected light, clacking angrily and waving their claws. I counted fourteen before I had to turn and help Hubert pull the other trap aboard. It held only two crabs and two big, ugly toad fish with full sets of sharp teeth and jaws powerful enough to inflict serious wounds.

We continued up the creek searching for the third and last trap.

"You don't suppose somebody would have stolen it, do you?" I asked after we had gone a considerable distance without spotting its milk-jug marker.

"Maybe," said Neal. "They do sometimes."

We came upon it a little later. It held another half-dozen crabs, mostly big jimmies, as adult male crabs are called, as well as a couple more toad fish.

Back at the dock, we eased the traps into the canal, safe from tides and poachers. There the crabs would remain alive until the next day when they would join the clams and oysters in big steamer pots to provide us a glorious feast, consolation for the fish we hadn't caught.

I love an ocean that finds a way to feed you even when the fish aren't biting. I love an ocean that's stormy, that's cold, that's rough on me. We think the pleasures the beach has to offer are summer-time things. But if we stop there, pack up the cooler and the umbrella and the lounge chairs, and head back inland till spring peeks over the mountains and sets us to thinking sand and surf again, we are cheating ourselves of at least half the charms the shore has to offer. Winter at the beach may well be one of nature's best kept secrets.

I lifted my reddened body from the steaming waters of the whirlpool and stretched out in the sunshine that streamed magnified and reheated through broad sheets of glass. Beyond the windows and the nearby shivering palms, I could see a few people bundled in heavy coats and hats, walking on the beach. The ocean was calm, a soothing lover, caressing the land with gentle strokes.

"Isn't it nice to see water that isn't frozen?" said Linda.

I had been trying to forget that.

"Not again," we had cried as the lights flickered and went out during the second big ice storm in less than a week. When I went to the power company the next day to report our dark, helpless situation and found the employees working by candlelight, I knew that this failure was going to be even worse than the last. After two nights of huddling over candles, with no relief in sight, we loaded the meat from our freezer into two big boxes, hauled it to a locker with its own power source, and fled southward 175 miles to Myrtle Beach.

Our hotel had not only lights, hot water, a functioning TV, and a beautiful view of the beach; it also offered an enclosed, heated pool, a hot tub, and a solarium, where it was possible to stretch out and pretend summer had arrived.

It may well be that Myrtle Beach is at its best in winter. Most of the hotels and motels and all of the amusement parks, arcades, and souvenir shops are closed. Many of the hotels that do remain open have enclosed pools and low rates. There are no traffic jams, no lines at restaurants, no crowds on the beach.

Bundled in heavy coats, Linda and I walked the beach reveling in splendid isolation. At Springmaid Pier, where I fish amidst mobs each fall and spring, we encountered only two hardy fishermen testing their luck at midday.

"Usually, I fish for trout," one told me. "Caught some nice ones last Wednesday. But today I'm fishing for croakers."

They had been keeping him busy, stealing his bait. But as he spoke, a yank on his line produced a nice specimen, flopping sluggishly. He showed it off proudly before we left him to resume our walk.

Shells that can't be seen in other seasons litter the beach in winter, along with driftwood and other debris tossed high on the sand by storms. But no ghost crabs skittered at our approach, and at water's edge no mole crabs scurried from the sand in frantic pursuit of the fleeing surf. Coquina clams, so active in summer, were nowhere to be seen, but they must have been there, we figured, for sandpipers rushed about, pecking at the sand, feeding nervously and endlessly.

The beach belonged to gulls. They stood about everywhere, fluffing their feathers against the wind, looking confident and in command, unconcerned about a few bundled humans encroaching on their territories. The gulls kept sensibly away from the water, but it proved an irresistible lure for a Labrador retriever that raced across a dune and into the gentle breakers, followed joyfully by a boy, maybe seven or eight, who charged in behind the dog, gloriously oblivious to the frigidity of the water soaking his heavy clothing to the thighs.

Not for me, thanks. I chose the steaming whirlpool, the rewarmed sunshine under glass. There, for a while, at least, I could forget that back home the trees remained ice-encrusted, the power was still off, the telephone out of order, and that at least a week's work clearing downed trees and limbs awaited me. There, for a little longer, I could escape.

Jimmy Buffet has a song about trying to reason with hurricane season. Its tone is ironic, of course, for there is no way to make sense of something as furious and as powerfully chaotic as a hurricane. Still, with my love of a stormy beach, the news of a hurricane approaching the stretch of coastline closest to me is an almost irresistible temptation. Whether its reasonable or not, I find myself longing to be at the heart of the storm. On occasion this urge has been strong enough to pull me across the miles to the sea, where I sit and wait for the storm to hit. I know most people take the opposite path, head inland to sit out the beating the coast is likely to take. But I've never been one to do the obvious if I have a choice.

I left the balcony door open so that I could hear it when it came. I didn't want to miss it, not after all the buildup. I wanted to get out in it, feel the wind, and watch the surf crashing over the sea wall.

All day I had followed reports of the tropical storm's progress up the East Coast. It was off Brunswick, Georgia, when I left home in early morning, heading for Atlantic Beach on North Carolina's Bogue Banks, just across the sound from Morehead City. As I drove eastward in the rain, the storm moved up to Savannah. The prediction then was that it would come ashore at Charleston in the afternoon, and I felt a twinge of disappointment. So I admit to having been a little pleased at hearing that Dennis had veered seaward, bypassing Charleston. I knew chances were good that it would come ashore on North Carolina's jutting coast and that I could be in it.

My second-floor room at a beachfront motel would be a front-row seat, I hoped. It was only thirty feet from the sea wall, and it had a sliding glass door that opened onto a seaside balcony. Rain was falling hard when I checked in, the clouds dark, turbulent, and clinging. The radio kept reminding me of the possibility of tornadoes. But soon the sky brightened, the rain stopped, and a few determined vacationers ventured into the surf, which wasn't as disturbed as I thought it might be.

When I watched the evening TV news, the storm was approaching Myrtle Beach, a couple of hundred miles to the southeast, still headed for the Outer Banks. I was sure then that I wouldn't miss it.

A thunderstorm hit after dark as I was eating fried flounder at a waterfront restaurant in Morehead City. Sharp lightning rent the sky, and rain streaked the windows as I watched fishermen struggling to secure their boats at the adjoining docks. Back at the beach, the surf had grown violent. Huge waves rolled in, sending walls of spray racing along the curls of their crests, as they broke with thunderous crashes. Waves were breaking well beyond the end of the fishing pier just down the beach from my motel.

The eleven o'clock news made it certain. The storm was entering North Carolina waters. The eye was supposed to pass over

Morehead City at six A.M. Although winds were only fifty-five mph, the storm was not to be taken lightly, the weatherman said. The tide was high then, and the waves were lapping at the dunes and splashing up to the sea wall that protected the motel. There was little wind. The rain came and went with varying intensity.

At midnight, I saw a group of people in rainsuits shining flashlights at something on the beach. During a break in the rain, I went to see what it was. Some tourists were torturing a frantic ghost crab and laughing wildly. One man grabbed it by a hind leg and held it aloft. In its struggle to free itself, the crab pulled off its leg, flopped onto the sand, and skittered toward the safety of the dune with several people yelping in pursuit. Disgusted at the cruel and mindless spectacle, as well as at myself for doing nothing to stop it, I trudged back to my balcony and sat watching the show the surf was putting on.

The wind had begun to pick up a little when I went to bed about one-thirty. The storm was off Cape Fear, according to the last TV report I heard, a hundred miles away. I left the balcony door open so that the storm would be sure to awaken me when it arrived. Because I was keyed up, I didn't doze off until after two. When I awoke, it was with a start, the kind of awakening set off by fear of being late, of having missed something. I looked at my watch: five-fifty. The storm should be raging, but all I could hear was the steady pounding of the surf.

I stumbled sleepily onto the balcony in my underwear to be greeted only by light wind and rain. Could the storm have turned out to sea and missed me? Had I slept through it? No television station had signed on yet, so I couldn't find out.

The sky was beginning to lighten. The tide was out, and the beach had reappeared. I pulled on my clothes, donned a poncho, and went to walk the beach to see what the big surf had washed in. Mostly beer bottles, soft-drink cans, plastic containers, shards of Styrofoam, and other such pervasive and indestructible relics of our society. A few dead jellyfish lay here and there. Except for the busy sandpipers and prowling ghost crabs, I had the beach to myself. But as I neared the pier, two teenaged boys carrying surfboards darted across the dunes and raced into the still-tall breakers.

I found a whale bone and a fishing knife before I turned back to my room for a cup of coffee. On TV, a fellow was explaining that the storm was now off Cape Hatteras. It had passed over Morehead City at four A.M., he said.

Ungracious. That was the word for this storm. I left the door open, and it didn't even come in.

You invite nature to hit you in the face, say, in essence, come on and give me your best shot. What does she do? She passes you by. She's got better things to do than toy with you. So you accept it, adjust, realize your relative unimportance in the overall scheme. Then you set out on an innocent excursion, a simple boat ride. And what does nature do? She hits you with her best shot.

The fish were biting—wouldn't you know it?—when the wind suddenly died, as if sucked into a vacuum, and an eerie silence foretold storm. The day was viciously hot, so hazy that earlier we couldn't even see across Bogue Sound to the mainland just a few miles away from our rented beach house at Emerald Isle, and I heard thunder rumbling far in the distance, barely audible, hardly discernible from the thump of artillery that frequently rumbles over the Bogue Banks from the big marine base at Camp Lejeune twenty-five miles away.

"We'd better head back," I said, reeling in my line.

We were on our first real excursion in our little-used motor boat, a fifteen-footer with a fifty-horsepower motor. We had started in the morning at Emerald Isle—Linda and I and our friends Stan and Kay Swofford, all of us boating novices—and headed east toward Morehead City and Beaufort.

I had been very pleased with the trip so far. We'd been stranded only once in the sound's shallow waters, if you didn't count having to walk the boat across the dredge shoals to get it into the intra-coastal waterway on the north side of the sound. I had even docked for lunch at a Morehead City restaurant without smashing either boat or pier. Remarkable achievements all, I thought.

After lunch, we headed out into the shipping channel, past Radio Island to Beaufort Inlet. Rounding the point into Beaufort Channel, we cruised past that town's picturesque waterfront before beaching on Carrot Island, across the channel from Beaufort, to search for the wild horses that live there. The horses were nowhere to be seen in the fierce heat, so we made our way back across the baking dunes to the boat. Stan and I tested the fishing while Kay and Linda cooled in the shallow water until we sensed the approaching storm.

The wind picked up as we passed the Beaufort waterfront, and a couple of raindrops splatted against the boat. But we were in the relatively calm waters of the protected channel, and the storm still seemed far away. I was certain that we'd have plenty of time to get back to Morehead City, where we could wait it out in safety. Not until we'd passed the dangerous underwater jetties and the Marine Corps loading docks on Radio Island and rounded the point into the shipping channel did I realize how badly I'd miscalculated. Before us lay a frightening panorama.

A bank of rolling, angry clouds, black and savage-looking, was heading straight for us, moving fast. The murky brown waters of the channel had suddenly turned an eerie, tumultuous green, frothed with white. The wind came in a rush, ripping my hat from my head and carrying it away. It brought big raindrops and small, stinging hailstones. Lightning creased the sky ahead of us with a frightening crack. The boat strained and shuddered as it crashed into each wave, spraying us with sheets of water.

My first thought was of Linda, who can't swim. She was seated directly behind me. "Get a life jacket on, Babe," I shouted.

"I don't think we should be out here," Stan said from the seat beside me.

"I don't either," I said, "but we are."

"Maybe we should turn back."

I know next to nothing about navigation, but I had heard that you should always head into waves. If we tried to turn and got broadside to them, we might be capsized. If we got them to our backs, we might be swamped.

"We're committed now," I said grimly, clinging to the wheel with a grip that would've taken crow bars to pry loose.

At this point, I was as frightened of the lightning as I was of the waves, and I kept telling everybody to keep low. But that was soon to change. Ahead of us, in the driving rain, I saw a huge Coast

Guard boat cut across our path, heading from Radio Island to the Coast Guard station at Fort Macon. Within moments, I saw towering dead ahead a wall of water, the wake from the Coast Guard boat.

There was no time to think about it, nothing to do. We hit the gigantic wave and took flight. The entire boat, motor and all, left the water. It seemed that we were flying a long time. I remember looking down at the water, trying to think what would happen when we crashed. We slammed back to the surface with a neck-wrenching jolt. Water washed over us. Linda began struggling from the back seat to get a life jacket over my head, but I knew that miraculously we were still moving, pounding the waves, intact.

I have never been so happy to see the Morehead City waterfront. We beached the boat and ran to a nearby motor lodge for shelter. Only then did I realize that I was trembling, that we were all ashen-faced. As we waited out that storm and another that followed close behind, we condemned ourselves for being caught in it, for being so foolish that we were not wearing life jackets. We marveled that the little boat had brought us through, that it hadn't broken apart, that none of us had been knocked out of it, and, perhaps more than anything else, that I hadn't panicked and done something stupid. We were very lucky, we all agreed.

Not until the next day did we learn just how lucky. Two inlets away, at New River, four men in a much larger boat, a twenty-one-footer, had been caught in the same storm, but their boat broke up. Three drowned.

The sand is cool underfoot, fine as flour, a welcome contrast to a few hours earlier when we fairly had to dance across it to keep from burning our feet. It is a sparkling clear end-of-summer night, and we are closing the season, Linda and I, in a fitting way, with a last barefoot walk on the beach. Morning will bring back the heat and the long, dreaded drive home.

We must find our way by flashlight. No moon brightens this night. The stars are an ostentatious display of diamonds strewn across black velvet. I can't remember when I last saw the Milky Way like this. To the southeast, a string of lights marches out to sea, illuminating the stark skeleton of a fishing pier. To the northeast are the lights marking the entrance to the channel in the inlet leading to Morehead City and Beaufort. Far beyond them, the Cape Lookout lighthouse flashes its insistent warning. A ship is out there taking heed, for we can see its diminishing lights, red and green.

The weekend crowds are gone, and only a few lights brighten the windows of the sprawl of condominiums lining the beach. Except for a few tiny figures leaning on the railing of the fishing pier, no people are to be seen. The beach is ours. Well, ours and the ghost crabs'. They are out in force, feeding at the surf's edge. Night creatures, they are rarely seen in daylight, then only to skitter sideways from burrow to burrow, fleeing the aggravations of children, heat, and light.

The larger ones now flee before us, not to the safety of their burrows, but to the unseen dangers in the closer surf. The smaller ones, caught in the ray of the flashlight, freeze like rabbits exposed in a car's headlights. They remain motionless no matter how close we come. But as soon as the light is directed away, they dash furiously for the deeper sand.

Except for an occasional jet fighter passing low over the beach, rending the night on the way to land at Cherry Point Marine Station, some miles inland, all is quietness. Even the surf rouses no more than a murmur. The ocean appears, in fact, as placid as a farm pond. Only the slightest hint of a breeze stirs from the south, far too frail for the hardy work of making waves. Its effort is feeble indeed, creating breakers hardly deserving of so strong a word. Lappers would be more suitable. They fold at the last minute with a little whoosh and gently kiss the beach, barely foaming around our feet as we splash along, ankle-deep.

The tide is high, flooding the wide expanse of smooth, firm sand that is so good for walking and running when the tide is out. The sand where we walk now at the high-water line is not nearly so hard. Behind us we leave a zigzag trail of footprints that the lazy surf takes its time erasing.

As we approach the fishing pier, it gives me secret satisfaction to notice that nobody is catching anything (I haven't had a nibble this trip), but as I watch one of the little waves breaking as green as an emerald in the lights from the pier, I see three fish flash through it. Whiting, no doubt. And obviously not the least bit interested in the enticements offered by the patient souls above.

At the pier, we turn back toward the darkness. Holding hands and saying nothing, we splash along, admiring the brilliance of the sky. I break my silence to repeat, as I have on so many similar nights, my regret at never having studied astronomy. Just as I am about to zero in on the Big Dipper with Linda's patient help, I hear something cutting through the dark water beyond our view. Simultaneously the word comes to our lips: "Shark." I shine the flashlight over the water, but we see nothing and continue on our way, thinking of dark presences and rare end-of-summer nights, keeping well away from the water. We are ready to head home.

Fellow
Travelers

*T*he safe, contained world of our mountainside is my home, and I believe that living there provides me with strengths and insights that I would never have if I were a city dweller, for instance. But I also believe that the lines between city dwellers and us country folk aren't nearly so rigid as we sometimes pretend. We are all part of a larger world; we have all been set upon a journey together. The concept of the melting pot nation certainly hasn't been perfected in these two hundred years or so of our great experiment, but there is something fundamental that we share with those around us, I believe, something that makes us more alike than different.

When the United States celebrated her two-hundredth birthday in 1976, I was far from my North Carolina farm — in miles and in atmosphere. I experienced the bicentennial celebration on Atlantic Avenue in Brooklyn, the perfect place for that occasion. If any street exemplifies America, surely it is Atlantic Avenue. There Arabs and Jews, blacks and whites, Latins and Orientals, long-haired radicals and blue-suited conservatives live and mingle. One side of the street borders the well-to-do section of Brooklyn Heights; the other side is the northern boundary of the poor area of South Brooklyn. It is a street of exotic smells, shops, people, and sights — an only-in-America street.

Shortly after sunset on that anniversary fourth of July, the street became a funnel for this great variety of citizens. They came in throngs, all moving toward the river just down the hill. It seemed that every building was being emptied.

Earlier in the day, the heralded tall ships had sailed up the river, but there had been no parade down Atlantic Avenue to watch them. Except for the occasional popping of firecrackers, the street had been quiet all day. But now everyone was marching toward the river to see the fireworks. It was a festive parade that grew steadily as darkness gathered, thousands of people marching happily.

They assembled in the streets on the bluffs overlooking the docks, grouping wherever there was a clear view of the Statue of Liberty, standing proud in the glow of spotlights across the harbor. Traffic jammed as the numbers swelled. Police watched helplessly as cars were abandoned mid-street, blocking even the emergency entrances at a hospital. People were still coming when the first rockets burst over the harbor, and some began running to get into better position.

The fireworks were as spectacular as had been promised, great sprays of color and light that set everything aglow. The crowd gasped at several of the more ostentatious bursts and occasionally broke into applause. Then came the finale. The whole sky was filled with rocket bursts, and suddenly, high above, a big American flag materialized, as if by magic, glowing against the darkness.

And the crowd began to cheer, a sustained cheer of unabashed pride. The cheering stopped when the flag flickered out, and for just a moment an eerie silence settled, as if all of those people had been surprised to find themselves cheering and were embarrassed to be caught with their patriotism showing so blatantly.

The crowd began to break up as soon as the display ended. Red lights flashed, horns honked, sirens wailed, cops shouted, fire-crackers popped. People began moving away in groups, and here and there a few started singing. It was a spontaneous thing. Others began to join in, they were joined by more, and soon there were big groups, hundreds of people, marching up Atlantic Avenue singing joyously. They sang "It's a Grand Old Flag" and "America the Beautiful" and "The Star-Spangled Banner."

All of them, strangers to one another, marched up the avenue singing together. It was a rare and beautiful experience, the kind that brings a lump to the throat. I didn't see any tears of pride, but I did hear some very sophisticated people joking about it, trying hard to make it appear that they, too, hadn't been moved by the experience. But their true feelings were obvious. A little later, I stood on a roof at a party on Atlantic Avenue watching as the people of South Brooklyn celebrated with fireworks displays of their own that made it look as if one whole end of the city were at war.

A friend of mine, a fellow known to be far more critical than laudatory of his native land, stood looking down on all of the people still moving about in a festive mood on the street below us and remarked, "You know, this really is a hell of a country."

During my years in the newspaper business — a profession that depends on people and the things they do to create its product — I have found myself repeatedly arriving at the same conclusion my friend did on that once-in-a-lifetime night of celebration in Brooklyn. This *is* a hell of a country. Maybe it's more obvious during a big-time celebration like the bicentennial, but if you look carefully, day in and day out, in the course of living your life, you see the same things. The dramas of human experience, played out all around us, teach us gratitude and humility, provide us with entertainment and food for thought, draw us closer in sympathy and compassion and celebration.

I for one am more than glad not to be traveling through this world in isolation. Of course I want my family and friends, those I love and work with, the people at the core of my existence, with me. But I also want the others — most of them people whose names I'll never know. I want their stories, their lessons, their joys and sorrows. Life is too short to rely only on the small vistas available to an individual soul, however alert and engaged he tries to be. It is through our fellow travelers that the limited personal vista can become a wide panorama of experience. It is through them that we can live our fullest lives.

America is a machine, a big, gawky, noisy machine that requires constant attention to keep it running. If she were a car, some of that attention would be her tune-ups and oil changes. But sometimes more is required — body work, major engine overhauls, rebuilding. Part of that more serious work involves the judicial system, and part of that system involves us, ordinary folks. We make up the juries that make the judiciary work. We don't always enjoy it. We some-times look for ways to avoid it. We complain about the time it takes away from our more important and personal activities. But we do it. We have to, not just because it's the law but because it's the only way to sustain what we are and want to be.

When I was summoned for jury duty, my first thought was to try to find some way to get out of it. It was an annoyance; it would break my routine. But then I thought about it. Words like *responsibility* kept careening through my head. So I found myself listening to a judge telling us that we were participating in what might be the most important civic duty any of us would ever perform.

That sounded good, sounded important, but mostly it turned out to be an exercise in boredom. Sitting and waiting. Crossing and uncrossing the legs. Squirming in a futile attempt to make the hard bench a bit more comfortable. It's really better to be called for a trial. Then you must listen. And the chairs in the jury box are a lot more comfortable than the bench where you wait to be selected for a case.

I was well into hearing my first case before it struck me just what an awesome responsibility this was. I sat and watched the witnesses traipse to the stand, and for the first time I realized that I must determine who was lying, who telling the truth, and that whatever I decided would have a great effect—especially if my decision were wrong.

On trial were a sixty-year-old woman, her middle-aged son, and her divorced daughter. Good, churchgoing people without blemishes against their names, they were charged with obstructing three sheriff's deputies who had come to the old woman's house to arrest another of her sons, an alcoholic. One deputy said that the old woman had grabbed at his gun, that the man had pushed him. The other said the daughter had jumped on his back. It was not a simple case. The deputies had previously been to the house many times to arrest the alcoholic son without interference. This time, said family members, the deputies started beating him.

In the jury room, one juror immediately revealed that he had once been a sheriff's deputy in the county for nearly six years, that he had known one of the prosecuting deputies for most of his life, and could not vote against him.

During the debate a woman juror stated that she didn't believe in jury trials, that anybody who had been arrested had to be guilty of something or he would not have been arrested in the first place, that police officers would not lie, commit mistakes, or do any wrong, and that drunks deserved to be beaten now and then on general principle.

The case quickly became a political matter. If we did not convict, then we did not support our police. We would instead be supporting people who commit all sorts of unspeakable criminal acts. These people had to be made examples, regardless of their guilt or innocence. Three did not agree.

Vote after vote, the result was the same. Sometimes we just sat silently after our votes, anger simmering in the majority. Finally, we sent word to the judge that we were deadlocked. He brought us out, talked to us, sent us back to try again. It was no use. After several hours, a mistrial was declared.

On the third day of my week of service, I sat on a second case. The solicitor called it a "neighborhood incident." Two fifteen-year-old boys and a nine-year-old girl in a pickup truck camper parked in a backyard. The charge: assault with intent to commit rape.

The boys were clean-cut and nice-looking. They had never been in trouble before. The girl was very pretty and physically mature for her age. She had been allowed to play tackle football with the boys and other neighborhood kids. This incident had taken place after one of those games. The girl went home crying and told her grandmother that the boys had tried to have sex with her. She was not injured physically and had not been examined by a doctor. The boys denied touching her.

While the trial wore on, I searched the faces of those involved hoping for some clue, but there was none. The boys seemed frightened. The girl was calm and bright-eyed. The families were grim-faced. It was not a pleasant thing for anybody involved.

With the evidence complete, we retired to the jury room. Nobody said anything for a while. Then a man said he thought that we ought to pray. He prayed aloud, asking guidance. After finishing, he said that he thought we should do what Jesus might have done. Not guilty, he said.

"Frankly," I said, "I wouldn't mind if we wound up a hung jury. I know that's selfish, but if I could, I would gladly pass the responsibility for deciding this to somebody else. But I have to vote guilty. According to the judge's instructions, if we think the boys touched her, we have no other choice."

We talked. We reasoned. We voted. The vote remained divided time after time. We sent word to the judge that we were stymied. He brought us out to encourage us to try anew and sent us back. The man who had done the praying was first to change his vote. It was getting close to lunchtime, he said, and he didn't want to stay all day. He'd just been thinking about the boys' future, he said, but he could go with the majority. A little later, two others decided simultaneously that they, too, could vote guilty.

That left only one holdout—the woman who in the earlier case had said that she didn't believe in jury trials. I had thought that she was out to hang everybody. I was wrong. Clearly, this was an agonizing experience for her. Her thin hands twisted a tissue. Her head was bowed.

"Come on, honey, go along with us," said the man who had done the praying. "Let's get out of here."

"Don't pressure her," somebody said. "It's her conscience. She has to live with it."

She sat in silence for long minutes then almost reluctantly nodded her head. "Okay," she said softly.

It was noon, time for lunch.

The judge told the boys that he wanted them to get together with their families and lawyer and have a long, prayerful session during the lunch recess. When they returned, before he decided on their sentence, he wanted them to tell him the truth about what had happened in the pickup camper. I thought that the boys would change their story, plead for mercy. I wanted to hear them admit their guilt. Beyond reasonable doubt, after all, is not beyond all doubt. I wanted to know that I had been right in my decision about their lives. But when they returned to court, the boys swore that they had told the truth. They hadn't touched the girl. She had made up the story. The judge gave each five years and suspended the sentences.

Later, I watched as the boys left the courtroom with their families. Their faces, I knew, would be with me always. I had affected their lives, and, to a far lesser extent, they had affected mine. One of the boys looked up and saw me watching. He offered a small, forgiving smile and a wave of farewell. I guess my face will be with him for a long time, too.

Lots of the stories I come across in my work or that I hear about on the news deal with this conflict within us all about the best, fairest, most constructive attitude to take toward those who violate the rules of our society. The conflict is so deep that, at times, it threatens to divide the country itself into separate camps. These factions wear different labels, depending on the circumstances of the moment: liberal and conservative, civil libertarians and law-and-order partisans, bleeding hearts and hard-liners. But no matter what the labels, the issue rises up, subsides, festers, only to rise up again. We ponder the merits of victims' rights versus the need to protect the accused until he or she is proven guilty. And even the guilty, under our Constitution, have their rights. It is murky territory even in theory. When it hits home, even in a relatively minor way, the murkiness engulfs us.

Tracy Saunders, who lives just across the field from us called with the first report. Linda told me about it when I came in late from a meeting. Somebody was going onto our land and cutting wood, she said. There had been a little excitement. Tracy had caught the guy cutting across his property on a three-wheeler and had tried to stop him. The guy almost ran over him and kept going.

I was too tired to worry about it and went to sleep in a chair watching the TV news. Early the next morning another neighbor, Robert Saunders, Tracy's uncle, whose land also adjoins ours, called. The trespasser had been cutting across his property, too. Robert had seen him several times. The day before he'd heard him running a chainsaw on my land.

"He cut across me down there, and then he went up along your creek," Robert said. "I don't know whether he's building a deer stand or cutting wood for a still."

A still? That was an intriguing possibility. And not so far-fetched, actually. A still had been destroyed by law enforcement officers — busted, they prefer to call it — in our county only a week earlier.

"You think somebody could have a still up in that hollow?" I asked Linda after talking with Robert.

"I don't know," she said. "It's looked awfully smoky over in there the last couple of mornings."

I got dressed, took my glass of orange juice outside, and summoned the dogs. They were frisky and ready to go, as always. We cut across the pasture to the creek and started upstream. Picking my way slowly through the thicket along the creek's lower section, I considered the possibilities. A still seemed unlikely although I'm almost certain that these woods and this creek have accommodated stills before.

Not so long ago, deer hunting could have been ruled out without consideration. For the first dozen years that we lived on this place, I saw lots of wildlife but never deer. Then I saw two one morning not far from our house, and neighbors told me of seeing others nearby. Only a few weeks before Tracy had seen deer signs along our creek, a big buck, he was sure. I knew then that trespassing hunters surely would follow, and anything and anybody might end up shot. Country dwellers soon learn that most people in the woods with guns are anything but sportsmen. Chances were good that the trespasser was one of the bad guys.

But the intruder might also be somebody stealing wood to sell or burn, I figured. Or perhaps, since Christmas was nigh, somebody cutting cedars or gathering greenery for decorations. Tracy had already lost a pretty cedar to Christmas tree poachers. We have plenty of cedars and wild hollies, and somebody might covet them for Christmas. I was particularly concerned about our patch of running cedar, which makes the most beautiful Christmas wreaths. It fetches a handsome price in the holiday season.

It always irritates me that I can't walk my own land without feeling endangered, but that's the case in hunting season. Deer hunters are particularly prone to mistaking wandering country folk and other hunters for their prey. I made a lot of noise as I went, huffing and blowing, whistling and calling to the dogs, so that a trespassing deer hunter perched in one of my trees wouldn't think I was a buck. I wasn't sure that would help, though, because anybody who would build a deer stand on somebody's land without asking permission might just as soon shoot a landowner as a deer.

I found nothing amiss below the remains of the old stone dam that was washed out decades ago, but above the dam two big trees had recently been toppled by the creek in its ambition to claim wider banks. Could it be aspiring to riverhood?

Several times I stopped to listen. The creek gurgled over little falls. Wind rattled the brown leaves on the beech trees, which refuse to give up their warm weather attire until new buds force them to in spring. I could hear the huge cruncher groaning at the county landfill a few miles away, a truck passing on the highway, the whining of a distant chain saw. The early morning sun sliced through the trees and turned the clinging fog to gold, a scene worthy of poetry.

At the old stone tractor crossing, where the creek disappears underground, I found the tracks of the three-wheeler and followed them back to Robert's land. I returned to the creek and fought my way through vines and briers looking for damage or signs of hunting but found nothing until I came to a bog created by a small spring. There in the mud were the deep hoofprints of a deer, a big one, no doubt the reason for our trespasser.

I searched a small branch of the creek and checked my running cedar patch (it was unmolested) before calling in the dogs and heading back for my morning cup of coffee. I felt a little disappointed, to tell the truth. I was hoping to find a still, I guess, something we could take care of and laugh about later. As it was, we might never catch the trespasser. In fact, we didn't. And as long as he was free to make himself at home on our property, we couldn't feel entirely free and safe to enjoy what was ours. Hunting season would pass, we knew, and things would return to normal. But we would remember, and doubt would linger, tickling some dark corner of the mind whenever we set out to walk the woods we love.

Few things are more frightening than the violation of a home, the place we call ours. Perhaps violation of our bodies, physical injury of any kind, is more feared, but little else. But violation is one thing.

It means a temporary disturbance, one that will be remembered but that doesn't necessarily alter things irrevocably. What real experience could be more nightmarish than witnessing the total destruction of your home? What can an outsider who happens upon such an event say or do to help?

It was two A.M., and I was twenty miles from home. The red speedometer needle touched sixty-five. The heater was humming, the radio playing soft, lulling music. The interstate highway was all but deserted. Only occasionally did another set of headlights whiz past. Most of the world, like the child on my backseat, was sleeping.

The night was cold and bright with a full-faced moon high in the cloudless sky. To the north, just above the blackened treeline, a faint orange glow appeared. It looked like a fire. Closer, there was no question. It was a fire. A big one. Black smoke roiled from the glow and drifted toward the highway.

Up ahead a fire truck raced across a bridge. The exit loomed, and curiosity turned the wheel to follow. There were other cars now, with red lights flashing in grills and windshields, driven fast by volunteer firemen just jolted from sleep.

In seconds, the fire was in sight. It was an old, two-story brick house with a big front porch. It sat back from the road and looked as if it were once the centerpiece of a big prosperous farm, long since gone to seed. Now the shabby house was completely aflame.

Firemen tumbled from their cars, pulling on protective coats and boots as they ran. Three men hurriedly dragged a hose toward the house. Flames danced from the windows and leaped from the attic. A small group of people milled about an old car parked in the front yard, a man and several boys. The man shivered in a short-sleeved shirt. The boys had sweaters and jackets draped around their shoulders, but they were barefoot and cold. The man was cursing bitterly.

"That goddamn woman," he muttered. "I swear I'll kill her if it's the last thing I ever do. It may be poison, or it may be a gun, but I'll get her."

His wife and several other children huddled inside the car. Firemen were playing water on the house. Glass shattered loudly. Something popped inside the inferno. Somebody ran up to ask the man if everybody had gotten out. Yes, he nodded.

"How many people in the house?"

"Me and my wife and six young'uns."

"How did it start?" an onlooker wanted to know.

"Goddamn woman set it afire," he said. "She called my wife a bitch and throwed a cigarette in the back room. . . . That's all right. I know who she is. I'll get her. I swear I'll kill her."

The boys were eager to tell how it happened.

"We'as in bed," blurted a little one.

"I was going to the store to get me a drink," interjected the teenager, the eldest. "I looked back and seen the house was on fire. I run back and hollered, 'Daddy, get 'em out, the house is on fire.'"

The mother emerged from the car. She was short and dumpy, wearing a dark skirt and faded green sweater stretched out of shape by excessive wear. Small children hung onto her legs as she stood looking at the fire and sobbing.

"Everything we got is gone," she cried. "The young'uns ain't even got shoes."

"That's all we got," said the man, motioning to a big pile of clothes in the yard near the car. "Everything's gone. Everything we got is gone. We ain't got nothin'. Ain't got no place to go. What we going to do?" He began crying, too, cursing as he turned away.

It was very cold. The fire was coming under control, but it was obvious that nobody would ever live in the house again. Other people were arriving. A fireman started asking questions and writing in a little notebook.

"Goddamn woman set it afire," the man told him.

The littlest boy had been watching wide-eyed through it all, shuffling his bare feet, shivering, wanting to say something.

"Goddamn woman," he blurted, breaking into tears. "I swear on my grandmother's grave I'll kill that woman."

Back on the road, the heater hummed again. The radio played soft music. The child still slept on the backseat. Two-thirty A.M. and fifteen miles from a home that would be warm and a bed that would feel good. Safe.

In the last few years, since garage sales and auctions have become participant sports, a lot of us travel from sale to sale searching through the remnants of total strangers' lives, looking for treasures and doodads to carry back to our own homes, many to reappear at a later date in the midst of our own garage sales. It's fun. It's relatively inexpensive. It's certainly harmless. Yet every so often at an auction or garage sale an item will catch your attention, and somehow you'll know that it's more than item. With it goes a story, a life, dreams and memories and feelings that were as real to the person who owned the item as anything can be. Maybe that's what we're shopping for—stories and dreams. Maybe those are the real treasures to be had.

That dress. It fairly shone. I should have suspected that a story lay behind a dress like that. But how was I to know?

Instead, we laughed.

"Looky here!" cried the auctioneer. "We got a purty dress here. What'll you give?"

It was a garish, slippery-looking thing made of royal blue velvet with some sort of burgundy trim. It seemed to pour from the box when the auctioneer's assistant held it up.

"Okay, what'll you give?" the auctioneer repeated. "The highest you'll give's the lowest we'll take."

I nudged Linda.

"Now there's just what you need," I said. "You want to bid on it?"

We laughed.

Soon, the dress was gone, and the auctioneer had moved on to some old dishes and cooking utensils. I didn't pay attention to how much the dress brought. Not much, I'm sure. Old dresses seldom do. I didn't even notice who bought it.

Auctions such as this are regular Saturday affairs in our county. An old country homeplace was changing hands, the personal property being sold. Never know what you might see at one of these things. The house was from another era, a rambling, two-story frame farmhouse set under towering oaks, its unpainted boards grayed to brittleness, its tin roof oranged with rust. It had a wide, wraparound porch with a hand-crank well on it. A bucket of cool water with a tin dipper in it sat atop the well.

The house had been emptied, and all the contents were on display in the backyard, where the auctioneer labored on the back of a pickup truck. In the front yard, the ladies from a nearby Methodist church were selling hot dogs, hamburgers, and homemade pound cake from a funeral home tent. There was a big crowd.

I had come hoping to pick up some old farm tools cheap, but the bidding was going too high. Dealers were buying the tools to resell as antiques, not to use. As I stood near the back of the crowd, despairing, an old man wandered up and stopped beside me.

"Did this old woman die?" he asked.

"I don't know," I said. "I don't even know whose place this is."

He told me then that it had belonged to an old woman everybody called Miss Lillie. She was up in her eighties, he said, and she had lived here alone. He lived not far away and had brought firewood to her now and then, he said, but a while back he had come by and found a note on the door saying that she had gone to visit somebody. He never saw her at the house again. He didn't even know the auction was scheduled until he happened by and saw the crowd.

"You know, there is an unusual story that they tell about this old woman," he said.

I asked him to tell it to me, and he said that he would as soon as he found out what had happened to her. He went off to question others and soon came back with the news that she had fallen ill and wouldn't be returning. She was in a nursing home. Her belongings were being auctioned to help pay expenses.

As the old man told me about Miss Lillie, several others gathered around who knew details of the story. This is what they told:

In her youth, Miss Lillie fell in love with a young local man of great promise. They courted for several years and planned to marry. But first the young man wanted to establish his career. He went to college and later to medical school while Miss Lillie stayed behind, waiting and dreaming about the life they would make together. She filled her hope chest, and on many of the items she embroidered the initials that would be hers when they wed.

During all of those years that he was away studying, the young man wrote long and florid letters to his intended, declaring his undying love, even in poetry. Miss Lillie kept every one. But while the young man was serving his internship at a distant hospital, he met another woman and broke his engagement.

When she recovered from the shock, Miss Lillie's anguish turned to anger. She sued the doctor for breach of promise. The doctor hired lawyers who used every legal trick to delay the case and keep it from coming to trial. When it did finally get to court, the doctor didn't show up to defend himself. Miss Lillie offered in evidence all of her love letters, and people came from all over the county to hear them read.

"You know, I wonder if that doctor's new fiancée came to the trial," said one woman listening to the story. "I know I would, wouldn't you?"

Miss Lillie became the only woman ever to win such a case in Randolph County, or so the story goes. The doctor had to pay her a considerable sum. He married the other woman and settled in another county, where he became a highly respected physician. Miss Lillie stayed at home and never really recovered from her hurt.

"I've heard that story ever since I was a little girl," said a woman who had joined in the telling of it. "You know, one of the first things they sold this morning was the dress she had bought to get married in."

It is partly my training as a reporter, partly natural inclination, I guess, but almost everywhere I go, I seek out a story. They're always there, waiting to be discovered. Everywhere. If we only look closely enough, listen clearly enough, we can take away much more than the surface reveals in most situations. Even a cemetery, silent and forlorn, has its stories to tell.

The cemetery was deep in the woods. We passed a few gray, sagging houses, beaten by the elements; a bright, fresh pasture, newly cleared; then only trees, strangled by thick growths of vines, lining the sandy road. The woods were pregnant with spring. Because we weren't sure exactly where the cemetery was, we missed the turnoff and stopped to back up.

A truck approached us from behind. It was a gray, four-wheel-drive pickup that sat high on its haunches. A young man was driving. A child sat beside him on the seat. A sad-faced dog—a bloodhound?—rode disinterestedly in the back. The truck was going fast, and it kicked up a spray of sand as it swung off the main road onto the narrower road leading to our own destination.

The cemetery commanded a broad, open field on a gentle incline. A few tall, widely spread pines offered it meager shade. It was fenced and well-tended, and there was no accounting for its presence in the deep woods. No church or dwelling stood in its sight.

As we drove slowly along the narrow road encircling it, I saw the gray truck parked beside a car near the gate. We parked close-by, and as we walked to the gate, we saw the man who had been driving the truck leaving the cemetery, walking hurriedly. A few steps behind followed a dark-haired young woman, walking slump-shouldered with her head down. The man looked anxious. The woman seemed near tears. We nodded, spoke hellos, and paid no more attention to them as the man climbed into the truck, and the woman got into the car and drove away.

We had come — my friend Ernie Wyatt, Erik, and I — to pay our respects at the grave of Marjorie Kinnan Rawlings, a writer we had known only through her works. Her books, including *The Yearling* and *Cross Creek*, had captured the life of backwoods Florida in the twenties and thirties. After a little searching, we found her grave marked by a stone set flat in the ground, a bushy azalea sprouting at the head of it. Somebody had left a single yellow porcelain rose on the stone.

Peggy Shaw, a writer working on a biography of Marjorie Rawlings, was with us, and she explained how Marjorie had come to be buried in this backwoods spot near Island Grove, not far from Cross Creek, which she had once called home. Marjorie attended a funeral at this cemetery and remarked to her second husband, Norton Baskin, that this was a place where she could be happy. When she died of a cerebral hemorrhage in 1953 at age fifty-seven, her husband remembered the remark and brought her here to be buried amongst the people she'd written about.

Our visit took place on a Sunday made beautiful by warm breezes, bright sunshine, and dogwoods opening on the edges of the woods, and we wandered about enjoying the day and reading tombstones. Near Marjorie's grave, we found the more recent one of Zelma Cason, once a close friend of Marjorie's, who sued her for libel in a celebrated trial after publication of *Cross Creek*.

As we were about to leave, we happened onto a fresh grave near the gate, a rectangular blemish of white sand in the manicured greenness of the cemetery. The plot had been meticulously raked, leaving patterns like those found in the sand of Japanese gardens. A single set of footprints marred the symmetry of the patterns. They led to a shallow, rounded depression near the head of the grave.

Suddenly, it struck me that the footprints had been made by the woman we had seen leaving as we arrived. She had apparently been sitting alone on the grave when the man in the pickup came for her. A small temporary marker had been placed on the grave by the funeral home. It revealed this to be the final resting place of a man thirty-eight years old, dead not yet two months.

We all realized that unwittingly we had happened onto a little drama as we arrived. What relationship had this man had with the woman who had come to sit on his grave on a beautiful Sunday morning? Who was the man who had come for her, and why had he come in such a hurry, looking so irritated, when she had a car of her own? Apparently, we had just missed the confrontation as we arrived, and perhaps our very presence had affected it.

"There's a story there," I said, looking at the footprints.

"Yes," said Ernie, "a sad one."

When you go to a quiet, peaceful place, like a cemetery, and happen upon a story that you'll never be able to finish, there is a feeling of poignancy surrounding the event in memory. When you are a young reporter sent out to cover a story, you sometimes make more of it than you should, everything appearing to be a matter of earth-shattering importance through the lens of your naiveté and eagerness to please and make your mark. The objectivity of time lets you laugh at this distortion later. But when you become part of the story, not as a tourist or an observer, the feeling is entirely different: you are moving within it, inevitably, possessed of all the emotions and reactions that any participant would have, but, at the same time, you try to keep up the old story-gathering habit that is second nature to you. That's a lot to do, especially if you find yourself in the middle of a tornado.

The sky looked menacing, dark clouds moving fast. Thunder set up a constant rumble. When I saw lightning, I said, "Man, we better get out of here, or we're going to get drenched." The truth was, of course, that I am scared of lightning and wanted to get someplace safe before it got closer.

We were at Atlanta Raceway, my friend Steve Deal and I, only about twenty miles from Steve's house in Conyers, Georgia, where I was a guest. It was late on the Saturday afternoon before race day, and we had stopped to chat with a fellow on the back of Richard Petty's truck as the storm drew closer. At my nervous urging we finally broke away and made a dash for Steve's car, arriving just as the rain began. It came in big drops that splatted on the windshield and beat a furious rhythm on the roof as the car shook from a sudden, fierce gust of wind.

The storm was so bad that we began to talk of tornadoes as we left the race track for Steve's house and supper. Years earlier, Steve and I had worked at a small North Carolina paper — he as photographer, I as reporter — where we covered a couple of small tornadoes that uprooted a few trees, turned over a couple of trailers, broke windows, ripped off roofing shingles. We laughed about how excited such small storms had made us.

The rain was falling so hard that Steve could barely see to drive. Several times we slowed to a crawl to pass through flooded spots on the highway. When the rain began to slacken, the lightning was so spectacular that Steve stopped and got out with his camera.

That may have saved us. A few minutes later, as we rolled down Interstate 20 into Conyers, I saw a police car, its blue lights flashing, speeding across a bridge ahead.

"Must be a wreck," I said.

"I think it's right up there," Steve said.

We could see cars pulling off the highway a short distance ahead.

"Looks like a bad one," I said, pointing out a huge green road sign crumpled on an embankment, well away from the highway. Then I saw the top of a huge pine tree lying in the grassy median, and it took a few moments for my brain to register that no pine trees grew there, or anywhere else along the highway right-of-way.

"Oh, my God, look!" Steve said suddenly. "There's been a tornado."

Obviously, it had just passed. Cars that had been traveling on the highway minutes earlier had been picked up and hurled through a chain-link fence onto an access road. A trailer park looked as if it had been stirred with a giant spoon; many of the trailers were turned upside down or smashed. Big factories and warehouses near the highway had been reduced to rubble.

"Those were new buildings!" Steve cried in disbelief.

We could see the path that the storm had followed as it approached the town. A great swath of pine forest had been cleared, every tree either uprooted or shorn, thick trunks snapped like twigs.

"Oh no," Steve said, his anxiety building. "That must have come right by the house. I live right over there!"

We had left his wife, Brenda, at home alone.

Steve weaved the car through the traffic and debris, then hit the accelerator and made for an exit. We raced toward his street but found it whole and quiet, spared by the storm, his wife at a friend's house. We got flashlights from his utility room and hurried back to town in Brenda's Volkswagen, figuring the smaller car would be easier to maneuver through the wreckage. Darkness was closing rapidly, and all was confusion. We could hear sirens coming from every direction. Streets were blocked by downed power poles, trees, and rubble. People kept yelling, "Watch the wires! Watch the wires!"

The destruction could not have been more thorough if bombers had undertaken the job. Houses lay in shatters, roofs gone, walls and windows exploded. In some, people still sought shelter from the rain. We could see candles burning here and there. The whim of the storm was difficult to understand. One house stood relatively undamaged between two that had been destroyed.

Headlights, flashlights, and the glowing tips of cigarettes punctured the darkness, adding to the eeriness of the scene. The air had become deathly still and heavy and enforced a strange quietness. People moved in silence and spoke in whispers, as if stunned or in awe. Sounds came only from the distance: sirens wailing, a dog barking forlornly, a transistor radio playing "Blue on Blue," a burglar alarm clanging excitedly to no particular notice.

Rescue teams had begun pouring into the area, volunteers from all around. Steve recognized one fireman, who was attempting to direct entangled traffic, and stopped to ask him how widespread the damage was. "I don't know, Steve," the fireman said. "Lithonia's flattened. C&S is flattened. Everything's gone."

At one point, we encountered a man in the street near a house that had been blown away except for the foundation. He was looking for an old man. "He always sat right there by the front door watching the cars go by," he said. "Him and me used to drink some wine together, if you know what I mean. He'd get my fishbait for me."

Up the hill and across the railroad tracks, a small group of businesses had been reduced to rubble, and the street was blocked by the roofs of the buildings. The counter stools, standing in defiant rank, were all that was left of Dot's Diner, which had closed before the storm hit. Next door at the fish market, the display cases stood in the open, still filled with fish. Five people had been in the market, and they had huddled behind a big freezer as the building disintegrated. The man who owned the market stood looking at the wreckage, his young granddaughter clinging to his legs.

"I thought we was gone," he said. "I said my last prayers."

Only one of the five, a woman in her twenties, the owner's daughter, had been hurt. She had a knot on her head and a cut over her right eye. She stood looking at the remains of her car and her father's truck, buried in the street by bricks and other rubble.

"Let's go home, Daddy," she said. "Please, let's go home." But her father seemed reluctant to leave.

Several hundred yards away, the huge Lithonia Lighting Company factory, principal employer of the town, had been ripped into two sections. Its big shifts of weekday workers were home when the storm struck. Only nine men had been working inside, and all had escaped safely. But a watchman in a glass-and-metal cage at the plant entrance had been injured.

A company official wearing a white hard hat arrived and sought out the foreman. "Are your men all right?" he asked.

"All but the watchman," the foreman replied. "They took him to the hospital. He was cut up pretty bad."

"I think we've got a watchman trapped over at the warehouse," the official said.

Rescue workers had begun setting up emergency lights at the warehouse. It had been a huge building, perhaps two hundred yards long, built of brick and cement blocks and steel, but no part of it was left standing. The watchman's white pickup truck, which had been parked at the loading dock, was flattened under the rubble, no part of the truck more than two feet high.

Some men had already crawled into the twisted rubble, calling as they went, stopping to listen for a response that didn't come. The watchman's time clock and book had been found, and I held the light while the rescuers thumbed through the book trying to figure where the watchman's last stop in the building might have been.

"If he's in there," one of them said, "I don't see how he could possibly be alive."

At a nearby trailer park, which had been completely upturned by the storm, a fire truck crept through with a fireman repeating over a loudspeaker, "Anybody who knows of any missing persons, please report to the fire truck." Several injured people had already been taken away in ambulances. Others, scorning treatment, were picking through the wreckage in the glow of headlights, salvaging what they could.

"I was just sitting there watching television, when I heard the wind picking up," one man paused to tell me. "First thing I knowed, there was a '57 Chevrolet sitting in the living room."

"I had a premonition," another man said. "I felt like something was going to happen. I just got restless. I got in my car and drove downtown, and when I came back a few minutes later, everything was gone. I reckon that proves you ought to pay attention to your premonitions."

My friends cover quite a spectrum. There are seasoned farmers, hotshot young reporters, good old boys, and intellectuals. They follow paths as varied as their personalities and interests, and just watching them broadens my own road toward wherever it is I'm headed at any given moment.

I once made a trip of some urgency with my friend E, an artist. He slung a package over his shoulder, in much the same way a GI on patrol would carry a mortar, and we headed for the subway. The package could have been mistaken for a short roll of linoleum. It was round, about four feet long, wrapped in brown paper. Inside, concentrated in paint and paper, was a man's life.

The paintings rolled inside the bundle were not E's. They were the work of an acquaintance, a young madman-addict-genius who would strongly disapprove, probably to the point of violence, if he knew what E was about this day. But E and other of the young man's friends had decided that something had to be done, and this, they thought, might be a beginning.

The young man had grown up in the slums, had been on heroin for years, had been in and out of mental institutions, undergone shock treatment, married twice, sired four children. Now he hopped from woman to woman, depending on theft and the generosity of friends for his fixes, always dodging the law, frequently becoming violent without warning. He considered himself dispossessed, a member of some vague underground.

All this came out in his art. He had been painting for ten years, and he did it with such ferocity and intensity that he had once burst a blood vessel in the act. The toll of his lifestyle had pushed him to a critical point. His friends thought that he couldn't last much longer. "He's one of these people who's just going to burn himself out—and fast," E said. E thought that if his talent and work could gain some recognition, some acceptance, it might be a stabilizing influence. Hence our trip.

We boarded the subway at the Court Street station. The destination: a hotel on Central Park, where, in room 605, awaited the director of one of the country's major art museums. Young artists do not get to impose on directors of big museums just by calling or showing up at their hotel doors with bundles of paintings. Such things are arranged.

In this case, the arrangements had been easy. The museum director is the father of a close friend of E's. Both E and Tom, the director's son, think that the tormented young artist is tremendously talented, that he may, indeed, be a genius. The night before, they had sat talking about what the old man's reactions to the paintings might be.

They pictured it as a confrontation between the art underground, represented by the young man's paintings, and the art establishment, represented by Tom's father. Tom had told his father about the young man, about the drugs, the emotional problems, the violence, the scrapes with the law. Tom and E were certain that these things would color the old man's judgment of the work, that because the old man was a retired Marine Reserve colonel who didn't approve of drugs and a counterculture lifestyle, he would dismiss the work without due consideration of its merit. They had agreed that it would be interesting to see what happened.

Tom, a burly, bearded writer and editor, was waiting in the hotel lobby, wearing a black leather motorcycle jacket and carrying his helmet. He accompanied us to his father's room.

The old man was in town for just a couple of days to look at paintings and other works he hoped to acquire. In his late sixties, he was balding, jowly, but still fit and strong. He had been one of the first Marine pilots. He started studying art when he took a job in a gallery as a young man. He went on to set up college art museums before becoming director of a large museum in the Midwest. Quite the dandy, he usually wore golfer's hats or berets and carried a gold-headed cane. He still caught women's eyes when he walked down the street.

Now he was in shirtsleeves, collar open, tie askew. His trousers were held up by red suspenders, his shoes as shiny as mirrors. Five to one, he was wearing garters. A grumpy sort, but agreeably so, he had the look of a cantankerous and eccentric favorite uncle. He growled his words, punctuating with snorts. Frequently he made his points with humor. His laugh was distinctive, close-mouthed, rushing up from the depths of his belly and skidding to a snorting halt as it puffed his jowls and expired in a harumph and a wheeze.

The amenities were observed, a bit of chitchat about flying and whatnot. E was a bit nervous and ill at ease. His own work didn't fit the bounds set by the art establishment, and he wasn't really comfortable around people he perceived to belong to it. It was a matter of thinking differently about art.

The subject turned slowly to the young man whose paintings lay bundled on the floor.

"From what I hear, he needs a psychiatrist," the old man said.

In the conversation about the young man's background that followed, the old man made several remarks indicating disapproval, a bad sign, E knew.

"All that aside," said E, "he's a damn fine painter."

"Prove it to me," said the old man.

E opened the bundle and began unfurling the paintings, spreading them across the bed. They were dark and violent and brooding, great splashes, swirls, sloshings, and drippings of paint, the kind of work that causes people who know little about painting to say, "My God, that's art?"

The old man grunted.

"I look at these things, and I think of a lot of other artists I've known who did things like this and resolved their problems," he said.

It was going about as E and Tom had expected.

The old man stood over the paintings, rubbing his chin. "He's got a lot of vigor. I can see a lot of experimentation, but everybody's doing that nowadays. . . . He's got talent, but it's unresolved."

This led to a vigorous discussion about resolution in painting, particularly in these paintings, and about what these paintings were saying.

"You've got to consider his background," E said. "He's lived five lives to my one."

Tom put in a word of agreement and joined E in talking about the harshness of the young man's life. It had to be considered, they said.

"Bullshit!" said the old man, quieting the room. "I can't be concerned with that, mmmmm? Can I? I can only see what's here. I can only be concerned with the final product. . . . And it's not art. It's unresolved."

Clearly that was it, but the old man thumbed through the paintings again, grumbling to himself. "Fuzzy drug dreams. . . . Maybe he's a genius and I'm just missing it. . . . I don't think I can do anything for this guy, or for the thousands of other artists like him. It's something they have to resolve for themselves. . . . How old is he?"

"About thirty-three."

"Oh, he's still a pup. He still has time to resolve it."

"I don't know," said E.

"But listen," said the old man, "don't take my word for it." He offered the names of others and said that he would help make appointments. E and Tom began rolling paintings back into the bundle.

We said our good-byes on the street outside. The old man, swinging his cane, sauntered off down Madison Avenue to see some Egyptian art he wanted to buy. Tom left on his motorcycle. I followed E, who struck out for the subway in his Texas gait, the paintings again slung over his shoulder. He said little about the encounter until we were back in Brooklyn.

"You know, it's funny," he finally said. "He turned it around on us."

Clearly, that was the case. He and Tom had used the young man's lifestyle to justify his work. They had done in reverse what they had expected the old man to do.

"*He* was the one defending art," E said. "I respect him for it."

The people we respect most are usually those who stand firm for the integrity of something we ourselves believe in fiercely. E and Tom's father might have been worlds apart in a million ways, but in one way that mattered most to both of them, they shared common ground. They both believed in the integrity of art. Ever since I've been a journalist, one of my idols, one of those with whom I have worked to share common ground is Ernie Pyle. I respect his work; I respect what he stood for as a writer and as a human being. Although we never met, he has had a profound impact on my life.

Beyond the Wabash, U.S. Highway 36, flat and straight, reaches for the Illinois line. Farmers on oversized John Deere tractors plow the rich black fields that stretch in intricate patterns to the horizon. The patterns are broken by square oases, each containing a white farm house shaded by tall trees, a barn, a silo, a collection of outbuildings, each oasis linked to the highway by a straight, narrow dirt road.

An official green highway sign advises: "Ernie Pyle Rest Park— 1 Mile."

The park is small, set in the corner of a farm field. The picnic tables have been freshly shellacked and are stacked by the single shelter, waiting to be set out under the trees for use by summer visitors. The state dedicated a big gray rock to Ernie here in 1946, a year after his death. A plaque on the rock reads: "In Memory of Ernie Pyle, America's Greatest and Best Loved War Correspondent." Another nearby rock honors Henry J. Schnitgius, the founder of Indiana's roadside park system.

Some of Ernie's friends and neighbors also erected a replica of the simple monument that stands on Ie Shima, the tiny coral island off the northern tip of Okinawa, where Ernie caught a Japanese machine-gun bullet in the head. The inscription: "At This Spot the 77th Infantry Division Lost a Buddy. Ernie Pyle. 18 April 1945."

The park is two-and-a-half miles north of Dana, which lies beyond a big red barn that urges passersby to chew Mail Pouch tobacco. The town rises from the plains looking like any other farm town along the highway: a clump of trees, a grain elevator, a water tower.

Ernie once described his home in a column. This is what he wrote:

> *U.S. Highway 36, the transcontinental road known as the Lincoln Highway, might be called the road of great men's homes. Practically every fifty miles from Kansas to Ohio you pass through a town where some remarkable figure was born or spent his early days: Jesse James, St. Joe, Missouri; J. C. Penney, the chainstore man, Hamilton, Missouri; General John J. Pershing, Le Clede, Missouri; Mark Twain, Hannibal, Missouri; Abraham Lincoln, Springfield, Illinois; and E. Trocadero Pyle, Dana, Indiana.*
>
> *If any of the above gentlemen, or their heirs or assignees, object to being mentioned in the same breath with Mr. Pyle, let them go ahead and sue. All these great men were memorialized*

> *in some way or other by their hometowns — all, that is, except the last one. On the crossroads where Highway 36 cuts past Dana, there might be a large marker saying:*
>
> *"Three miles south is the house in which E. Pyle, Indiana's great skunk-trapper, jelly-eater, horse-hater, and snake-afraider-of, was born. In his later years, Mr. Pyle rose to a state of national mediocrity as a letter writer, a stayer in hotels, a talker to obscure people, and a driver from town to town. The old house is in a good state of preservation, although the same cannot be said for Mr. Pyle. Historians say he has been falling to pieces for years."*

At the intersection of Highway 36 and Highway 71, Dana's main street, just across from an abandoned railroad-car diner, is a simple sign, short and humorless, with fading red and green letters: "Visit Dana, Hometown of Ernie Pyle — ½ Mile." Not one mention of jelly-eating or snake-afraider-ofing.

The town begins at the B&O Railroad tracks. It has changed little since Ernie was writing about it as a roving columnist in the late thirties. Its houses are maple-shaded, old, comfortable, well-tended. Several fly the flag from staffs attached to front-porch pillars. A single block of old brick stores, all of which were around when Ernie was a boy, many of them empty, forms the business district, all but deserted on a Saturday afternoon. A few people sit over coffee in Mag's Café. A couple of farmers in overalls stand chatting in front of the farm implement place. The only busy spot is the IGA Food Store.

"Dana's 'bout gone to pot," one resident told me rather forlornly. "A skeleton town anymore. We only got one grocery store. Used to be three. 'Course, the one we got is a nice one."

Ed Columbo, a Dana resident for twenty-five years, sat on a stool inside his soda shop next-door to the empty office of the *Dana News* (established 1885).

"Paper moved up to Cayuga," he said. "Been about a year ago, hadn't it?" he asked his wife, who nodded agreement.

"I saw Ernie Pyle, and I was well acquainted with his dad and Aunt Mary," he went on. "They don't have no more relatives here.

The house is still out here south of town. You seen it? Widow woman lives in the house, Mrs. Hasley ... what is her name?"

"Mrs. Hazen," said his wife.

Ed Columbo dug around behind the counter and found a folder that the Dames Club of Dana put out several years earlier about Ernie and the town and offered it along with directions to Ernie's house.

"You go down this road about three miles and take a left. It's the fourth house on the left, just before you get to this hill. We call it the mountain," he said.

"The house sets way back," Mrs. Columbo added.

"Oh, it don't set too far back."

"What about that Mrs. Bales that lives out there?" asked a young woman sitting at the fountain with two small children, all of them sipping soft drinks. "Wasn't she some kin to the Pyles? Aunt Mary was a Bales."

Aunt Mary. Ernie wrote a lot about her. She was a real character. People in Dana talk as much about Aunt Mary as they do about Ernie. She died ten or twelve years ago, according to Ed Columbo.

The Bales house is close-by the road, with tulips blooming in the yard. Nobody answered my knock for a long time. Then a small, graying woman with watery, frightened eyes peered from behind the louvered door.

Mrs. Bales?

Yes.

Was she related to Aunt Mary?

"She was my stepmother."

Would she consider talking about Aunt Mary and Ernie, perhaps telling a few family stories?

"I couldn't tell you any more than's in those books," she said. "It's all in those books."

The house where Ernie was reared, she points out, is just up the road in a yard filled with tall maples.

It is a white house, well preserved but listing slightly, as if pushed off base by the unrelenting wind that whistles through the trees and stirs eerie creakings in the old house. A story-and-a-half tall, the house has a green, shingled roof and a big front porch with a swing on one end. To one side is a weathered barn that somebody started painting white years ago without finishing and a collection of other outbuildings. Nearby rises "the mountain," actually an ancient Indian mound where kids still come to search for beads and arrowheads, as Ernie once did.

Carmen Hazen is just the person to live in Ernie's house — open and friendly and happy to talk. But not happy to have her photo made.

"Oh, God, no," she said, smoothing her windblown hair. "I look like holy hell today."

She had been living in the Pyle house for six years, renting it from Ed Goforth, who lived the next farm over. He bought it after Ernie's father died in 1950.

"It's a restful little place out here," Mrs. Hazen said. "Nobody bothers you."

She was living alone now. Her husband, Clyde, had died three years earlier while they were on a fishing trip in Michigan. "Just died sudden, never said a word, just died," she told me. She passed her time keeping house and babysitting for neighbors.

People were always coming by to see the house where Ernie lived, Mrs. Hazen said, even though no signs lead visitors to it. "They ask if I can sell them souvenirs. Well, I guess I could start something like that, but I never did. It'd be wonderful if they'd make a historical place out of it, but then I'd have to find another place to live, I guess," she said.

One fellow from Connecticut arrived to see the house in the middle of the night and wanted to take a picture of it, Mrs. Hazen reported. She told him to go ahead, and he spent an hour rigging up flashbulbs all over the place, even in the trees. When he set them off, the flash was seen all the way to town. Made some people think a thunderstorm was coming. When he got back home, Mrs. Hazen said with a laugh, the fellow wrote and told her that the picture didn't come out.

As she was telling her story, Ed Goforth arrived in his pickup truck and got out to feed the livestock behind the barn. A tall, lean, hard-jawed, friendly man, Ed was born and reared on the adjoining farm. He went away to teach school in Gary for forty years before coming home to farm. He had succeeded; he owned several big farms around Dana.

"Oh, yes," he said, taking off a work glove to shake hands. "I knew Ernie. Went to school with him. Of course, he was a little older than me. He'd have been sixty-nine this summer. I'm only sixty-six.

"We threshed together. He hated the farm, though. He had to do the plowing, had to do it by horses then. He'd get out here in these fields behind the house, and he'd get lonesome, you know.

"So he went off down to Indiana University, I don't know that he finished there, and got into the newspaper business. He'd travel around the country writing stories, just like you're doing.

"He'd put people's names in his columns. That's what the people liked, you know. He'd write where people could understand it. He was a very common man. His mother and dad were fine folks."

He points to a small shed at the back of the house. "His dad built that for him for his Model-T Ford," he said.

As Ed Goforth headed off to feed the pigs and cows, Mrs. Hazen showed off the interior of the house, drawing special attention to photos of her grandchildren and to the fancy flowered porcelain lighting fixtures.

"Aunt Mary bought those and put them here," she explained of the fixtures. "After Ernie started writing about her, people would send her money sometimes. She took it and bought those. Now there was a good old soul. She lived by me in Dana. Witty. A good old soul. She died ten or twelve years ago. Time gets away."

Back outside, Mrs. Hazen watched while I snapped pictures of the place. She looked toward the barn where Ed Goforth was finishing his chores and making ready to leave.

"He used to get up there by that old barn," she said of Ernie, "set up there and shoot groundhogs, and then come down here and grieve about it. I read that somewhere. I used to read his column in the *Indianapolis Times*. Never did dream I'd ever live in his home."

Ed Goforth said good-byes and left. I soon followed, a pilgrim who had come seeking a glimpse into the early life of a fellow newspaperman nearly a quarter of a century dead. Mrs. Hazen, who would have been a perfect subject for an Ernie Pyle column, stood waving from the porch. Two turns and U.S. Highway 36, now the Ernie Pyle Highway in Indiana, reached on toward Illinois and the homes of famous men. But I had already found whatever it was — a feeling of connection, I suppose — that I'd made my journey looking for.

Mine is a profession that requires travel. I've never been a war correspondent, but I have stayed on the move for much of my working life. You begin to take for granted the ability to move around, by car or air, to get where you need to be when you need to be there. It is an amazing power we have, here in the twentieth century, and a wonderful one, until something goes wrong. It doesn't take much — the slightest thing — and the lesson is again brought home that we move so freely only through the mystery of grace.

I was late leaving work, and it was far past suppertime. I hadn't eaten; my stomach was speaking to me about it. I had my meal all picked out. It entered my mind at some indeterminate point, but I'd already been thinking about it for some time, tasting it, savoring each dish. I stopped at the supermarket and picked up the necessary items, which now sat in brown paper bags, silent passengers in the backseat.

I eased the car down the ramp onto the highway and, gathering speed, made for home. It had been raining, still was a little, barely a drizzle, but the big trucks passed by in such a roaring hurry that they tossed a fine, dirty spray onto the windshield. The wipers struggled with it, but they never quite conquered. It was a dangerous night to be on the road, I knew, even though the traffic wasn't as heavy as usual.

Earlier in the day someone had made a remark during a casual conversation: "Everybody's gotta go sometime." It's one of those truths we live with but rarely think about. But, for some reason, the moment he said it, the idea penetrated — someday I wouldn't be around anymore — and churned a ripple of fear in my stomach. I quickly put it out of my mind, as I would any useless thought.

But when I found myself skimming along the slick, treacherous highway, the remark slipped back into consciousness. Instinctively,

I tightened my seatbelt and checked the speedometer. I was doing sixty, a murderous speed, but legal, and I felt safe. I let my thoughts wander back to the food that awaited my loving preparation. Funny, how hunger, just mild hunger, can so occupy the mind, how a meal can become so fixed in imagination that any deviation from your menu would destroy not only the meal but your hunger as well. By the time I ate my dream supper, I would have savored every morsel so thoroughly that the actual dining would be anticlimatic.

With supper still on my mind, I headed over a slight rise and in a small valley below saw the bright red glow of brake lights. It was a wreck, no doubt, not surprising considering the night and the traffic. I knew the intersection that lay ahead. It was a bad one; I'd seen wrecks there before.

I slowed down. Big trucks were pulling off the road. Cars were stopping. Clearly, the accident had just happened. There were no highway patrol cars or ambulances on the scene. A truck driver had lighted a red flare and was standing in the middle of the road, directing vehicles away from the wreckage. A bus had stopped on the other side of the four-lane highway; its passengers peered curiously from its long row of windows.

I found myself upon the wreckage with no place to stop. The truck driver waved me on, and I began to creep through what amounted to a maze of vehicles and debris. It was hard to tell what had happened. A truck blocked the intersecting road. A car was sideways in the median. Neither seemed damaged. Then I noticed people running toward a field on the right. There, outlined in the headlights, I caught a glimpse of what had apparently been a car but was now a clump of twisted metal. The road was strewn with broken glass, clumps of under-fender dirt, and stray pieces of wreckage.

On the side of the road lay a hulk that at first glance appeared to be a fender. With horror, I realized that it was not. It was a person. A young man, lying lifeless on the wet pavement only a few feet away, his legs folded beneath him like those of a Raggedy Andy carelessly cast aside. It took but one look to know that he was dead.

I started to stop but hesitated. Others were there. I could do nothing except add to the confusion. I'd seen too many of these things to become another wreck gawker. So I continued my journey, feeling suddenly sick and empty.

Only minutes ago that young man must have felt as safe and dry in his car as I felt in mine. Did he experience pang of fear about death today, as I had? It struck me, too, that had I not tarried at work, had I not been delayed that extra minute in the supermarket checkout line, I might have been in that place at that time and . . . the thought was too awesome to consider.

One thing was certain. I was no longer hungry. The mere thought of the meal I had planned and savored for hours had become repulsive.

I picked up speed, got back to sixty, turned on the radio, cinched my seatbelt. Within the hour, I knew, wreckers would have hauled away the smashed machinery from the awful scene then disappearing in my rearview mirror. The glass shards would have faded into the night. People would pass the spot without knowing that just a short time before a young man died there, crumpled on the pavement like a child's toy.

No person even half-awake could deny that the dangers around us are deep and unending. But to withdraw from life because of those dangers *is* to withdraw from life, to miss its rewards without ensuring that you will also be spared its terrors. There is finally no compromise to be made, beyond good sense and compassion, I suspect. So we move forward, as best we know how, and calculate when to take our risks and when to draw back. Those decisions are largely a matter of instinct, and maybe the best we can do is keep our instincts finely tuned.

I quit picking up hitchhikers after a frightening experience, but how could I drive past an old woman hitchhiking in the rain? The truck ahead of me passed her by, but I couldn't. I stopped.

She was a little ball of a woman wearing a shabby coat and a purple kerchief on her head. She slid onto the seat beside me, smoothing her thin cotton dress over heavy, veiny legs.

"What they need around here, brother, is a bus," she said.

I agreed, adding that there wasn't likely to be bus service anytime soon, especially not on country roads like this. She asked which way

I was going, and I told her. It wasn't the direction in which she was headed.

"If you could just take me up here to the highway, I would appreciate it," she said.

She had a round and deeply lined face and an obvious need to talk. She didn't like to hitchhike, she said, but she had no other choice.

"I know it's dangerous. There's so much meanness in the world," she said. "I don't think we've ever had any more meanness that we've got now, do you, brother?"

I said that there surely was a lot of it around and set the wind-shield wipers at a faster pace.

"I blame the old people," she said. "You have to set an example for young people. The way I look at it, we're all brothers and sisters. There's no reason we can't be kind to one another, is there, brother?"

"No, ma'am, there isn't."

"I don't like to have to hitch," she said again, "but I have things I have to do. I know it's not safe to stop and pick up people either, but if nobody ever comes to any more harm than they'll come to from me, they won't come to any."

We were at the highway now. I knew she was going on into town, several miles distant. I had an appointment in another town in the opposite direction, and I was in a hurry. But how can you put an old lady out on the highway in the rain?

"I tell you what," I said. "I'll just take you on into town."

"Well, bless you."

Again she said how she hated to have to get out on the road and depend on others to take her where she had to go. "I get Social Services," she said, "and I thank the Lord for it, but we don't draw much, you know, and you have to cut corners wherever you can."

She'd been living in the country for only two weeks, she said, in the small, run-down frame house near where I'd picked her up. Before that, she was in an apartment in town. Didn't like it. Too crowded and noisy.

"And," she said, "if you walked out in the yard, people'd look at you funny. I like to be out by myself. And the rent's cheaper out. I can sit on my porch and look at those little mountains, and it's so purty. I want to get me a swing. I love a swing on a porch, don't you, brother? And I want to set me out some tomato plants and squash and okra. Just a little bit like that'll help out, you know."

"Do you live alone?" I asked.

A little laugh of joy burst from her. "Oh, no," she said. "I have the Lord. He's in every room of that little house. And He's with me everywhere I go."

She said it with such conviction that I looked over my shoulder, halfway expecting to see Him smiling in the back seat.

"Do you mind if I ask your age?" I said.

"How old do you think I am?" She grinned mischievously.

"Oh, I'd say about sixty-five."

"Be seventy-three this Sunday next. My daddy died when I was eight year old, and I've been on my own ever since. Ain't been easy either, brother."

She told how she'd taken care of her brother until he died of cancer at thirteen, how she'd moved from South Carolina and spent more than forty years cleaning other people's houses, tending to their babies, their old and sick, until she reached the point that she just couldn't do it anymore.

"You never married?"

"No. My boyfriend died three weeks before we was supposed to get married. It liked to killed me when he died. I never could find another one I could love as much as him. Just the Lord."

We were at her destination.

"Would you mind if I included you and your family in my prayers?" she asked as she got out of the car.

"Please do. I would appreciate that very much."

I shifted gears, impatient to get going. "Look," I said, "do you think you'll have any trouble getting back?"

She smiled. "Oh, no. The Lord got me up here. He'll get me back. He'll ride with you, too, brother, if you'll let him."

We arrived as midnight revelers, denying the sacred aura of the night, summoning boisterous spirits to lift us above the pain of our mission. A motley crowd we were, hunched in heavy jackets, clumping onto the pier in threes and fours, wisecracking and laughing, testing the direction of the breeze with white puffs of alcoholic breath.

The full moon shone overhead, making patterns on the ocean's flat surface, illuminating even the horizon. The neon-adorned strip of high-rise condos and hotels glittered along the beach. Beyond our own raucousness, the only sounds were the far-off hum of traffic and the soft lapping of the surf.

We stopped short of pier's end, not wanting to disturb the solitary fisherman lurking there, and rested the small cardboard box on one of the high benches where fishermen perch. Inside the box was a plain metal can, not much bigger than a coffee can. A label identified the contents: Crematory Remains Number 261, Jimmy Lee McAllister.

To most of us McAllister had been friend and companion for a long time. He was a newspaper columnist and raconteur, a short, gray-bearded man with an impish sparkle in his blue eyes, who liked to wear strange little hats. Some said that he looked like Kenny Rogers. He loved playing poker, fishing, shooting pool, betting on jai alai, watching major-league baseball. He also had a high regard for women, laughter, tradition, banana pudding, and Cheerwine, a favorite sweet, cherry-flavored soft drink from his Carolina boyhood. He was harsh on mayonnaise and overly educated young editors who didn't know anything about life.

McAllister knew a lot about life. For one thing, he understood that friendship must be cultivated as vigorously as a garden, lest it wither and die, so he was the instigator of regular trips and events for widely separated friends. For fourteen years we had gathered twice yearly at Myrtle Beach for a rowdy weekend of fishing, poker, tale-telling, and laughter.

Nearly two years earlier, on one of our regular trips to the jai alai frontons of Florida, some of us had finally browbeaten McAllister into admitting that he needed to see a doctor. He had known for months that something was seriously wrong, but he wouldn't accept or admit it. His obstinancy was costly. He fought cancer with humor and impatience, and for a while — long enough to work in several more trips with friends—he seemed to wrestle it to a draw. He had died three months earlier on Labor Day weekend.

McAllister was not a man for ceremony. In his will he decreed that no service be held, that friends take charge of his remains. In his waning days, I asked what he wanted us to do with them.

"Just take me on a beach trip," he said, "and heave me off the pier."

The pier stirred memories, and as we waited for stragglers, we told stories of happier times there. Laughing, we did imitations of the dramatic way McAllister would pounce upon his rod when a fish nibbled, setting the hook as if a blue marlin were on the line instead of a tiny croaker.

One pier story had been retold almost every trip, to McAllister's chagrin, and it was only natural that it should be told again.

Margaret and Verlene were their names. They came onto the pier one afternoon when we were fishing for our supper. Margaret was heavy and beginning to show her age. Verlene was chubby and had bad teeth. They had come to the beach from an inland mill town intent on having a good time, and they seemed to be perusing the crowded pier for prospects other than cold fish.

I was standing near the pier's entrance, trying my luck in the surf, well apart from my friends. Maybe that's why they stopped and struck up a conversation. When I told them I was with a group, Margaret said, "Oh, which ones are you out here with?"

"Well," I said, pointing them out, "that tall ugly one over there, and that one in the green jacket, and that one in the toboggan, and that little bearded one with the funny hat." McAllister was wearing his Greek seaman's cap that day.

"You're not out here with *him*," Margaret said, indicating McAllister.

"Oh, yes," I said, thinking they had recognized him, for McAllister was famous in parts of South Carolina.

"Lord have mercy," she said. "We come by him a minute ago, and I said to Verlene, 'Verlene, the-e-e-re's your last chance.'"

We never let McAllister forget that, for he fancied himself a ladies' man.

"You know," Roy Rabon said after the story had been told again, "it's too bad ol' Verlene's not here tonight. It really would be her last chance."

The stragglers had arrived during the storytelling, and when the laughter died, I said, "Well, let's do it."

We tested the breeze again, moved to the opposite side of the pier, and hoisted a farewell toast of Cheerwine.

Earlier, during the poker game that we had interrupted for this chore, we had dealt McAllister a final hand of five-card stud. He won with trip queens. His winnings and a symbolic royal flush had been placed atop the plastic bag inside the can. We laid them aside now, and I ripped open the bag, curious to see the ashes. They looked like cornmeal.

Karl Hill and I had been closest to McAllister. We knelt together and emptied the can over the side, creating a slowly settling cloud of fine gray dust. The cards and chips went next, followed by Cheerwine from all the cups. The ashes formed a changing pattern atop the water, two white chips and two red cards floating facedown among them, hole cards and ante, drifting slowly northward, away from the pier.

"It's almost as if he's trying to spell out a message to us," Chuck Alston said, as we watched the milky patterns change.

"I think it says, 'Deal,'" Stan Swofford said.

The gulls seemed to come from nowhere, suddenly and eerily. When we had arrived, they were luminous apparitions bobbing on the swells in the black water off the end of the pier, a large flock bedded for the night. Without our noticing, they began paddling toward us, making soft chirping sounds I'd never heard from gulls, merging in harmonious hymn.

They approached the widening pattern of ashes and surrounded it, a welcoming host. One bird rose, skimmed over the ashes, and landed noisily on the other side. As the pattern drifted and dissipated, the gulls moved with it, slowly tightening the circle. When the ashes had disappeared, the gulls settled quietly again in the distance.

Harry Blair broke the silence that had overcome us. "I think that's the most beautiful funeral I've ever seen," he said, and we walked off the pier in hushed and reverent agreement.

Plume

THE FINEST IN SHORT FICTION

(0452)

There's an epidemic with 27 million victims. And no visible symptoms.

It's an epidemic of people who can't read.

Believe it *or* not, 27 million Americans are functionally illiterate, about one adult in five.

The solution to this problem is you… when you join the fight against illiteracy. So call the Coalition for Literacy at toll-free **1-800-228-8813** and volunteer.

Volunteer Against Illiteracy. The only degree you need is a degree of caring.